Praise for Richard L. Mabry's

Fatal Trauma

"*Fatal Trauma* asks big questions of faith, priorities, and meaning all within the context of a tightly crafted medical drama."—**Steven James**, best-selling author of *Placebo* and *Checkmate*

"Grab your heart meds! This medical suspense is guaranteed to raise your blood pressure."—**DiAnn Mills**, author of *Firewall* and *Double Cross*

Stress Test

"Packed with thrills, *Stress Test* is a lightning-paced read that you'll read in one breath."—**Tess Gerritsen**, *New York Times* best-selling author

"It is easy to understand why Mabry's popularity has been skyrocketing. He is a fine, fine writer."—**Michael Palmer**, *New York Times* best-selling author

"The plot moves along with plenty of action and empathy, and there's suspense and suspicion enough to keep readers zipping to the last pages. Mabry's novel arrives with a positive prognosis."—*Publishers Weekly*

"You are not going to want to miss Dr. Richard Mabry's newest thrill ride! Mabry combines his medical expertise with a story that will keep you on the edge of your seat."—*USA Today*

Heart Failure

"Vintage Mabry. *Heart Failure* weaves an intricate plot of mystery and suspense that will leave you guessing until the final page."—**Billy Coffey**, author of *When Mockingbirds Sing*

"*Heart Failure* is a well-written suspense story that sets you on the edge of your seat. Author of the Prescription for Trouble series, as well as *Stress Test*, Richard Mabry uses his background in medicine to his advantage as he draws the reader through this heart-stopping thriller."—*CBA Retailers and Resources*

Critical Condition

"A riveting medical suspense tale from an author at the top of his game. If you love thrillers then you must be reading Richard's books."—**Jordyn Redwood**, author of the Bloodline Trilogy

"Mabry has the uncommon ability to take medical details and make them understandable while still maintaining accuracy and intrigue. He will leave you asking whodunit until the end."—*RT Book Reviews*

MIRACLE
DRUG

RICHARD L. MABRY, M.D.

Abingdon Press

Nashville

Other Books by Richard L. Mabry, MD

Code Blue
Medical Error
Diagnosis Death
Lethal Remedy
Stress Test
Heart Failure
Critical Condition
Fatal Trauma

Miracle Drug

Copyright © 2015 by Richard L. Mabry

ISBN-13: 978-1-6308-8118-4

Published by Abingdon Press, 2222 Rosa L. Parks Blvd.,
PO Box 280988, Nashville, TN 37228-0988

www.abingdonpress.com

Macro Editor: Teri Wilhelms

Published in association with Books & Such Literary Agency

Library of Congress Cataloging-in-Publication Data

Mabry, Richard L.
  Miracle drug / Richard L. Mabry, MD.
    pages ; cm
  ISBN 978-1-6308-8118-4 (binding: soft back)
  I. Title.
  PS3613.A2M57 2015
  813'.6—dc23

                                                            2015016731

Printed in the United States of America

1 2 3 4 5 6 7 8 9 10 / 19 18 17 16 15

*For the unseen heroes of the publishing industry:
agents, editors, copyreaders, graphic designers, marketing
specialists, and everyone else working behind the scenes
to bring the reading public the best possible product.*

A Note to the Reader

Perhaps I should start by saying that although the story of the volunteers who became infected with the Ebola virus while serving in Africa captured the attention of all of us during the time this story was being written, the manuscript was essentially complete before that scenario played out.

Next, I want to point out that there is no such drug as robinoxine or RP-78. On a happier note, there is no *Bacillus decimus* either. Both are products of this author's imagination. It is true that all drug studies are done on volunteers, and it's possible there could be one where convicts sentenced to life with no prospect of parole volunteer to receive drugs to treat a potentially fatal disease. However, I have no certain knowledge of such testing in Colombia or anywhere else.

Authors of fiction walk a fine line between accuracy and literary license, and this book is no exception. I appreciate the assistance of Agent Robert Hoback of the United States Secret Service in my quest for authenticity. Nevertheless, the characters and actions I have crafted that involve those brave men and women are purely fictional. Both the University of Texas Southwestern Medical Center and Johns Hopkins Medical Center are fine teaching and treatment facilities, and I am honored to have been a faculty member at one and a Visiting Professor at the other. Be that as it may, the people and events portrayed here and their relationship to those medical centers are purely a work of fiction. The same is true of the doctors and facilities of the fictional Prestonwood Hospital.

As always, I count myself fortunate to have representation by a talented agent like Rachelle Gardner of Books and Such Literary. I'd like to express my appreciation to the Senior Acquisitions Editor at Abingdon Press, Ramona Richards, as well as to Editor Teri Wilhelms, for exercising their editorial skills on this manuscript. The Anderson Design Group came up with a dynamite cover. As always, Cat Hoort and her crew took the lead in making sure people know about the book. And, of course, without you, my reader, this novel would languish on bookshelves and storerooms without ever being read.

My wife, Kay, serves as my first reader and always makes a significant contribution to my work. In addition, and even more important, she continues to teach me how to smile and have fun once more. Thank you, dear.

My thanks to my family, for not only believing in me, but for expressing it so well and so often that I've never doubted their support.

I hope you enjoy this novel and any future ones God may grant me the ability and opportunity to write. Any praise for this or any of my work goes to Him.

Richard L. Mabry, MD
September 2014

1

Dr. Ben Lambert stood at the bathroom sink washing his hands. He sensed more than saw the movement behind him.

"You're not supposed to be in here," he said without turning. The intruder didn't respond. Lambert repeated the words, this time in Spanish. *"Se supone que no debe estar aquí."*

When there was still no answer, Lambert, his hands wet, the water still running, turned toward the intruder. That's when he felt it—a sharp pain in his left upper arm. Within seconds, a burning pain swept over his extremities. His vision became fuzzy. He tried to reach out, but the commands his brain sent went unheeded by his arms and legs.

With agonizing slowness, Lambert crumpled to the ground. He felt his heart thud against his chest wall in an erratic rhythm, at first a fast gallop, then slower and more irregular. He tried to breathe but couldn't satisfy his hunger for air. His calls for help came out as weak, strangled cries, like the mewling of a kitten.

Then the next wave of pain hit him—the worst pain he'd ever experienced, centered over his breastbone as though someone had impaled him with a sword. Lambert struggled to move, to cry out for help, to breathe. Through half-closed eyelids, he could barely see a patch of worn linoleum, topped by an ever-enlarging puddle beneath the soapstone sink. Then that vision and the world around it faded to black, and Ben Lambert died.

Dr. Josh Pearson tapped on the office door. "Nadeel, you wanted to see me?"

Dr. Nadeel Kahn half-rose from behind his desk. Kahn was a small man—almost five eight compared with Josh's six feet plus. His accent was almost non-existent, probably worn off through years of medical school, residency, and practice. Normally, Josh's interaction with the managing partner of the Preston Medical Clinic was limited to an occasional "Hi" as they passed in the halls, plus phone calls about hematology patients Josh referred to the subspecialist. This summons to Kahn's office had come as a surprise.

Kahn motioned Josh inside. "Thanks for coming. Close the door and have a seat, would you?"

Josh did as Kahn asked. "What's up? I think this is the first time I've ever been called into your office." He tried to summon up a grin. "Am I in trouble?"

Kahn's expression never changed. "We'll wait to decide that until you hear both pieces of news I have for you." He leaned back in his desk chair and tented his fingertips under his chin. His dark eyes fixed on Josh's. He took a moment, apparently deciding how to deliver his message. When he spoke, his tone had turned serious. "As you know, our colleague, Ben Lambert, left a few days ago to accompany former president Madison on a trip to South America. The delegation was to consider locations for a free clinic Madison's foundation was considering setting up. Before he left, Ben approached me and said he thought it appropriate, as he got older, to prepare a younger colleague to care for David Madison should the need arise."

An idea took faint shape in Josh's mind, but he quickly rejected it. *Surely not.* He shook his head.

"Yes. He named you," Kahn said. "Ben told me he had already discussed it with Madison. They'd known each other for years—actually grew up together—and Madison trusted his friend. He said he was willing to go along with Ben's recommendation."

"I'm . . . I'm flattered, I guess, but I have no idea why he'd choose me."

"Unfortunately, we can't ask Ben that question. I just got a phone call that he died earlier today of an apparent heart attack." Kahn rose from his chair. He reached across the desk and put his hand on Josh's shoulder. "I don't know whether to offer congratulations or sympathy. Josh, you're now the personal physician for David Madison, former president of the United States."

Tears formed in Rachel Moore's eyes as she stood on the tarmac of El Dorado International Airport in Bogotá, Colombia, watching the special metal coffin holding the earthly remains of Dr. Ben Lambert disappear into the cargo hold of the private jet. *Dr. Lambert, I'm so sorry. I wish I could have done more.*

An older man, the silver waves of his hair blowing slightly in the wind, stood beside her. As though he could read her thoughts, he said, "Don't beat yourself up, Rachel. No one could have predicted this. And you and the others did everything humanly possible. Ben was probably already dead when you found him." Then David Madison put his arm gently around her shoulders and hugged her.

"I guess I know that," she said. "But no one expected it. I mean, we all had physicals along with our immunizations before leaving, and he told me he was in tip-top shape for a man over sixty. Then, when we were eating lunch at the church, he was in the bathroom . . ."

"I know. It's a shock. Ben Lambert was an old friend. We grew up together. And now he's gone." Madison took his arm away and looked down at the nurse. "You know you don't have to be the one to accompany his body back to Dallas. One of the other members of the party could do it."

"No, I think I need this to achieve some closure. You'll be coming back in a couple more days, and if there's a medical problem after I leave, you still have Dr. Dietz and Linda Gaston."

The door to the cargo hold closed with a thud, and Rachel shivered despite the tropic heat. She lifted her carry-on bag and started to turn away, but Madison stopped her.

"Ben must have sensed something like this might happen, because before we left he spoke to me about another physician he thought should take care of me if he couldn't." Madison hesitated. "I think you know him. Matter of fact, I imagine he's the one meeting you at the airport after you land."

"You mean Josh?"

"When you see him, please tell Dr. Pearson I need to see him as soon as I return."

◆

The Preston Medical Clinic utilized cutting-edge technology in every aspect of its practice, and records were no exception. All the records were computerized, the information encrypted, ample backup in place. The primary difference between David Madison's records and others was that the former president's were more strongly encrypted and only available to the medical staff on a need-to-know basis. Now Josh had that need.

Most of the physicians had gone home for the day, but Josh was still at his computer studying David Madison's medical records, trying to prepare himself for what he anticipated was going to be his biggest job ever as a physician.

Did Ben Lambert have a premonition something like this might happen? Was that why he named Josh as his successor before leaving on the trip? Maybe there was a clue in his medical records.

Closing down Madison's record, Josh opened the one for Ben Lambert. His pre-trip physical had been just as thorough as the ex-president's . . . maybe even more thorough. Then why would he have suffered a sudden heart attack and died? Josh figured it was something weird like a rhythm disturbance. He shook his head. No need for him to agonize over something that had already happened. Maybe the autopsy would tell them, maybe not.

But, no matter what was in Ben Lambert's medical records, whatever his autopsy would show, one thing remained a certainty. Dr. Ben Lambert was dead, and Josh Pearson was now the personal physician for the immediate past president of the United States.

❖

It would be wonderful to get back home to Josh, Rachel thought. They'd been dating for a year, and this was the longest they'd been apart. A mutual friend had introduced them, warning her that he was still a bit fragile from the death of his wife a couple of years earlier. But Rachel rationalized that since her fiancé had dumped her before she moved to Dallas, perhaps she and Josh would be kindred spirits. They proved to be more than that, though. And this absence from him cemented it— her feelings for him were more than friendship. She'd fallen in love with Josh. And she could hardly wait to see him, to pick the right time to let him know.

Rachel looked out the window of the plane, trying to discern landmarks below. She'd always envied people who could look down at the metropolitan sprawl that was Dallas and say, "Oh, I can see my house" or "There's the building where I work."

Sometimes, if she was lucky, she might recognize the sprawling campus of the University of Texas Southwestern Medical Center. On rare occasions, she might even be able to spot the Zale Lipshy Hospital where she worked—but not today. She wished she were there right now, checking on patients in the ICU, instead of escorting the body of a colleague back to his loved ones. A wave of guilt washed over her like the rain that streaked past the windows of the plane. *Get over it, Rachel. You did all you could.* But if that were true, why did something about it all simply feel wrong?

The plane dropped lower, and through the rain she was able to make out street lamps and car headlights. The touchdown was relatively smooth, and soon she heard the roar of reverse thrusters and the squeal of brakes as the pilot brought the jet to a slow rollout. This area of Love Field was reserved for VIPs, and certainly a plane chartered by former president David Madison qualified. She wondered who would meet her—besides Josh, of course. Exactly how would she accomplish the handoff of Dr. Lambert's body?

The jet rocked to a stop and the engine noise died. Rachel looked out the window and saw that the plane was probably a hundred yards from the terminal building. The male steward unfastened his seat belt and made his way back toward her. "Miss Moore, we're here. Are you ready to deplane?"

Rachel rose from her seat, took her carry-on bag from the steward, and moved toward the forward door, which had already been folded downward to form a short staircase. She grasped the wet handrail and descended the steps, which were already slippery from the rain. She avoided looking to her left as the airplane's cargo door opened. Dr. Lambert's coffin would be off-loaded soon, and she knew that seeing it would tear at her heart.

Then she saw Josh hurrying toward her, oblivious of the rain. His raincoat flapped behind him, the rain on his bare head turned his sandy hair to a helmet from which water streamed down a handsome face. Josh opened his arms toward her, and for the first time in what seemed like days, Rachel felt the clenched muscles in her shoulders relax.

◆

As Josh had prepared for his trip to the airport to meet Rachel, he once again took a personal inventory and realized how blessed he was to find love once again. When Carol died two years ago, Josh felt as though his world ended. He was certain he'd never love again. But Rachel changed that. She'd brought sunshine into what had been, to that point, a dark world. Josh was determined not to let her go.

In his vehicle, he tried to imagine how she must feel. Josh knew it was up to him to comfort her and guide her through the next few hours and days. He just hoped he could do it.

He snagged a parking place in the short-term garage at Love Field. Despite a few wrong turns and false starts, Josh managed to navigate the route to where the private jet bearing Rachel would land. He planted himself where he had a good view of the tarmac outside, then stood peering through the large, rain-streaked plate glass window, as though by his actions he could make the plane arrive more quickly. Finally, he saw the small private jet land, traverse a couple of runways, and come to a stop. As soon as the plane door opened and the steps unfolded, he hurried across the tarmac to Rachel, ignoring the rain. He kissed her, then pulled her close to him and clasped her tightly, her head resting comfortably on his shoulder. He nestled his face in her soft brown hair and whispered, "I've missed you so."

"And I've missed you." He held her as though he'd never let go. Eventually Rachel pushed back and said, "I . . . I guess I should see about—"

A middle-aged man in a black trench coat and dark felt hat approached them. He opened a black umbrella and held it over Rachel to shield her from the spring shower as he talked.

"Excuse me," he said, in a voice as somber as his attire. "Miss Moore? I'm Bill Smith. President Madison's office arranged for us to meet the plane and take the body of Dr. Lambert."

"Oh. We . . . we hadn't talked about the details." She looked uncertainly at Josh. "I guess it's okay."

"Could we see some identification?" Josh asked.

"Of course." Smith pulled out a wallet, which he opened to show a Texas driver's license bearing his name and photo. Then he brought out a card identifying him as a member of the National Funeral Directors Association.

"Thank you," Josh said. He turned to Rachel and gave a small nod.

Smith raised a clipboard in the hand not holding the umbrella. "If you'll just sign this form, we'll do the rest."

Rachel took the pen from under the clip and signed the paper. "And that's all?"

"Do I need to call someone to pick you up? Anything else we can do?" the man asked.

"I'll take care of her," Josh said.

As the hearse pulled away, Josh took Rachel's arm. "Let's get in out of the rain. What about your luggage?"

"I only have this carry-on. Mr. Madison said not to worry about the rest of my things—someone would pack them and send them back. I guess all I have to do right now is clear customs." She took Josh's hand. "I thought that once someone else took charge of Dr. Lambert's body, I'd feel some relief, but I don't . . . I . . . I . . ."

"Later. We'll talk about it all you want, but right now let's get you home."

As they arrived at the glass door into the terminal, it slid back to reveal an older man wearing a black suit and a somber expression. "Miss Moore?"

"Yes. Did President Madison arrange for you to meet me?"

The man nodded and stepped back so Josh and Rachel could enter. "I apologize for being a few minutes late. There was an accident on Mockingbird Lane that held us up." He handed her a business card, then reached into the breast pocket of his coat and produced a three-page document. "I'm Vernon Wells with Sparkman Hillcrest Funeral Directors. The coach will be pulling around next to the plane in a moment. If you'll sign this, we'll take possession of Dr. Lambert's body."

2

Josh looked at Rachel, who stood in stunned silence, her mouth forming a tiny O. At this point, he figured the less said, the better. "Mr. Wells, there's been a mix-up." He gestured with the business card Wells had given him. "Someone will be in touch."

Wells said something about "mistakes happen, I guess." He left, a somewhat puzzled expression on his face.

Rachel looked as though she might throw up right there. "Oh, Josh. What have I done?"

Josh put his hand on her elbow and urged her further inside the terminal. "Obviously you hadn't been briefed on the hand-off of Lambert's body. Smith, if that's what his name was, showed proper identification. There was no reason to suspect the encounter was anything but routine. I don't think you could have handled it any differently."

An official waited for her a dozen steps further into the terminal. "Miss Moore? Mr. Madison asked me to meet you." He nodded toward Rachel's carry-on bag. "Do you have anything to declare?"

"What? No. No," Rachel said, in a distracted voice.

"Then you're free to go."

"I . . . I have to make a call first," Rachel said.

The official said, "Follow me. There's a meeting room down here you can use."

Once they were inside the room, Josh thanked the man and closed the door behind them. Rachel took one of the swivel chairs arranged around an oval table and pulled out her cell phone. "I have the number of the satellite phone Jerry Lang carries."

As she punched in the numbers, Josh asked, "Who's Jerry Lang?"

"The head of the Secret Service detail assigned to guard the former president," Rachel said. "He's—" She cocked her head. "Jerry, this is Rachel Moore. I need to speak to Mr. Madison."

She listened for a moment. "I see. Well, please ask him to call me back at this number ASAP. It's urgent." She read off her cell number and ended the conversation. "He'll get back to me in a few minutes."

After a moment's silence, Rachel asked, "Should we notify the police?"

"I suppose," Josh said. "I guess stealing a body is a crime. Probably Agent Lang or someone on Mr. Madison's staff will know. I suggest you let them take care of that." He motioned her to take a seat. "In the meantime, I know you're concerned about what just happened, but it's not your fault."

"That's what Mr. Madison said about Dr. Lambert's death, but I still felt bad that none of the medical workers on the trip could save him," Rachel said.

The ring of her cell phone interrupted her. "Mr. Madison? This is Rachel. Something terrible has happened. It looks as though someone has stolen Dr. Lambert's body."

Rachel sketched the details of the bogus mortuary pickup, then listened for a moment. "I see. Thank you. I'm really sorry—"

Josh couldn't hear the other side of the conversation, but obviously it was designed to help settle Rachel. Finally, she said, "I see. Yes, I'll be here. And I'll give Josh the message."

"So?" Josh asked.

"Agent Lang will contact the Dallas Police. I'm to wait here for them. And I have a message for you."

"For me?"

"Yes. When I left, Mr. Madison told me he wanted to meet with you as soon as he got back." Rachel frowned. "Now he's changed his plans. The rest of the group will be returning to the U.S. in a few more days, but he's arriving tomorrow. And he said it's extremely important that you meet his plane."

◆

"Are you okay this morning," Josh asked when Rachel answered her phone.

"I didn't get much rest, but it's good to be home. I haven't heard from the police yet about Dr. Lambert's body."

"I'm afraid that may take a while," Josh said. "I need to meet Mr. Madison's plane this afternoon, but I can come over this morning if you'd like. I don't have to go into the clinic."

The silence stretched far too long. Finally, Rachel said, "Josh, please don't take this the wrong way, but I'm still processing all that's happened. Why don't you call me after your meeting with Mr. Madison?"

Josh spent the morning catching up on reading journal articles he'd brought home for that purpose and then neglected. He wasn't hungry, but forced himself to eat part of a sandwich for lunch. The day seemed to drag, but at last it was time to leave for the airport.

At Love Field, Josh discovered that access to the former president required being cleared past a number of checkpoints, even if your presence had been requested. "I'm supposed to meet Mr. Madison's plane," Josh said for what seemed like the hundredth time. This time he was speaking to a security guard at a door leading to the tarmac. Through the windows that flanked the doors Josh saw private planes sitting in staggered rows like rank upon rank of soldiers awaiting orders. Several hundred yards away he could barely discern the runway on which Madison's plane would land.

The guard consulted a clipboard. "I don't see your name."

"Mr. Madison's staff was supposed to—"

"Hang on," the guard said. "Here it is. It was added at the bottom of the list."

"Thank you," Josh said. "Shall I wait here?"

"In there with the others." The guard inclined his head toward a nearby room where several men and women sat waiting. All but one of them were studying their smart phones, scrolling through messages and posts as though the fate of the free world depended on their up-to-date knowledge. The one exception was a man who sat staring quietly into space.

The solitary individual was a husky middle-aged man whose off-the-rack medium brown suit did little to conceal the slight bulge under his left armpit. His thinning hair, mainly brown with some gray at the temples, was combed across his scalp in what was apparently an attempt to cover a bald spot. The man's thick-soled, brown lace-up shoes were scuffed and slightly run-down at the heels. Josh recognized him as the detective to whom Rachel had talked last evening at the airport—a common name, what was it? Williams? West? Warren. That was it—Detective Stan Warren.

"Mind if I take this seat?" Josh asked.

"Suit yourself," the detective said, with no hint of recognition.

"We met last night." Josh offered his hand. "I'm Dr. Josh Pearson. I was with the nurse, Rachel Moore, who reported the . . . whatever you call it when someone steals a body."

"Oh, yeah. I'm not sure what the legal term is, but I call it body snatching, and we're investigating it. I've heard lawyers called ambulance chasers, but I've never before heard of crooks being hearse chasers." Warren displayed a brief, crooked grin.

The detective reached into his pocket, pulled out a crumpled pack of gum, and offered it to Josh, who declined. "Trying to quit smoking," Warren said. "I go through these things faster than I ever smoked cigarettes. But they don't cause cancer." He shoved a stick of gum into his mouth and returned the pack to his coat pocket.

The security guard stuck his head into the room and said, "The plane has just arrived."

Warren pushed to his feet. "Well, I've got to report our progress—or, more accurately, our lack of progress—and then get back to work." He looked toward the men and women who'd been waiting. "Madison will have to speak to these reporters after he deplanes." He pushed his sleeve back and consulted his watch. "You've probably got half an hour to wait. See you."

Josh followed Warren out of the room where they'd been waiting. He stood at the window and watched as the former president appeared in the open doorway of the private jet. Madison looked almost like the pictures Josh had seen of him—a tall, silver-haired man, usually with a faint grin on his face, the perfect image of a kind grandfather or a respected political figure. The main difference was that today the grin was absent. Instead, Madison's features were fixed in a somber countenance. It was a sad day, and his demeanor reflected it.

Detective Warren met Madison at the foot of the jet's stairs. The detective, with a few gestures including shrugs and uplifted palms, gave his explanation and, Josh figured, assured Mr. Madison that the police were on top of the disappearance of Ben Lambert's coffin. After Warren shook hands with Madison and started away, the ex-president walked briskly through the gathered reporters, trailing "no comments" behind him. When he spotted Josh, Madison detoured toward him. "You must be Dr. Pearson. Thanks for meeting me. Come on. We can talk in the limo."

A man in a navy blue suit, his red hair cut short, a look of utter concentration on his face, strode ahead of Josh and Madison toward a stretch limo idling nearby. Josh realized this was the man who'd preceded Madison through the crowd of reporters, parting them like Moses at the Red Sea. He opened the passenger door, stuck his head inside, and looked around. He did the same for the back of the limousine. Then he stood back and motioned for the two passengers to enter. Once they were inside, the man climbed into the front seat and the car pulled away.

"Who's that?" Josh asked, indicating the red-haired man who now sat in the passenger seat of the limo.

"That's Jerry . . . Agent Jerry Lang. He's the head of my Secret Service detail. I'd better introduce you since you'll probably be seeing a lot more of him." Madison leaned forward and tapped on the glass partition separating him from the front seat. When it slid back, he said, "Jerry, this is Dr. Josh Pearson. He'll be taking over as my personal physician."

Lang extended his hand across the seat. "Doctor, good to meet you. Can we come by your office tomorrow and dispose of a few formalities before you see Mr. Madison—things we need to know about you and vice-versa?"

"Sure. Shall I—"

"We'll make the arrangements. Don't worry." And Lang slid the panel closed.

"Things moving a bit too fast for you?" Madison smiled. "Get used to it. What Jerry can't arrange, Karen can."

"Karen?"

"Karen Marks. She was my chief of staff when I was in the White House, and she followed me into retirement . . . although neither of us seems to have slowed down much."

"Was she on this flight with you?" Josh asked.

"No, she'll be coming back later. I've returned early because of recent events. And that's why I wanted you to meet my plane."

Josh decided he might as well ask the question that had been foremost in his mind since talking with Rachel last night. "Sir, why do you need to see me so urgently?"

Madison looked up to make certain the partition separating them from the driver and Lang was closed. Then he leaned close to Josh and said in a soft voice, "Because I think someone is trying to kill me. And I'll need your help to make certain they don't succeed."

◆

Rachel studied her reflection in the mirror in the front hall of her apartment. She wondered if there was any truth in the old wives' tale about people turning gray overnight. If so, she was an ideal candidate to have at least a few strands show up. She fluffed her short hairdo and saw no light strands among the brown ones—not yet, at least. Her hazel eyes were still a bit red rimmed, but she could fix that with a few drops of Visine. As for the dark circles under them . . . well, maybe a good night's rest would help. Last night had been full of nightmares. She hoped tonight would be better.

Rachel was going over the events of the past several days in her mind when her doorbell rang. Through the frosted glass panel beside the door, she could see a familiar outline of a tall man with light hair—Josh was here. Last night she hadn't felt like doing anything but relaxing in a hot bath and trying to put recent events out of her mind. Today, she was ready to lay out the story in detail to see if her fears were reasonable or simply the product of an overactive imagination.

Rachel opened the door for Josh. "I'm glad to see you."

"Me, too," he said. Still standing in the open doorway, he enfolded her in an embrace that seemed to last forever. He bent down to kiss her, and without thinking she responded. When she realized what she was doing, she pulled back. *I let myself get carried away at the airport. I've got to be careful—certainly until Josh knows the whole story.*

She took Josh by the hand and they walked together into the living room.

"I don't ever want you to be gone like that again," Josh said.

"And I don't want to experience anything like what I've been through."

As though by common consent, they moved to the couch and sat side by side. "I've had an interesting and sort of unnerving conversation with Mr. Madison," Josh said.

"Tell me about it."

He hitched himself closer and put his arm around her. "He thinks someone is trying to kill him. It seems that, although he's no longer in office, he wields a great deal of influence, both here and abroad. There are people who don't want him to exercise that influence. And in the past several years he's done things that made a number of people hate him—some apparently enough to try to kill him."

Rachel coughed. "Excuse me." She took a few deep breaths. "In other countries?"

Josh shook his head. "Not only in other countries."

Rachel thought about that. "You mean—"

"Yes, there are people in the U.S., as well as throughout the world, who'd like to see David Madison out of the picture . . . totally."

"That's probably true of all former presidents," Rachel said.

"I gather it's truer of Mr. Madison than most of the previous ones," Josh replied.

He went on to explain that Madison had learned of a couple of projected attempts on his life that had never come to fruition. "The latest was a plan to assassinate him while he was making a public appearance. The local police nipped that in the bud. There have also been rumored attempts to infect him with anthrax or something equally deadly. I think that's why he feels so dependent on his personal physician."

Rachel paused to cough again and clear her throat. "And since Dr. Lambert is dead, now that responsibility is yours."

"I guess," Josh said. "One more thing I probably should share with you. Madison thinks someone may have killed Dr. Lambert."

"Josh, that man had a heart attack. He was in the bathroom just off the room at the church where we were eating lunch. We heard him fall. I helped give him CPR."

"I'm going to have to do some research, but as I recall, there are drugs that can cause a death that's clinically indistinguishable from a heart attack. And remember, Ben's body disappeared from the airport."

"What—"

"Normally an autopsy would confirm whether Ben died of natural causes," Josh said. "But now, there's no body. That means no autopsy."

The waiter moved silently away, leaving Josh and Rachel alone in a quiet corner of the restaurant. Josh reached across the table and put his hand atop Rachel's. He'd planned this evening since the time Rachel left. Now it was finally here.

After the limo had delivered Josh and Madison to the former president's home, Lang asked another agent to drive the doctor back to Love Field for his car. By the time he'd made it to Rachel's apartment and told her about his meeting with the former president, it was getting late. She'd offered—almost insisted—that she could make dinner for them, but Josh wouldn't hear of it. "I want to take you out." So now, they were sitting here in the back of the almost deserted restaurant.

"Your hand is shaking," Josh said. "Is something wrong?"

"I . . . I need to tell you about something that happened on the trip." Rachel coughed, then took a sip of water. "And it may fit in with what President Madison told you earlier this evening."

Josh felt as though things were coming at him faster than he could process them, but he composed his features as best he could and said, "Sure, let's hear it."

Rachel picked up her water glass but put it down without drinking. "It was quite a thrill accompanying Mr. Madison on a trip like this. More than that, he actually seemed to value my opinion and that of the other medical people in the group. We talked about the location for the clinic he wanted to build— about the size of facilities, staffing, all the things you'd expect."

"Was this in a primitive area?" Josh asked.

"Yes and no," Rachel said. "It was a small town with perhaps seven hundred people in it and another two hundred or so living in the countryside around it, but the nearest medical facility was about fifty kilometers away."

Josh automatically translated the distance: approximately thirty miles. "I'm assuming the Madison Foundation was going to fund this. Was there opposition?"

"No overt signs of any. But President Madison told us he'd heard rumblings. I asked him about details, but he didn't want to go into them."

"But the trip was going along okay—"

"I'll give you an example. We were quartered in the homes of members of a local church. The women cooked our meals, and we ate them together at the church. One day Mr. Madison complained of stomach pains after a couple of bites. He left the table, and Dr. Lambert gave him some medication for his symptoms. At the time I figured it was just a bug, although no one else had any trouble."

"That doesn't mean much," Josh said.

"One of the women serving us scraped the remains off all our plates into a bowl she left outside the kitchen door to feed some of the dogs that hung around the church." She stifled a cough. "The next morning, someone in our group found one of the dogs about sixty yards away from the church . . . dead."

"Okay, that's troubling. What did Lang do?"

"Lang was concerned, but Mr. Madison dismissed it as coincidence, and I guess it could have been. The dogs were wild, and I take it they had a sketchy existence. Anyway, Madison didn't want to make a fuss. But two days later, Dr. Lambert, Mr. Madison, and I were looking at a proposed site for the new clinic when a woman in a long dress with a scarf over her head and a cloth covering the lower half of her face ran into the room where we were. Mr. Madison asked her in Spanish if he could help her. Without a word, she drew what looked like a flask full of yellow liquid from the folds of her dress and showered us with the contents. Then, still without a word, she ran out."

"Strange, but—"

"No, it doesn't end there," Rachel said. "The next day each of us had a raw throat and mild cough. At first, we attributed that to irritation from the environment we were in."

"When was this?"

"The exposure—and I think that's what it was—took place five days ago. Two days ago Ben Lambert died of what we thought was a heart attack. That's pretty well occupied our thoughts and actions since. Did Mr. Madison say anything to you tonight about coming back with respiratory symptoms?"

"He asked me to see him in my office tomorrow, but he led me to believe it would only be a routine, get-acquainted visit."

Rachel held her napkin to her mouth to smother a violent cough. When she stopped, she said to Josh, "I think you'd better check him over pretty carefully." She coughed again. "And maybe someone should have a look at me as well."

3

Jerry Lang spoke softly, but the state-of-the-art two-way radio picked up his voice loud and clear. "Cowboy is leaving his house now. ETA to Preston Medical Clinic is 0930."

"Roger that."

"Do we always have to go through that Dick Tracy wrist radio stuff?" David Madison asked from the backseat of the town car. The question was the same one he always asked, and his grin took any possible sting out of the words.

Lang turned from his position in the front seat. "Sir, you're at liberty to cancel your Secret Service protection at any time, but if I were you, I'd speak with Mrs. Madison before doing anything that rash."

"I know, I know," Madison said. He coughed and cleared his throat. "But you'd think, after a couple of years out of office, I wouldn't be worth much to any terrorist who's out to kidnap me."

Lang didn't answer. He kept his eyes moving, quartering the area as the car rolled through the streets of Dallas. This assignment to guard the former President might not be as glamorous as his former post at the White House, but he was determined to carry it out to the best of his ability.

His wife—actually, his ex-wife—had told him repeatedly he had to stop making the Secret Service his life, but it was hard to do, especially after that incident at 1600 Pennsylvania Avenue. Shortly after that, he got this assignment to follow Madison into retirement. Say what you will, despite his boss's calling it a lateral transfer, in Lang's mind it had been a demotion. Now he was determined to prove to everyone he was still at the top of his game.

The car pulled to a stop in the circular drive of the four-story white stone building that housed the cadre of doctors—both generalists and specialists—that made up the Preston Medical Clinic. An agent hurried from the area of the front door and assisted Madison from the car.

"I think I'll be safe in here, fellows," Madison said as he strode through the sliding glass doors.

Lang fell in beside him. "Agent Gilmore there has already done the sweep of the clinic building. I spent the morning checking out Dr. Pearson. I'll hang out in the waiting room while you're in there with him. Give me a heads-up when you're ready to leave, and I'll have the car pulled around."

◆

Dr. Josh Pearson shrugged into a crisply starched white coat. He wasn't sure why he'd changed before seeing this patient. After all, David Madison put on his pants one leg at a time. Maybe the difference was that the pants were part of a suit worn by a man who was the immediate past president of the United States.

Josh tapped on the exam room door before opening it. "Good morning, Mr. President."

Madison was perched on the edge of the examining table, a faint smile on his face. He'd shed his suit coat, which hung on the back of the exam room door, a tie peeking out of one pocket. The collar of his dress shirt was open.

"I've reviewed your chart, so let's get right to your present status. Last night you said some things were bothering you. I'd like to hear more about them." Josh pulled out a rolling stool and sat. "While you're telling me, would you please slip out of your shirt?"

Madison unbuttoned his shirt and shrugged out of it. "Let's drop that 'Mr. President' stuff at the door if we can. In here, I'm David . . . or, if you prefer, Mr. Madison. Treat me like any other patient. Okay?"

Josh knew that, despite Madison's attempts to put him at ease, he'd always be aware of this man's status, of what he'd been, and what he'd done. But he appreciated the gesture. "I'm flattered, Mr. . . . Madison. Now, how can I help you?"

Madison coughed. "This has to stay between us."

"Everything you tell me is in confidence. Your records are doubly encrypted, and I'm the only one with access to them."

Madison went on to relate the scene Rachel had described to Josh the night before. "Rachel's pretty good at hiding things, but I had a hunch she was getting sick about the time they were loading Ben Lambert's coffin on the private jet for the return to Dallas."

"I can tell you that Rachel related this same story to me last night. One of the other clinic doctors is examining her this morning. And, before you ask, I'm sure we can trust Dr. Neeves to be discreet." Josh rolled his stool forward a bit. "Now let's talk about you. After that incident, what kind of symptoms have you developed?"

"I didn't say I had symptoms," Madison said. He coughed again. "Well, I might have picked up a little respiratory infection while I was gone."

"I noticed that. You have to be honest with me."

"Even if it's nothing serious?" Madison asked.

"Yes. Because you're used to being invulnerable. I suspect chiefs of state, even those no longer in the limelight, feel that way." When Madison started to speak, Josh stopped him with an upraised hand. "Don't worry. It's the same with doctors."

Madison gave a wry grin. "You got me. All right. I had a raw throat a few days ago—probably two days after the incident with the native woman. A day or two later I developed a mild cough. I still have it. And I might have a bit of a fever."

Josh nodded. "Well, let's have a look at you." When he'd finished, he stowed his stethoscope in the pocket of his lab coat. "I'm going to take a swab from your throat and ask our lab to culture the material and also to make a slide, stain it, and look for bacteria. I want to get a chest X-ray and some blood work. The nurse will assist you and bring you back here when you're done."

"What do you think?"

"It may be nothing more than a routine viral or bacterial respiratory infection, but I want to be certain." He smiled.

"Sounds like you're being extra thorough, but you're the doctor," Madison said. "I can see why Ben Lambert thought so highly of you."

As Josh exited the exam room, he wondered if that confidence was misplaced. Was he overreacting? He hoped not. But the incident with the woman flinging liquid at Madison troubled him. It could be that she was just someone angry with the Americans who'd come to their small town. But perhaps there was more to it than that.

Meanwhile, he wanted to double-check something in Madison's medical records. And maybe he could catch Allison Neeves and see what she thought about Rachel.

He'd asked Allison to see Rachel because, of the half-dozen internal medicine specialists at Preston Medical Clinic, she was probably the sharpest. Besides, she was female and something told Josh that Rachel might prefer a doctor of the same sex.

He and Allison had done their residency at different facilities, so much of what he knew about her he'd learned after she came to Preston Medical Clinic. Allison had always been hesitant to reveal details of her personal life, but Josh finally learned that she'd married during her first year in medical school. However, she and her husband had been divorced about the time of her graduation. Allison's natural beauty plus her bare ring finger had quickly made her a target for most of the single doctors at the clinic as well as a couple of the married ones. She'd gently rebuffed these approaches, some more gently than others, but had never been anything but cordial to Josh.

Allison was closing the door to the exam room when Josh rounded the corner heading down the hall toward her. She ran her fingers through her short blonde hair and smiled at him. "Josh, I was going to see if I could find you, but you found me first."

Josh nodded. "I'm concerned about Rachel."

"I saw her a few minutes ago. Now she's gone for some lab work and a chest film."

"And . . ."

"My philosophy is to expect the common diagnoses but check for the worst-case scenarios, too. That's what I'm doing here."

A nurse, escorting an older woman, came down the hall toward them. Josh was itching to continue his conversation, but waited until they passed by and entered one of the several exam rooms that lined the hall. Then he said, "Rachel and President Madison were on the same trip to South America. I presume she told you about the incident—"

"With the woman who showered them with an unknown liquid? Yes. Ordinarily, I might not be too concerned, but when I look in her throat—"

"You see not just redness but a few tiny patches of exudate. Right?"

Allison nodded. "And she has cervical lymph nodes that are more prominent than you'd see with a run-of-the-mill pharyngitis. So I'm getting a throat culture and smear."

Josh grimaced. "I'm doing the same thing. And while we wait, I'm going to go over the list of immunizations the group received again."

As Josh walked away, he tried to ignore the ominous thought that kept popping up. Surely this wasn't— No, it couldn't be.

◆

Josh sat before the computer in his office and scrolled through David Madison's medical records until he came to the visit before the former president left for his South American trip. Madison had undergone a complete physical, even though his previous one had been only nine months earlier. That included a cardiac stress test, which he passed with flying colors. Josh pulled a notepad toward him and jotted down a reminder to recheck Ben Lambert's cardiograms. Maybe there'd been something there that had been missed.

What about immunizations? Before the trip, Madison had received multiple immunizations, including a tetanus-diphtheria booster and preventive shots against hepatitis A, typhoid, and yellow fever. That made what Josh was concerned about less likely, but then again, no immunization is 100 percent effective. And there was always the possibility of a rare type of infection, not covered in the routine spectrum of immunization. He'd double check that—another note to himself.

Dr. Ben Lambert hadn't provided the ex-president with any prophylactic antibiotics at the time of that visit, but since Lambert was part of the group that would be traveling, he might have planned to give those out to everyone at the time of departure or even while on the plane. Josh would have to look into that. Rachel or Madison should be able to tell him. He scratched out another reminder.

His intercom buzzed. Josh pulled his eyes away from the screen long enough to hit the button. "Yes?"

"Doctor, Ethan Grant at the lab just called. He's made a smear of the throat swab you took and thinks perhaps you should look at it yourself."

"Tell him I'll be right there," Josh said. For reasons of security, the specimen had been sent with a code instead of a name, but he figured it wouldn't take long for word to get around that it belonged to David Madison. Josh closed down the open medical record on his computer—he'd have to get used to the extra layers of security in place for this special patient—and headed out the door of his office.

In a few moments, he was seated before a binocular microscope in the lab with Ethan Grant, the chief lab tech in the bacteriology section, standing behind him. Grant rubbed his shaved head nervously. "I think you'll see what I mean," he said.

Josh focused the microscope on the glass slide prepared from a swab from David Madison's throat. There was the usual trash: mucosal cells, white blood cells, but in among it all were dark rods. Their cell walls had absorbed the Gram stain—that is, they were Gram positive—and the organisms were elongated, with a few showing the characteristic clubbing at one end that confirmed the diagnosis Josh had feared.

"This is the best slide you have?" he asked Grant. He knew it was, but he had to ask.

"I made three, and they're all like that." Grant leaned closer and almost whispered. "Doctor, I know who your patient is, but don't worry. I'll keep it quiet. I also know that Dr. Neeves is seeing Rachel Moore this morning. We got her throat swab at almost the same time as this one came in."

"And?"

"It shows the same thing. The morphology isn't quite typical, but I've seen the real thing, and it's my opinion that both these patients are infected with a variant of *Corynebacterium*."

Josh nodded silently. The cultures would take days to grow out. Should he wait for them, or treat for something of which he wasn't quite sure?

It had been years since Josh heard or read the information. Although he, like most doctors, never expected to see a case of this infection in their lifetime, he knew what came next. If the smear and clinical picture fit, start treatment. Better to be safe and wrong than take a chance by waiting for a confirmatory culture. Both he and Allison would need to hospitalize their patients and begin treatment for diphtheria.

◆

Jerry Lang felt the familiar vibration of his cell phone. Was Madison ready for his car? No, the caller ID showed an unfamiliar number.

The agent rose from his seat in the waiting room of the Preston Medical Clinic and moved toward the door, answering as he went.

"Mr. Lang, this is Vernon Wells with Sparkman Hillcrest."

"Beg your pardon?"

"Sparkman Hillcrest Funeral Directors."

"Oh, yes. Sorry. At first the name didn't click." Lang stepped through the door and moved toward the end of the circular driveway, angling away from a middle-aged man helping an older woman out of a Lexus parked there. "How can I help you?"

"I . . . I really don't know what's going on, but since you're the one that originally asked us to pick up Dr. Lambert's body at Love Field, I thought I should call you."

"Have the police found Dr. Lambert's body?" Lang wished he still smoked. This would be an ideal time for one, as he stood in the sunshine doing what his job often entailed—waiting.

"No, the police haven't called us. But we have Dr. Lambert's body. At least, I think we do."

"Explain that."

"This morning I found a wrapped package on our doorstep. It was simply addressed to 'Funeral Directors'—nothing else."

"And—" Lang wished Wells would hurry, but evidently one of the characteristics of a funeral director was the delivery of every word slowly and carefully.

"And, given the mysterious nature of the package, we called the police."

"Mr. Wells, can you skip to the end of this story? I'm waiting for Mr. Madison and don't want to miss him."

"Oh, yes, of course. Well, the police bomb squad unwrapped the package and opened the box. Inside was a plastic container containing what appeared to be cremated human remains. Taped to it was a card with one computer-printed word: 'Sorry.' There was also a small plastic bag with a watch, a wedding ring, and a wallet."

Lang knew where this was going, and he didn't like it. "So—"

"We have . . . that is, I think Dr. Lambert's body has been cremated and delivered to us."

"Thank you, Mr. Wells. Hang on to the material, and keep this information to yourself. I'll get back to you." Lang ended the call and headed back toward the waiting room, but before he could get the instrument into his pocket, it vibrated once more. Was this a call from the police, asking how to proceed with the disappearing/reappearing body of Madison's personal physician?

No, caller ID indicated this was from Josh Pearson. "Yes, doctor?"

"I'm afraid I have some bad news about Mr. Madison."

Lang listened for a full minute, his mind racing to assimilate the meaning of this latest development. All thoughts of the hunt for Dr. Lambert's body were pushed aside. Now Lang and his colleagues had a new challenge. Then again, that's what his job was about, wasn't it? Meeting challenges.

4

I can't be in the hospital," David Madison said. Although he was clad in a skimpy exam gown and sitting in a treatment room on the edge of an examining table, the man still managed to exude both authority and dignity. "I don't feel that sick. Can't you just put me on some medications and look in on me every day or two?"

Josh had known this might be coming. Now here it was, on his first day as physician to a former president. "Mr. President." Seeing Madison's lips open, he started again. "Mr. Madison, you've been in charge of the most powerful nation on earth. You've had to make decisions that involved millions of people. And most of us feel you made the right ones. But here, in this situation, in this circumstance, you've put your trust in me, effectively saying I'm the person most qualified to make decisions involving your health. Well, my decision is that you should be hospitalized."

"So what's the treatment?" Madison asked. "IV antibiotics?"

"Actually, there are a couple of antibiotics, penicillin and erythromycin, that are effective against diphtheria. Either can be given by injection or by mouth."

"Then why can't you give me some pills and send me home?"

"We'll give you an antibiotic, but the treatment of choice is antitoxin, and there's not a lot of it around. I have to locate some and start you on it." *And Rachel . . . I can't forget Rachel.* "And we need to watch you carefully."

"Why?"

Josh studied Madison's face, but the man seemed calm enough. Then again, what would you expect from a former president? Crisis? Deal with it. *Okay, here comes the rest of the story.* "The main reason to keep you in the hospital is that we need to be ready to do emergency surgery to open your windpipe if we can't halt the progress of the disease. You could die of airway obstruction."

Madison was silent, but Josh could tell he'd succeeded in shaking the man. When the ex-president spoke again, it was in a softer voice. "Okay. You're the doctor. Call the CDC or whoever you need to and get the ball rolling to locate some antitoxin." Madison was moving ahead, once more the man in charge. "And you'd better call Jerry Lang and make him a part of the planning. At hospitals like Bethesda where they take care of presidents and high-profile patients every day, they're set up for this kind of stuff. I'm not sure you know what you're letting yourself in for."

I have an idea . . . and it won't be any picnic . . . especially if the response to treatment doesn't go well.

❖

Allison Neeves wasn't certain whether her job was easier or harder than the one Josh Pearson faced. It was never easy to give a patient the news that they had a serious illness and would have to be hospitalized. But what if the patient was in the health care field? What if they could read between the lines and imagine the worst?

Before she could tap on the exam room door, Allison was brought up short by Josh's voice behind her. "Allison, hang on a moment."

She watched Josh hurry down the hall. When he reached her, she said, "I was about to give Rachel the news."

"Would you rather I do it?" Josh asked.

Allison took a deep breath. Technically, Josh outranked her, since he'd been at the clinic a year longer, but for practical purposes they were equals professionally. If this was going to be a problem, it was better to settle it now. "Josh, Rachel is your girlfriend—from what I've seen the past few months, probably even more than that—but that's the very reason you shouldn't be her treating physician. I am. And I'll tell her."

She saw him absorb this, accepting the fact, but uncomfortable with the implications. "Look, you can see her as soon as I've told her our findings," Allison said. "And we'll consult with each other on treatment. But you've got to take a step back. Trying to manage her treatment would be the worst possible thing you could do."

"Okay," Josh said. "I'm getting ready to hospitalize Mr. Madison. I presume we're both thinking the same treatment: isolation, antibiotics, diphtheria antitoxin just as soon as I can get it, tracheotomy tray at the bedside."

"Right," Allison said. "We can cross-check each other's orders in case we forget something." She put one hand on the treatment room doorknob. "Now get on the phone and find some antitoxin while I tell Rachel what's going on."

❖

David Madison might be an ex-president, but he didn't think he was displaying much gravitas sitting on the end of the exam table. He smiled when he realized the wide-open back of his patient gown was displaying something, but it wasn't dignity and seriousness. Nevertheless, sitting in the Oval Office for eight years had taught him to take control of any situation, and even though he was forced to accept Josh Pearson's decisions about his treatment, he could at least control his environment while hospitalized.

"We're getting things lined up, sir," Jerry Lang said. "You'll be in a private room, and there'll be an agent outside your door at all times. Only a limited number of medical personnel will have access to you."

"I presume I'm being registered under a false name."

"Woodrow Wilson."

"Very funny. Does my wife know yet?"

"I just got off the phone with her," Lang said. "She wanted to cancel her luncheon speaking engagement, but I convinced her it would be best for her to go ahead with it before coming to the hospital. I'd like for her to continue her normal activities as much as possible. It will keep the media from suspecting anything."

"Good. Who on my staff besides you knows about this? The more people who are in the loop—"

"Sir, only the agents, your wife, and Karen Marks know right now."

Madison frowned. "How does my administrative aide know? She's still in South America."

"She called me a few minutes ago. Somehow, she found out you were ill, so she's flying home today."

"And the rest of the group?"

"They'll arrive back this weekend, on schedule." Lang held up one finger. "But there's something else you need to know. Right before Karen called, I got a phone call from the funeral directors we asked to pick up Dr. Lambert's body. It's reappeared."

"Maybe you'd better explain that."

"It seems that someone left it on their doorstep this morning."

Madison had a mental picture of a casket, or even worse, a body on a gurney deposited on the porch of a funeral home. "I beg your pardon?"

"Actually, what they got was a box with cremated remains, plus Dr. Lambert's personal effects."

"That's all?"

"That and a note that said simply, 'Sorry.'"

Madison thought about what this latest development meant. Maybe it was all a big mistake, but maybe it was deliberate. The first thing that came to mind was that cremated remains couldn't be autopsied. He'd have to check, but he doubted they could even be tested for DNA to confirm an identity. That brought to mind a whole new series of questions.

Well, it looked as though he was going to have a bit of time to think those questions through in the next few days.

◆

Rachel had never been to this hospital before. She'd graduated from a nursing program in Houston and fully expected to be there for years. Then her fiancé dumped her, her life fell apart, and she jumped at the opportunity to take a position at Zale Lipshy University Hospital in Dallas. Working with faculty physicians from Southwestern Medical Center seemed perfect for her. And it had been, until this happened. Now she found herself in the unfamiliar territory of Prestonwood Hospital, a patient rather than a caregiver. How quickly things could change.

Of course, if she'd stayed in Houston she'd never have met Josh, and that would have been tragic. It was becoming clear to her that he was the man she'd like to spend the rest of her life with. She thought Josh felt the same—actually, she'd expected him to tell her that when she got back from this trip, but—

A tap at the door of her hospital room interrupted her thoughts. She looked up, expecting another nurse or maybe a lab tech. Instead, she saw Josh. At least, she thought it was Josh. A surgical mask covered the lower part of his face. He wore a disposable gown, and thin purple gloves covered his hands.

"Rachel." His voice was slightly muffled by the disposable mask he wore. He advanced to her bedside and covered her hand with his own, careful not to disturb the IV running into the back of it. "I'm so very sorry this happened to you."

Rachel shook her head. "Don't worry about me. How's Mr. Madison?"

"Doing okay." Although his mask hid his features, Josh's eyes told her more than his words.

"Something's wrong. Tell me."

"Actually, his illness doesn't seem quite as pronounced as yours. But don't worry. I'm going to get hold of some diphtheria antitoxin. We may be able to start treating you both with it as soon as tomorrow."

"What about antibiotics? Am I getting those?"

Josh nodded. "You are, but diphtheria is so rare now that the latest study on which ones work best was done almost twenty years ago. Children now get diphtheria-pertussis-tetanus shots, and many adults get a diphtheria-tetanus booster periodically, usually when they have a tetanus scare. When patients do turn up with the infection, we depend on diphtheria antitoxin."

Rachel shook her head. "That's something I don't understand. I got a DT booster before the trip. Matter of fact, I got it here. Dr. Lambert's nurse had just given Mr. Madison his shot, so she still had the bottle of vaccine out. Why did we get sick?"

"That's one of the reasons I wish Ben Lambert were still alive," Josh said. "I could question him about that." He frowned. "Did you get much of a reaction to your shot?"

"Now that you mention it, no. And usually I get a red, sore arm from almost any type of immunization."

"We've ordered a test for immunity against diphtheria on both you and Madison."

"To answer the question of whether the shot gave me protection?"

"Not really. An elevated diphtheria antibody titer could be due to either your recent immunization or to a current infection."

Rachel started to ask Josh why he ordered the test, then she got it. There was one more possibility. If the titer was very low, she hadn't been immunized, but what she had wasn't really diphtheria—and the problem got even more complex.

"Josh," she asked. "How about you? When I arrived, you hugged and kissed me. You did it again yesterday, although I tried to keep my distance. Why aren't you taking precautions?"

"About six months ago, I stepped on a nail while working at a Habitat for Humanity project. I asked Nell, my nurse, to give me a diphtheria-tetanus booster, and I had a marked local reaction to it. I'm guessing I have plenty of antibodies right now." He touched the crook of his left arm. "I had an antibody level drawn earlier today, but I think I'm pretty well protected. Besides," he added, "I've already started prophylactic antibiotic therapy with erythromycin. I'll be fine."

Rachel realized Josh was gambling a bit, but she also knew he wasn't going to go into isolation right now . . . that wasn't in keeping with his nature. In his mind, as in that of so many doctors, he couldn't get sick—he was invulnerable. She looked at him and said so softly that Josh probably didn't even hear it, "I hope you are."

Karen Marks climbed into the rear seat of the limo and had her phone out even before the trunk slammed shut on the suitcases her escort had shepherded through customs. It was amazing how much power David Madison's name carried. Although it was more than two years since he'd sat behind the desk in the Oval Office, he still had clout.

Karen punched in a speed-dial number. Before it could produce a ring, the driver turned toward her and asked, "Where to, Miss Marks?"

"I'll tell you in a moment. In the meantime, just sit here and—" She signaled for him to close the soundproof glass partition, and at the same time said, "Jerry? Karen Marks. I'm on the ground in Dallas. Give me a sitrep."

She'd never dropped the habit of using abbreviations that were standard procedure in government. Lang would know she meant "situation report." And he'd give it concisely, without added verbiage. Given her choice, she preferred to deal with people who had worked in the White House. Barring that, at least let them have government experience. Those people were familiar with the chain of command, and most of them knew when to keep their mouths shut. She missed that in post-government life.

As she expected, the report Lang gave her was short and to the point. When he'd stopped speaking, she said, "So, who knows Madison's sick and in the hospital?"

"I talked with Madison's wife, of course, and she'll be here later today. Other than that, not many people know. The doctors treating Madison and Rachel Moore, a few nurses, maybe one or two other medical personnel—all vetted by me and all sworn to secrecy."

"So what can I do?"

"You can help with a problem with Dr. Lambert's body," Lang said.

Karen closed her eyes in order to concentrate as he told her about the cremated remains that had turned up. "Have you been able to keep this information quiet so far?"

"I've told the president about it, but so far no one else knows except the funeral director who called me. I haven't even had time to notify the police. And I don't know what we're going to do about Mrs. Lambert."

There was always something, wasn't there? Then again, Karen knew that was what she did. Now she'd handle this problem the way she had done so many others. She sighed into the receiver, not caring if Jerry heard it. "You keep things buttoned up there at the hospital. I'll take care of this. Give me the name and address."

"Are you—"

"Jerry, have I ever let you or the president down? You'll hear from me soon."

Karen closed the phone and tapped on the glass partition. "I need to make a phone call. While I'm doing that, take me to this address." She gave him one in the University Park area. Before the car was moving, she had her phone open again and was dialing.

When David Madison was admitted to Prestonwood Hospital, not only were a number of security measures necessary, but accommodations for his family and his medical staff were put into place. One of those measures was the designation of a small office for the exclusive use of his physician.

Now Josh sat in that office, the door closed. He'd given strict orders that he wasn't to be disturbed. He had none of his material from his own office at the clinic at his disposal, but fortunately he had all he needed: a computer and a phone. He used the first to find a number, then the second to make the call to the Centers for Disease Control and Prevention . . . the CDC.

This was his first direct contact with this agency, although he'd heard about it since medical school. Josh hoped he would be able to navigate the labyrinth of departments without too much difficulty. Then again, it was a government agency.

After his call was transferred several times, Josh was finally connected with the appropriate duty officer. He identified himself and said, "I need enough diphtheria antitoxin to treat two patients."

"We don't get much call for that," the doctor on the other end said. "Let's talk about the indications for DAT treatment of patients."

Josh patiently provided information until at last he said, "Look! I'm a board-certified internal medicine specialist. I've examined the patient. I've looked at the slides. These people have airways that are at risk. Now, how soon can I get the DAT?"

"I'll have to check the database to locate it," the duty officer said. "Let me get back to you shortly."

Josh was caught on the horns of a dilemma. If he hid the identity of his patient, it might take a day, even a couple of days to get the antitoxin. On the other hand, he was certain David Madison wasn't anxious for the whole world to know the details of his illness. "Let me emphasize that this is a genuine medical emergency," Josh finally said. "I need that antitoxin today. ASAP. Stat. If necessary, I'm prepared to send a private jet to pick up the antitoxin and fly it back here."

"Sounds like either you or your patient have resources most of us don't."

Please don't let this guy throw a monkey wrench into the works just because he's envious. "I'm not at liberty to disclose the identity of the patients involved," Josh said. He hardened his voice. "I'm going to say this once more. This is a medical emergency. Give me your name and your direct number. I'm going to call you back in thirty minutes, and I want you to get me sufficient diphtheria antitoxin for two patients. Do you understand?"

After Josh hung up, he wondered if he'd handled the situation the right way. Should he have used Madison's name and invoked his influence? Maybe he should have checked with Jerry Lang before making the call. Josh reached for his cell phone, where he'd entered Lang's number. If Ben Lambert weren't dead . . . but he was, and Josh was on his own. *I guess I have a lot to learn about caring for an ex-president.*

Karen Marks exited the limousine as soon as the driver opened the door for her. "Wait here. I shouldn't be long," she said.

The neighborhood where they were wasn't in the same league as the estate where David and Mildred Madison lived, but it certainly wasn't a poor one, either.

The home was a rambling, one-story house in a nice neighborhood—not pretentious, not opulent. Probably bought it as soon as they could after Ben graduated from med school. If there were children, they were long since gone.

She squared her shoulders and rang the doorbell. Karen had done lots of difficult tasks for David Madison at all his stops in government service. It never got easier, but she'd learned that a direct approach was best. It was sort of like ripping off a bandage. Get it done and move on.

The woman who answered the door was probably in her mid-sixties. Her black hair was neatly combed and styled. She'd made no effort to hide the streaks of gray that ran randomly through it. The woman wore a simple black dress, and reading glasses with red horn-rimmed frames dangled from a chain around her neck.

"Yes?" the woman said.

"Mrs. Lambert?"

"Yes."

"I'm Karen Marks. I'm David Madison's administrative aide—sort of a chief of staff, I guess you'd say. May I come in? I need to give you some news about your husband."

The woman stepped back and gestured Karen into the house. "I don't know how much worse any news could be than that my husband is dead," she said. There was neither rancor nor self-pity in her voice. This was a woman who'd already shed her tears in private. Perhaps her husband's relationship with the ex-president had schooled her in facing the world in good times and bad.

"Is there somewhere we can sit and talk?" Karen asked.

Mrs. Lambert nodded and escorted Karen into a living room, where she took a side chair and Karen perched on the couch. "What have you come to tell me?" Mrs. Lambert asked.

"One of our party—a nurse who participated in the attempts to revive your husband—escorted his body home. After Mr. Lang, the head of the Secret Service detail, talked with you, he contacted Sparkman Hillcrest and arranged for a funeral director to meet the chartered aircraft and take charge of the body. But another hearse got there first."

"What are you saying?"

"Someone took your husband's body."

Other than a sharp intake of breath, Mrs. Lambert showed no emotion. "I called Sparkman Hillcrest this morning," she said. "They told me Ben's body wasn't ready for viewing and I should call tomorrow. I guess that's why."

"There's more," Karen said. "This morning, cremated remains were left on the doorstep of the funeral home, along with your husband's watch, wallet, and wedding ring."

Mrs. Lambert slowly shook her head. "Why would anyone—"

"My guess is there was a terrible error. For instance, the body these people expected to receive might have been someone who died of a highly communicable disease. Immediate cremation was called for and carried out. In the meantime, the police had been in contact with every funeral director in town, looking for your husband's body. When these people went through the personal effects that accompanied the body, they realized their error. It was too late to stop, so they did what they could. They delivered the cremains to the right funeral home with the personal effects and a note that said they were sorry."

Mrs. Lambert sat silent, shaking her head, her lips pursed. Then she said, "You said the personal effects were a wallet, a watch, and a wedding ring?"

"Yes. The wallet was your husband's, with identifying material inside. The watch had his name engraved on the back, apparently a gift of some kind. And the wedding ring bore his initials and yours inside it."

"What about his class ring?"

Karen shook her head. "All we have is what I've described."

Mrs. Lambert looked away. "Ben did his pre-med at Texas A&M. That senior ring was more precious to him than his wedding band. He never took it off." She fixed Karen with a steady gaze. "If there was no A&M senior ring with the personal effects, I can't believe that those cremated remains are those of my husband."

5

Karen climbed into the backseat of the limo and said, "Prestonwood Hospital. And close the partition, please."

She dialed Jerry Lang. "Okay, I broke the news to Mrs. Lambert."

"How did she take it?"

"We may have a problem. She insisted that if there was no Texas A&M class ring with the personal effects, she couldn't be certain the remains were those of her husband."

"So . . ."

"I told her the police would investigate further and get back to her. Can you take care of talking with them?"

"Sure," Lang said. "The detective in charge is a guy named Warren. I'll ask him to keep a lid on it for a few days."

"Have him contact the funeral director who has the cremains we think are Lambert's, and tell him to keep his mouth shut until he hears from us."

"Already did that when he called me," Lang said.

"Now what else?"

Lang's sigh came over the phone clearly. "I've got a situation here."

"Tell me about it." *I've been back in the U.S. for less than three hours and I'm already solving problems. Maybe one day David will realize how much I do for him.*

"President Madison's doctor needs diphtheria antitoxin to administer to both his patients. He's talked with the duty officer at the CDC and is due to call him back in a few minutes. Frankly, he's not sure whether to reveal Madison's identity. If he does, it may start a rumor about Madison's health. On the other hand, if he doesn't, he thinks he risks getting a runaround for what I understand is a vital treatment. He was about to ask Madison, but I suggested he wait until I talked with you."

"Do you have the name and number of the person he talked with?"

Karen jotted the information down on a small notebook she pulled from her purse. "Tell the doctor I'll call and straighten this out. And I should be at the hospital soon. Be certain I'm cleared for immediate access to the boss."

She leaned forward and tapped on the glass partition until the driver opened it. "If I'm still talking when we get to Prestonwood, stop in the emergency room area and keep the motor running so the air conditioner keeps it cool back here."

"But if the guard asks me to move—"

"If he does, I'll handle him. Now I have to make a call." As soon as the glass was closed, Karen dialed the number Lang had given her. Actually, she didn't mind doing battle like this. She'd had very little of it since leaving DC. It was good to get back into action.

"Dr. James," came a voice in her ear.

"Doctor, this is Karen Marks. I'm the administrative aide for former president David Madison. I believe you spoke earlier to a doctor who needed diphtheria antitoxin for two patients. I'm calling to get that done—we need it in Dallas ASAP. How are we going to do that?"

"I . . . I was expecting Dr. Pearson to call back."

"And instead you have a woman calling on behalf of the ex-president. I hope you understand what this means."

"Is . . . is this for President Madison?"

"Let's say that Mr. Madison feels it's very important for this request to be expedited. Now, where is the material, and how do we get it here in the next few hours?"

"Uh, there's a small supply of DAT at the CDC Quarantine Station in Houston. Their location is actually at Intercontinental Airport there. I can authorize the issuance of the vaccine as an investigational drug to Dr. Pearson."

"Tell me what you need from this end. I'll have a plane at Intercontinental Airport in two hours to pick it up." She spent a few more minutes clearing up details. Her last words to the duty officer were, "Thank you for your cooperation, Dr. James. I'll make certain your superiors know how you assisted President Madison."

You've still got it, Karen. Ask how "we" are going to get this done, so the person feels they're part of the solution. And always dangle the carrot once you've shown them the stick.

◆

Josh sat at the desk in his hospital "office" and wished he could turn back the clock. Three days ago, he'd been like any other doctor, happy with his role in the Preston Medical Clinic's hierarchy, looking forward to his girlfriend's return from her travels. Then, as though someone had waved a wand to accomplish the change, he was the personal physician of one of the most important men in the world. And his patient had a real problem.

Now, although he wanted to be at Rachel's side, to watch over her, to do everything possible to guard her from the consequences of her illness, he knew his primary duty lay with the patient in the room across the hall from Rachel's. Never before had he so wished he could suspend the laws of physics and be in two places at one time.

Then there were his other patients. Despite Nadeel Kahn's assurances to him that his patients would be covered, Josh couldn't shake the obligation he felt toward them. "Just take care of President Madison," was what Kahn said. What he really meant, of course, was "Give your best efforts to caring for the ex-president. The publicity will be good for Preston Medical Clinic."

Josh looked at his watch: a bit after four in the afternoon. Lang had suggested he wait to call the CDC duty officer back until the agent could run the situation by Karen Marks and discuss whether to invoke Madison's name. It seemed Karen was the "get it done" person on the ex-president's staff. Well, Josh hoped—

His thoughts were interrupted by a brisk knock at his closed door. Josh brought his swivel chair upright and planted his feet squarely on the floor. He shrugged to ease the fit of his white coat—it had never seemed so uncomfortable—and took a deep breath. *What now?* "Come in," he called.

The woman who entered was striking, to say the least. Josh's gaze was immediately drawn to sparkling blue-green eyes accented by a just a hint of mascara. Her pale blonde hair fell to her shoulders in soft waves, framing a beautiful face. A faint amount of make-up was applied to porcelain-like skin.

At first glance, Josh decided she could have been a model or a movie star. But when he looked more closely, he saw something more. There was ice in the sparkling eyes. Her features were exquisite but displayed no emotion. Josh sensed she would be a dangerous enemy.

She stepped forward and extended her hand. "Dr. Pearson? I'm Karen Marks. Nice to meet you."

Josh took the proffered hand. At first, he wondered if he was supposed to shake it or kiss it. He settled on the former, and she gave him what he decided was a politician's handshake—grasp the other person's hand as far in as possible, to avoid getting your own hand crushed; one quick squeeze, neither too strong nor too gentle; then release.

He figured that Karen Marks was probably slightly on the far side of forty, but she could easily be mistaken for thirty—that is, until you looked into her eyes. Within them he could see experience and something more. He wasn't sure what else he saw, but it told him he didn't want to challenge this woman.

"Please, sit down," Josh said, indicating one of the two side chairs opposite his desk.

She smoothed the skirt of her perfectly tailored navy business suit and lowered herself with ease. "Jerry Lang explained you needed some . . . what did he call it? Oh, yes. Diphtheria antitoxin. DAT, I think he said. Anyway, I've talked with the CDC. Your antitoxin is in Houston. I arranged for Agent Gilmore to fly down, pick it up, and deliver it here." She reached into her handbag and extracted a sheaf of papers. "I had these faxed here. After you've signed them, give them to Jerry or me and we'll see they're faxed back. The last two pages are instructions for administering the DAT."

Josh had that feeling again, the same one he had in the limo when he first met David Madison. Things were going too fast for him. On the one hand, he thought he needed to regain control of the situation. On the other, he appreciated this new-found ability to simply say, "I need something" and it was done. No question, this was a different world.

"Thank you," Josh said. "Did you have to use President Madison's name?"

"I used his influence, but there was never any suggestion that the drug was for him," Marks replied. "You'll learn how to do that, too."

Yes, and probably to lie and cheat a bit if I'm not careful. "Look, I'm happy that you got the DAT for President Madison and Miss Moore, but let me be clear. All I want to do is practice the best medicine possible. If there's any political maneuvering to be done, I want to know about it ahead of time."

Marks gave him a sweet smile that was totally devoid of mirth. She rose, smoothed her skirt, and picked up her purse.

"I think you're telling me to stand aside. Well, I promise I won't challenge your medical judgment or interfere with your treatment. But I guess I should warn you, if you haven't already got the message. I'll do anything for David Madison." At the door, she turned and said over her shoulder. "Anything!"

Josh found Allison Neeves in her office at the clinic. She was working her way through a pile of charts, dictating from a stack of notes scattered across her desk. Allison looked up when Josh tapped on the frame of the open door.

"Come in," Allison said. "I checked on Rachel and she seems to be holding her own. But if we're going on a presumptive diagnosis of diphtheria, we need to get her started on some diphtheria antitoxin." She put down the chart she was holding. "And the same for President Madison, of course."

Josh dropped into a chair across the desk from Allison. "Look," he said, "this could get awkward, and I don't want it to be. I'm Madison's doctor. I didn't lobby for the position, but I've got it. You know that he and Rachel probably have the same infection. I'd like to treat her too, but I agree that would present something of an ethical problem. However, you and I need to stay on the same page. Can we do that?"

"I think what you're saying is that you'd like to call the shots for both patients, with me acting like your intern on Rachel's case—writing the orders, reporting to you." She leaned back in her chair and sighed. "I'll try to cooperate, but you should realize that Rachel is my patient, not yours, and I have to make the final decisions about her treatment."

Josh rose. "I don't think we need to argue right now. That DAT should arrive—" He looked at his watch. "It should be at the hospital in a couple of hours. Is it okay if I write the orders for both patients to receive it?"

Allison shook her head. "Just call me when it comes in. I've already reviewed the protocol. I'll check Rachel and write the orders for her; you take care of Madison."

"If that's the way you want it," Josh said. He rose, turned, and headed for the door. *I don't know what I did to step on her toes, but I can't worry about that. I've got to give David Madison the best possible care. And Rachel, of course.*

◆

"Mr. Madison," Josh said as he entered the ex-president's hospital room. "How are you feeling?"

"Not great," Madison admitted. "My throat's getting pretty sore."

Josh noted a raspiness in his patient's voice—something that hadn't been there before. "Any difficulty breathing?" he asked.

"Not . . . well, maybe occasionally."

"Okay. The diphtheria antitoxin has arrived, but before we give it to you, I have to ask you some questions, then do a skin test." Seeing the confusion in Madison's eyes, Josh said, "The DAT is made from horse serum, so I have to be certain you won't have a reaction to it."

Josh went through the litany, using the checklist he'd made so he wouldn't forget anything. Hay fever? No. Asthma? No. Hives? No. Madison couldn't recall previously receiving any products made from horse serum.

The skin tests were negative, as Josh expected. Now it was time. A nurse brought in a small bag of sterile saline and Josh added DAT to it. He attached a needle to the tubing and piggy-backed the mixture into the IV already in Madison's hand, then started the material flowing.

"Will you be checking back on me from time to time?" Madison asked.

Josh inclined his head toward the upholstered chair in the corner of the room. "No. That chair reclines. I'm going to sit in it for the next several hours." Madison didn't realize it, but Josh knew that if anything went wrong, minutes—no, seconds—would count. He looked at the crash cart in the corner. It contained everything needed to treat emergencies, including an anaphylactic reaction. Atop it was a wrapped set of sterile instruments for an emergency tracheotomy, an operation to open the obstructed airway of a patient. From its external appearance, the red-painted Craftsman rolling cabinet didn't look particularly unique, but at this moment it was the most important piece of equipment in the United States. And Josh was the most important person.

◆

As Ethan Grant prepared to leave for the day, he went through his usual routine, scanning the petri dishes one by one, looking for anything out of the ordinary. He knew that, like that of an airline pilot, his job here in the bacteriology lab of Prestonwood Hospital might be routine most of the time, but it had the occasional moment when he needed every ounce of skill and experience, because he was dealing with, quite literally, a life-or-death situation.

The round, flat glass dish he lifted from the incubator contained a gel-like substance on which scattered colonies of bacteria grew. This was the culture from a swab or specimen that would help him identify the organism and then define the antibiotic to which it was sensitive.

This particular set of plates wasn't even twelve hours old. It would probably be tomorrow or the next day before Ethan could definitively name the species of bacteria growing on them and say with certainty what antibiotics would work best to treat the patient from which the specimen came. But despite the short time involved, these colonies were already growing more vigorously than usual. Ethan toyed with the idea of making a slide to see if the organisms on the petri dish were the same as what he and Dr. Pearson saw earlier that day.

Before he could act on his thought, the phone rang. Ethan replaced the petri dish in the incubator and reached for the phone. The call was from a physician who suspected his patient was suffering from septicemia—bacteria infecting the blood-stream. Could Ethan check the blood cultures drawn the previous day?

Ethan looked at each of the three specimens carefully. It was too early to call them negative, but he could see no growth. He replaced the bottles and returned to the phone. "Doctor, they look negative. There's no growth in any of them."

"You're sure?"

Of course I'm sure. I've been doing this for . . . Never mind. "Yes, sir."

"Well, keep an eye on them."

Ethan's routine was the same followed by most, if not all, laboratories in the U.S.: monitor specimens for five days. If there was any indication of growth, he'd do a slide and Gram stain it. He could explain this to the doctor, but there was no need. The man was worried about his patient. Ethan could understand that.

After he hung up, Ethan wondered if he should follow through with making and examining another slide from the culture taken from Josh's patient. Then he looked at the clock. It was already almost six, nearly an hour past time for him to leave. He decided to put that on the back burner until morning. It probably wasn't important, anyway.

6

The next morning, Josh stood in the bathroom of his temporary hospital office and studied his reflection in the mirror. Finally, he shook his head and looked away. A night spent at the hospital watching a patient wasn't unheard of for him, but it had been a while. He decided he hadn't looked this haggard since pulling his last all-nighter as a senior medical student. Eyes red, a day's growth of beard, his clothes wrinkled, and developing a definite scent that told him he needed to shower soon. Josh was a mess. *That's not the way an ex-president's doctor is supposed to look.*

Maybe later this morning he could visit the surgeon's lounge and clean up, perhaps put on a clean scrub suit. But for now, Josh needed to get going.

He splashed water on his face, finger-combed his hair, and took a deep breath. Josh might hate the way he looked, but even more he hated the way he felt. He moved out of the bathroom, through his office, and into the hospital corridor. He'd grab a cup of coffee, check one more time on Madison, look in on Rachel, then make a quick trip home to shave, shower, and change.

A vibration in his pocket told Josh those plans might have to be put on hold. He pulled out his cell phone and saw the call was from a number inside the hospital.

"Dr. Pearson."

"Doctor, this is Ethan Grant in the bacteriology lab. I've got something here I think you'll want to see."

"Can it wait?" Josh said. "I need to—"

"Sir, if it could wait, I wouldn't have called," Grant said.

Josh recognized the hint of peevishness in the technician's tone. Grant had turned up something important, and now Josh was ignoring it. *This man is trying to tell me something. I should listen to him.*

"I'll be right there," Josh said. "Thanks for calling."

There'd been no need to ask who the patient was. Since Josh only had one patient—well, two, if you counted Rachel—anyway, this could only have something to do with the cultures he'd sent to the lab yesterday. Despite telling Grant he'd be there shortly, Josh decided to make a quick stop at Madison's room before he headed for the bacteriology lab. True, he'd only been out of Madison's room for less than half an hour, but he felt as though he needed to keep a close eye on the man. If Josh let something happen— No, he didn't want to think about that.

As Josh moved toward the elevator, part of him was curious about what the bacteriology technician had found. However, since it probably wasn't good, the other part of him dreaded finding out.

◆

Rachel slowly emerged from a troubled sleep and started to stretch, only to discover that she could move her left arm only a short distance. She opened her eyes and looked around. It took a minute for her to orient herself, then it all came back to her. She was in a hospital, and the reason her left arm was restrained was to keep her from inadvertently pulling the IV out of the vein in the back of that hand.

Rachel's eyes traveled to her left, up the IV tubing to the plastic bag of fluid, then to the smaller bag hanging next to it on the other arm of the twin pole. It was empty, which meant she'd received the full dose of diphtheria antitoxin. Were the proteins, at this moment, circulating through her body doing battle with the toxins released by . . . what was the name of the bacterium? She'd learned it in nursing school, but it danced just outside her memory. Was inability to remember another side effect, either of the infection or the treatment?

"Good morning. How are you feeling?"

Rachel was frustrated with having to look beyond the mask and face shield and depend on voice recognition to identify the speaker, but she hoped that wouldn't last much longer. "I guess I'm all right, Dr. Neeves. Is everything looking okay?"

Rachel wished she could see the doctor's expression. Instead, her answer came in the form of a shrug. "I'll know more after I have a look at you," Dr. Neeves said.

As she prepared to examine Rachel, Neeves said, "Look, Rachel, we both know this is serious. You're a health care professional. I'll level with you all the way. And in the meantime, why don't you call me Allison?"

Rachel nodded and sat up straighter in bed in preparation for Allison's exam.

First, the doctor used the flashlight and one of the tongue depressors from a jar sitting on Rachel's bedside table. "Not so much exudate," she said, "but the throat's still pretty red— maybe a bit redder than before. And there seems to be a bit more swelling back there. Any problem breathing or swallowing?"

"Not really," Rachel replied.

Allison picked up the stethoscope that hung at the foot of Rachel's bed. "Let's have a listen to your chest."

Rachel went through the routine she knew so well—except she usually was standing by to assist the doctor instead of being the person following commands to take deep breaths. She watched the doctor's eyes, which were about all Rachel could see of Allison's expression over the mask, but there was no clue there.

"It's probably too early to expect much change," Allison said after hanging the stethoscope on the foot of Rachel's bed again. "I'm troubled that your fever's still hovering around a hundred and four. Every time we give you something to knock it down, it climbs right back up within a few hours." She frowned—that expression was easy for Rachel to see. "But so far, even with increasing swelling in the throat, your airway seems okay. Let's see if the diphtheria antitoxin makes some difference today."

"How long will I have to be in isolation?" Rachel asked.

"Conventional wisdom is to isolate patients with diphtheria until they've been on antibiotics for at least two days." Allison shrugged again. "I'll see if Dr. Pearson agrees. If he does, maybe we can discontinue the precautions tomorrow." She made a half-turn toward the door. "Any other questions?"

Rachel felt foolish for asking, but the question had been niggling at her since the doctor came in. "Just one," she said. "What's the name of the diphtheria organism? I can't remember it, and it's driving me crazy."

<hr/>

"Mr. Madison, how do you feel?" Josh asked as he entered the ex-president's hospital room.

Madison managed a smile, but it was evident to Josh it was a politician's gesture, with no real emotion behind it. "I'm still here, so I guess that's something."

Josh moved quickly to the side of his patient. The main IV continued to drip at a "keep open" rate, but the smaller bag that had delivered the diphtheria antitoxin was empty and its line was turned off. "Let's have a look at you."

After the exam, Josh said, "I'm sorry to say I don't see much progress, but it's still early. Let's see how the diphtheria antitoxin affects you today."

"Do I get another dose?" Madison asked.

"No, everything I've been able to find says one dose is all that's necessary. We'll continue the antibiotics to kill out any residual organisms. And if your temperature comes down and there's less redness and swelling of your throat tomorrow, I'll think about discontinuing the isolation precautions."

"Good," Madison said. "The rest of the group that went to South America with me should be on their way back soon, and I want to confer with them. It'll be a lot easier if they don't have to go through this silly mask/face shield/gown/gloves drill."

"I don't like it any better than you do, Mr. Madison, but that's the routine that's called for."

After a few more words, Josh stepped outside and began to divest himself of the isolation garb. He scrubbed his hands a little longer than usual, although there was really no reason to do so. Josh hoped he could discontinue the isolation precautions soon. Madison had been on antibiotics for twenty-four hours, which was probably long enough to destroy all but the hardiest of the *Corynebacterium diphtheriae* in the average patient's body.

Josh pondered whether he should look in on Rachel, but decided he'd have to delay that until he checked out what the bacteriology technician had found. And, after all, even though Rachel was his girlfriend, Josh couldn't escape the knowledge that his primary allegiance was to his most important patient . . . the one he'd just left.

He headed toward the lab, wondering if his unease was related to guilt at not being attentive to Rachel or to the news he was afraid he would receive from the lab technician. As Josh punched the elevator button, he decided he'd know soon enough.

◈

Ethan Grant looked up as the lab door opened and Dr. Josh Pearson walked in. *He's not going to like what I have to show him.*

"Okay, I'm here," the doctor said. "What's this I need to see?"

Dr. Pearson, unshaven, his clothes wrinkled, showed evidence of long hours with no sleep. The lab tech felt sorry for him. What he had to show him wasn't going to make Pearson any happier, either.

Ethan rose from the counter where he'd been using a binocular microscope to scan a Gram-stained slide. "Let me show you," he said. He moved to a large cabinet with glass doors, opened one of them, and removed a petri dish.

Pearson made no move to take the shallow, covered glass dish Ethan held out. Instead, he bent until his face was a foot from it and studied its contents. Finally, he straightened and said, "I'm afraid it's been too long since I had bacteriology. It looks like this is a blood agar plate, and it's almost completely covered with bacterial colonies. What about it?"

"To begin with, it's totally unusual for *Corynebacterium diphtheriae* to grow this rapidly. I would normally wait twenty-four hours, then inoculate tellurite-enriched agar with some of the material from the original culture. That would further enhance colony growth. I'd eventually do a stain, basing the final identification on colony characteristics and microscopic morphology of the bacteria."

"Didn't we already confirm a diagnosis of diphtheria?" Pearson asked.

"True, the morphology of the bacteria we saw on the slide from the original throat swab are Gram-positive bacilli with clubbing at one end. That, combined with the clinical picture, is generally enough to justify starting treatment for diphtheria. But I don't stop there. I keep going until I have the diagnosis nailed down. That's why I'm still working on this."

"And have you found something more?" Pearson asked.

Ethan put down the plate and picked up another, this one with perhaps a dozen filter paper discs scattered around its surface. "We know that the diphtheria bacillus should respond to penicillin and erythromycin, sometimes to a few other antibiotics, although that varies, but 'should' isn't always dependable, so I do sensitivity studies, seeing how various antibiotics prevent bacterial growth."

Grant held out the new petri dish for Pearson's inspection. "This one was plated less than twenty-four hours ago, and as you can see, the colonies have already grown so rapidly they almost fill the dish." He used his pen to point. "Each of those white filter paper discs is impregnated with a different antibiotic. Normally, a sensitivity study isn't ready to be read this early, but this one's unusual."

Pearson looked at the petri dish, then he took it from Ethan's hand and studied it more closely. "Where are penicillin and erythromycin?"

Ethan pointed. "There and there. But it really doesn't matter, does it? There's no zone of inhibition anywhere."

"So that means—"

"Yes, sir. That means the organism infecting your patient is growing so much more rapidly than the *Corynebacterium diphtheria* that it's covering over that bacteria. And whatever this other organism is, it's resistant to every antibiotic in our arsenal."

◆

David Madison awoke from a fitful doze when he heard the door of his room open. Despite good eyesight, he couldn't identify the person who entered. He'd complained to Dr. Pearson about the face shield, mask, and gown all his visitors had to wear, but until now, using height and mannerisms, he'd generally been able to identify the few people cleared to enter his room: two nurses, one orderly, and his chief of security, Jerry Lang. This new visitor was taller and thinner than Lang, and his walk was different from Dr. Pearson's. Madison didn't recognize him, and he had a bad feeling about it.

He felt silly challenging the person like a sentry on post, but then again, he'd learned in his years in the White House to have a high index of suspicion in some situations. This one qualified. Madison cleared his throat and said, "Who are you?"

The intruder—because that's what Madison was beginning to think of this person as—didn't respond, but continued his slow advance across the room. When he was six feet from the foot of the bed, his hand disappeared for a moment beneath the hem of the yellow isolation gown he wore.

"What are you doing?" Madison asked. He was concerned not only by the visitor's failure to respond to his question, but by the raspy tone he detected in his own voice. Pearson had warned him to watch for difficulty breathing. Was what he was experiencing now due to fright or to a progression of his disease?

The man's hand emerged holding a small pistol with a long, thick barrel. Still without a word, he pointed it at Madison, who thought he could see the man's finger tighten on the trigger.

It was probably useless to make a grab at the weapon, but Madison determined to try. He gathered himself for the effort. His left hand was encumbered just enough by the IV in his vein that Madison leaned a bit to the left as he tried to sit up. Then gunfire shattered the relative hush in the hospital room.

7

Mr. President, are you okay?" Jerry Lang stood half in and half out of the doorway of Madison's room, his service pistol in his right hand. The smell of gunpowder hung in the air. Lang addressed his question to the man in the bed, but his eyes never left the shooter who lay facedown on the floor, his pistol near his outstretched hand.

"I'm not hurt, if that's what you mean." David Madison's voice was weak, but still bore a hint of its commanding tone. "But you can't come in here like that, not gowned and masked."

"I'll gown up in a minute," Lang said. "First, I want to be sure that man is dead."

"What's going on here?" Dr. Josh Pearson, an untied gown covering his white coat, a mask loosely in place, grabbed Lang by the shoulder and spun him around. "I heard gunshots and shouting."

Lang inclined his head toward the corpse on the floor. "Even after that man showed Agent Rutledge a hospital badge at the door, I had a feeling there was something not quite right with him. He went into the room, and when I opened the door for a closer look, I saw him pull a gun and fire at Mr. Madison." He used his pistol to point at the gowned and masked figure on the floor. A pool of blood was slowly spreading around the assassin. "That's when I shot him."

Pearson jerked his head toward the stack of isolation gowns and masks in the hallway. "Get one of those on. Put on some gloves."

"I will," Lang said. "But until I get back, watch that man. If he moves, yell."

There was more commotion in the hallway as Lang backed out of the room. "Stay back," he said to the group that was gathering. He hurried to don the required garb.

"I'll call 911," an older woman, a nurse, said.

Lang stopped her before she could turn away. "No. Call the Dallas Police." He finished tying his gown and picked up a mask. "Give them this message: Agent Lang needs Detective Warren at the hospital as soon as possible. He should bring one police officer and probably the coroner, but other than that we need to keep this to ourselves."

Once he was gowned, gloved, and masked, Lang stepped back into the room and closed the door. He motioned for Madison to stay where he was in the bed. He directed Dr. Pearson to a corner of the room where he'd be out of the way. Then, his pistol pointed toward the man lying on the floor, Lang crept forward. He'd seen enough dead bodies to know his bullets had found their mark. This man was no longer a threat. But he'd handle this by the manual. That was the only way—the only safe way—to deal with the situation.

When he reached the side of the would-be assassin, Lang searched with his gloved left hand for a carotid pulse in the neck and found none. He gently moved the pistol well away from the dead man's outstretched hand. Then Lang stood up and announced, "He's dead."

"Who is he? Why did he try to do this?" Madison said.

"Dr. Pearson," Lang said, ignoring the ex-president's questions, "check Mr. Madison and make sure he's okay. Don't come near the body, though. We leave everything as it is until Warren gets here."

Lang opened the door of the room wide enough to hold a brief whispered conversation with Agent Rutledge, who stood guard outside. In hushed tones, he told the man what had happened and asked him to call a couple of agents to beef up the security around the ex-president. Someone had tried to shoot Madison. The shooter was dead, but they couldn't relax. The danger wasn't over.

◈

Rachel stirred and slowly came awake. It took a few moments for her to realize where she was . . . and why. Her dreams had been a troubled mishmash of sights and sounds, and when she tried to recall their content, it was like trying to catch a butterfly with her bare hands—it danced just outside the reach of her mind. It seemed that she'd heard shouting and loud noises. Did they represent gunshots? She blamed it all on the fever.

She knew she still had fever. Actually, although her time perception seemed to be skewed, she thought her fever was worse than when she was admitted. How long had she been here? Her watch was on the bedside table, and by carefully rolling over she was able to reach it. She had to squint a couple of times before she could see the tiny numbers and letters in the date window at the edge of the dial.

The watch told her it was Friday noon. Surely that couldn't be right. If it were, she'd been in the hospital for only about twenty-four hours. She looked at the IV pole above her head. Yes, the empty bag that had held the diluted diphtheria antitoxin was still hanging there, although the piggyback line that had been plugged into her IV dangled free. So maybe the fever she felt was due to the effects of the DAT, the antibodies doing their job. When she'd received immunizations in the past, she'd sometimes had low-grade fever along with arm soreness. That, in turn, made her wonder why she hadn't experienced any of those symptoms when Dr. Lambert administered her recent immunizations.

The process of her selection to join the group was a bit hazy in her fever-ridden mind. She'd received a call from President Madison's administrative aide, asking if she'd come to Preston Medical Clinic after her shift ended in the ICU at University Hospital. A nurse had dropped out of the group scheduled to leave in a few days for South America. Rachel's colleague at the medical center, Linda Gaston, was going on the trip and recommended her as a replacement.

Rachel wondered if she should have talked it over with Josh Pearson before saying yes. But she'd had to make a decision right then. Of course, afterward, they'd discussed it, and Josh told her it sounded like a great opportunity. In retrospect, Rachel wondered if she'd made a wise decision.

She rolled back onto her side and closed her eyes. Maybe the fever would be gone when she woke this time. Maybe if she prayed hard enough . . . she was still praying silently when sleep overtook her.

"Are you okay?" Josh said in a low voice, bending over David Madison's bed. He noticed two bullet holes in the pillow where the ex-president's head would have been had he not sat up and leaned to the side.

"I'm shaken," Madison replied, "but other than that I'm okay."

Josh assured himself that the ex-president hadn't been harmed before he straightened up and conveyed the message to Lang.

The agent nodded. "Good. Now we need to preserve this room as a crime scene, so I think it's best to move Mr. Madison, if you can arrange it."

Josh considered that for a moment. "We'll still need to maintain isolation precautions."

"For how long?"

Until I can figure out what else is infecting Madison and Rachel and get it under control. "I don't know yet," Josh said. "Let me see if we can do some shuffling and move Mr. Madison to a room across the hall, next to Rachel."

"And the assumed name?" Lang asked.

"Despite our best efforts, gossip spreads here, the same as it does any other place. You saw the crowd that gathered outside this room when they heard shots in here. I think that ship of anonymity has sailed, don't you?"

"Okay, but I think we should keep trying. I'll ask Warren to keep the number of police personnel in here to a minimum. If we restrict access to this area of the hospital, I think we can maintain security and a degree of secrecy. That is, unless you'd rather transfer Mr. Madison to another medical facility."

Josh had already considered this. That would entail giving up control of his patient to another doctor, not to mention the effort of bringing another medical team up to speed and the possibility that information would fall through the cracks. And what about Rachel's treatment? For better or worse, the care of the two patients was linked, and Josh felt it was his responsibility to bring it to a successful end. When he was honest with himself, he realized he didn't want to let go of the case. Despite the bleak outlook, he thought he could handle it.

"If you're suggesting we airlift Mr. Madison to Bethesda, I don't like the idea," Josh said. "The same goes for the special isolation unit the CDC supports at Emory Hospital in Atlanta."

"How about the university medical center here in town?"

"Again, I think it's best we continue the care started here," he told Lang.

"Okay. Step outside and set the wheels in motion for the move to another room. Keep this as a 'need to know' situation."

Josh had taken a step toward the door before he stopped. Should he leave Lang here alone with Madison? When he'd come into the room, Lang had just shot the gunman. Had that taken place before or after shots were fired at Madison? Was Lang part of a conspiracy, or part of the solution to it? Josh knew the idea was crazy—after all, Lang was there to protect Madison. If he couldn't be trusted, who could? Nevertheless, for whatever reason, Josh couldn't bring himself to leave the agent alone with the ex-president right now.

"I'll do it this way," Josh said. He pulled out his cell phone and punched in a number. "This is Dr. Pearson. I need to speak to the head nurse on two south."

In a few moments, there was a tap on the door and a masked and gowned nurse entered, followed by a similarly garbed orderly pushing a wheelchair. "Mr. Madison," the nurse said, "I'm Mary Wynn, the head nurse on this floor. Let's get you into this chair and take you across the hall. After the police are through in here, we'll get your belongings and move them."

A few moments after Madison was wheeled out the door, a stocky man in isolation gear entered the room. Josh didn't recognize him behind the mask. Then he heard the man's voice and recognized it as the one he'd heard at Love Field when he first met Detective Stan Warren.

"Okay," the detective said, swiveling his head between Josh and Lang. "What do we have here?"

Josh decided he had nothing to contribute to this conversation, so he edged into a far corner and listened as the Secret Service agent described the attempt to shoot ex-president Madison. "I saw the shooter go into the room. Of course, with that isolation garb, I couldn't tell who it was, but somehow I had a feeling things weren't right. I opened the door and peeked in, and I'm glad I did."

"Did you call out to him? Tell him to stop? Say something like, 'Police, freeze'?"

"There was no time," Lang said. "He had his gun aimed at Mr. Madison. I think I may have fired just a fraction of a second after the shooter did."

Warren nodded. "I see." He looked at Josh. "You got anything to add, Doc?"

"No," Josh said. "I got here after it all happened."

"Okay. We'll get your statement later, then," Warren said.

"We have Mr. Madison in a new room, right across the hall. I suppose you'll want to talk with him, since he was the only other eyewitness," Lang said.

Josh's cell phone vibrated in his pocket. He eased it out and looked at the caller ID. The call came from inside the hospital. Well, whatever it was, it would have to wait a bit.

Warren nodded once as he knelt beside the body. "We'll get Mr. Madison's statement in good time." He fixed his gaze on Lang. "I realize this is really a Secret Service situation, but if you want to keep a lid on this information getting around, I suggest you let me try to backtrack the shooter. I can use Dallas Police Department resources to do that."

"Fine. We'll coordinate and share information." Lang pulled his pistol from its holster beneath his isolation gown. He grasped the barrel and held the weapon out butt-first to Warren. "Will you need this?"

"I'm supposed to take it, but it seems to me you might need it again before you can pick up a replacement. Keep it for now."

"Thanks," Lang said softly. "I did what I swore to do—protect the ex-president, even if it meant risking my own life."

Warren edged closer to the pistol the gunman had dropped, but didn't touch it. "Looks like a Type 64 silenced pistol. It's a one-piece handgun, with the silencer built in."

"That's why I only heard two shots," Josh said. "The ones fired at Mr. Madison were from a silenced weapon."

"Probably no more than a loud *fftt*," Warren said.

"Does the type of pistol tell you anything?" Josh asked.

This time Lang answered. "Unfortunately, no. The Chinese military used this pistol a lot for clandestine operations, but that was maybe fifty years or more ago. Now, assassins of all nationalities seem to like it. Sort of an equal opportunity piece."

"Are you going to check his identity?" Josh asked, pointing to the fallen gunman.

"They'll take the shooter's prints at the morgue, and we'll see if we can get a hit on them," Warren said.

"What about his ID badge?" Josh asked.

Warren reached under the prone gunman and pulled out the badge clipped to his isolation gown. "Terry Forester. Ring a bell?"

"I'd have to check with the personnel office, but I think that's the guy who was fired recently for stealing supplies," Josh said.

"Well, let's see if the identity matches his face." Warren slipped his gloved hand under the gunman's head and turned it slightly, then used his other hand to pull down the mask.

Despite himself, Josh took in a sharp breath.

"What about it, Doc?" Warren asked. "Recognize this guy?"

Josh nodded slowly, wondering if this new information made things clearer or muddied them even more.

◆

Jerry Lang turned his head with a jerk when the door to the room opened a crack. He still held his service pistol, but let his arm drop when he heard the words from the hall outside. "Mrs. Madison, that's a crime scene. You can't go in there."

"That room is my husband's." The voice was a quiet but intense contralto. "Is David all right? If it's a crime scene, I need to know what happened."

Lang immediately recognized the situation. He held up one finger in a "just a second" gesture and moved toward the door. In the hall, Mrs. Mildred Madison tried to free herself from the gentle restraint applied by the uniformed Dallas police officer stationed there, while two men in dark suits tried to interpose themselves between her and the hospital room.

"Mrs. Madison," Lang said, trying to keep his voice down while portraying a sense of urgency. "Your husband is in the room across the hall now." He nodded toward one of the agents. "Gilmore, please take Mrs. Madison in to her husband." He looked at the stack of supplies by the room's door. "Remember that anyone going in there will have to observe isolation precautions."

Mildred Madison pointed to the door of what used to be her husband's hospital room. "But if that's a crime scene . . ."

"I'm sure your husband will explain it all to you. As soon as I'm finished with the police here, I'll come across the hall and answer any questions you might have."

He waited until the agent escorted Mrs. Madison into the ex-president's new room, then ducked back inside. "Sorry. Now, Dr. Pearson, you were saying you recognize this man. Can you explain?"

Josh crept forward to look more closely at the face of the dead gunman. "I'm not sure what his real name is. Maybe the fingerprints will help you there." He turned away from the body, as though by doing so he could distance himself from the case and the associated problems that seemed to be mounting. "When I met him, he called himself Bill Smith. This is the man who drove away in a hearse from Love Field with Dr. Ben Lambert's body."

8

Josh edged his way around the would-be assassin's body to where Warren and Lang stood talking. When he reached Warren's side, he said, "If you don't need me right now, there have been some new developments in the medical aspects of this case, and I have to make some calls."

The detective nodded. "We know where to find you, Doc." Then he resumed his conversation with Lang.

In the hall, Josh divested himself of his gown and mask, stripped off his gloves, and washed his hands at the sink in the hall. He was in the process of turning away when he heard someone call his name.

"Hey, Josh." Dr. Sixto Molina, dressed in scrubs, smiled at his friend. "I know surgery is a specialty that includes excitement, but it looks like you've managed to generate a bit yourself." He inclined his head toward the two men in dark suits standing in the hall across from the room Josh had just left.

"You might say that," Josh replied. "Right now I'd trade specialties with you, because I've got a problem I need to solve, but I can't attack it surgically."

"I guess I need to teach you the surgical method," Sixto said with a laugh. "If in doubt, cut it out. Then move on."

"Unfortunately, in this case that's not possible," Josh said. "I wish I could stay and talk, but I've got to make some phone calls."

"No problem. Let me know if I can help."

Promising to talk later, Josh moved down the hall. He pulled out his cell phone and checked to see what his missed call had been about. The in-hospital number meant nothing, but he saw the caller had left a message.

"Dr. Pearson, this is Ethan in the bacteriology lab. There's something you need to know, and it's important."

What now?

When Josh entered the bacteriology lab, he found Ethan Grant with his nose in a textbook. The tech looked up and grimaced. "I think I've identified the bug that's choking out the *Corynebacterium diphtheriae* in the culture, but I'm not sure it's going to help you."

Josh looked over Grant's shoulder. He didn't recognize the title, but from the appearance of the textbook, it was several years old. Whatever he'd found, Ethan had really done some digging to uncover it. The page to which the book was open was headed "Gram variable bacilli."

"I thought all the bacteria on the slide we saw were Gram positive," Josh said.

"When I couldn't figure out what was overgrowing the diphtheria bacillus, I remembered that some organisms vary in their Gram-staining pattern," Grant replied. "This one took up the Gram stain when I looked at it the first time, but I did another slide, and this time it's Gram negative. That's what sent me looking for a Gram variable bacillus."

"And you found it."

"That's the good news," Grant said. "The bad news is what I found about it." He pointed to a paragraph headed *Bacillus decimus.*

Josh followed Grant's finger and read: *Gram-variable bacillus, found primarily in Central and South America. When existing as Gram-positive rods, may have a club shape that makes it difficult to distinguish them from* Corynebacterium diphtheriae.

"That's your secondary infecting organism," Grant said.

Josh continued to read. *Infected patients display a diphtheria-like membranous pharyngitis that may result in airway obstruction. The usual course of the infection is high fever, followed by internal bleeding, convulsions, and ultimate death This bacterium is resistant to all common antibiotics.*

Josh closed the door of his hospital office and dropped into the chair behind his desk. He absolutely had to make a quick trip home to shower, shave, and change clothes—but first, he needed to get some help.

He ran through his mental file of people he could call. His mentor during residency, the chief of the medicine service at the hospital where he trained, had now retired, as had the man who headed the infectious disease service at that time. Were there others somewhere in the country who would know about the super-bacteria? Probably—but who would he call?

And could they be trusted to keep what Josh told them in confidence? It had been something about which David Madison was insistent, and Josh had to respect his patient's wishes.

Josh picked up the phone and was about to call Allison Neeves, but he hung up without dialing. He and Allison had trained at about the same time, although at different hospitals. There was no reason to think she'd know more than he about *Bacillus decimus*. Sure, she'd have to know soon, because undoubtedly Rachel was infected with the same organism. But Josh had the lead role in this, and he felt it was up to him to find a way out of what looked like a dead-end situation.

Maybe he could find someone at the National Institutes of Health. Then he saw the notes on his desk, written when he was contacting the CDC to obtain diphtheria antitoxin. If anyone would know about infection by this organism, they would.

He considered and discarded the numbers he'd written—they were for the duty officer who controlled diphtheria antitoxin. Now he needed someone who was familiar with unusual infections. What had the book said about the bacteria? It was found in Central and South America. So he'd start with whoever was expert on those regions.

Before he could pick up the phone again, there was a light tap on Josh's door. Without waiting for a response, Karen Marks walked in.

"Doctor, we need to talk," she said.

"I'm sorry, but it'll have to wait. I'm trying to save your boss's life," Josh said. *And Rachel's as well. Don't forget her.*

Marks pulled out the chair across the desk from Josh, eased into it, and crossed her legs. "That's why I'm here. Don't forget I'm the one who got you the antitoxin you needed. But from what I can gather, it's not helping. So I'm here to grease the wheels for whatever else you need."

"Look," Josh said, "I appreciate your offer, but—"

Marks dropped her purse on the floor beside her with a loud thud. "Josh . . . You don't mind if I call you Josh, do you? Josh, you're going to have to get used to having the power of a former president behind any request you might make. And I'm the one who can make those things happen. So what do you need?"

Josh thought for a minute. To this point, he'd felt like he was trying to move a brick wall. Hadn't Marks described herself as the person to get things done? Well, why not let her help? "Okay," he said. "Here's what I need."

◆

Rachel felt the fever rising within her. Her head pounded. Her joints ached. But worst of all was the realization that, despite all she could do to prevent it, her airway was gradually closing down. She made a concerted effort to breathe slowly and gently. So far there was no stridor—the semi-whistling sound that accompanied airway obstruction. But it couldn't be far away now.

She wasn't sure whether the gentle tap at the door of her hospital room was a product of her fevered imagination, along with some really weird dreams that had troubled her off and on through the night, or if it was real. When Rachel heard it again, she tried to call, "Come in," but produced only a faint croak.

Apparently, that was enough. The door opened and a man entered. His clothes were almost covered by the gown he wore. His face was virtually hidden behind a mask and face shield. Paper booties covered his feet, while on his hands were the purple Nitrile gloves that had replaced conventional latex ones in this hospital.

As the man advanced toward her bed, Rachel's heart sped up even beyond its fever-fueled rhythm. She felt for the button that would call for the nurse, all the while wondering if this intruder might accomplish what he came for before anyone could respond. Visions flashed into Rachel's mind of the woman in South America who had started all this by throwing the contents of a flask in her face. Was this someone sent to finish the job? Had they already been in President Madison's room, or would he be next?

The figure stopped at her bedside and reached out a gloved hand. Rachel squeezed her eyes shut like a little child who felt safer if she couldn't see the fearsome shadows around her. Then she heard Josh's voice, speaking softly. "Rachel, I'm so very, very sorry I've neglected you." He stroked her cheek and bent closer. "I know how sick you are. And I want you to know that I'm willing to move Heaven and earth to make you better."

Rachel opened her eyes and tried to smile. When she spoke, her voice was faint and breathy, but her words were easy to understand. "Oh, Josh. I know how tough this must be on you. How's Mr. Madison?"

"I think he's a bit better than you are." He went on to explain that, although both Rachel and Madison had received diphtheria antitoxin and appropriate antibiotics, there was another factor at work. "We're pretty certain you have a secondary infection with a bacteria no one thought was around . . . certainly not in the U.S."

As a nurse, Rachel could immediately see the implications of what Josh was saying. "So the DAT wasn't the whole answer," she said. "Do you know yet how to treat this other infection?"

Josh shook his head. "I've got someone calling the CDC to get the latest information about treating it. Believe me, I'm checking every source, doing everything I can."

Rachel managed a slight shake of her head, even though the movement exaggerated her headache. "I suspect you haven't tried one source."

"Tell me, then," Josh said. "I'll try anything."

Rachel reached out and grasped Josh's gloved hand. "Pray about it. That's what I always do when I don't see a way out. And so far, God's brought me through."

She half-expected an argument. After all, during the year they'd been going out, Josh had never said much about his relationship with God, even though she'd given him opportunities. However, his reaction this time surprised her. Silently, Josh dropped to his knees at her bedside.

❖

In the hall outside Rachel's room, Josh once more encountered his friend, Sixto Molina. He almost wished he hadn't seen the surgeon, because now it would be more difficult than ever for him to ignore what his eyes and ears told him. Part of him, the very human part, wanted to do just that. But the doctor in Josh kept coming back to one of the first lessons he'd learned in medical school. *If you think about it, you need to do it.*

"Sixto, do you have a minute?"

"Sure. I was just hunting for you to see if I could help. What's up?"

Josh looked around him. Two Secret Service agents stood guard in front of Madison's room. The door across the hall, the entrance to the room that was now a crime scene, was closed, but voices issued from behind it. "Let's find someplace a bit more private," he said.

He and Sixto found an empty patient room at the end of the hall and ducked inside. "You know my girlfriend, Rachel, don't you?" Josh asked.

"Yes. We've met a couple of times. Why?"

Josh wondered how much he could confide in his friend. In the end, he decided he had to trust Sixto's discretion in order to get the help he needed. In as few words as possible, he sketched out the events that led to the former president and Rachel occupying adjacent rooms in this wing of the hospital. "Between the antitoxin and the antibiotics, their diphtheria should be coming under control, but the secondary infection is getting worse. Right now, Rachel seems to be nearing the point of airway obstruction. I'm working on treating the infection." Josh shook his head. "That's not true. Actually, Allison Neeves is treating her, but I tried to call her a minute ago. She's back at the clinic, tied up with an emergency. Meanwhile—"

"Meanwhile you think Rachel needs a tracheotomy," Sixto said.

"She may need one," Josh said. "But I can't make that decision dispassionately. And even if I could, I'm not the person to do it."

"I presume you have a trach tray at the bedside."

"It's all there. If you think it needs to be done, I can assist."

"No, you stay out of this. If I need to do a trach, I'll get someone else to assist me. It should be simple . . . if I do it before it becomes an emergency."

"I'm hoping it won't come to that, but if it does . . ."

"If it does, I'll handle it." Sixto clapped Josh on the shoulder. "Meanwhile, why don't you see about finding out how to treat your patients?"

Josh turned without a word and strode away, wondering which one was supposed to make him feel better—praying with Rachel or asking his friend, the surgeon, to take over the burden of deciding when and if she would require surgery to keep her airway open.

◆

"Thank you. You've been quite helpful." Karen Marks cradled the phone. She scanned her notes, then pushed away from the desk and tilted back in the chair to think. Since Dr. Pearson had left her in his office, she'd managed to cut through about a mile of red tape at the CDC. Now she pondered her next move.

The door opened and Pearson entered. She thought briefly about moving from behind his desk, but he didn't give her a chance. He dropped into the chair across from her like a marionette whose strings had been cut. "Please tell me you have some good news," he said softly.

"Yes and no," Karen said. She consulted her notes. "I'll leave out all the times I was transferred or had to call a different number. The bottom line—I hate that expression—the substance of what I learned is that the only place this bacteria of yours is still found is in some of the less urbanized areas of South America. The CDC knows about a few cases of individuals infected by it over the past half-dozen years, and all have been fatal."

Pearson was half out of the chair. "I need to research this. There's got to be an answer."

"Please sit down," Karen said. "I may already have your answer." She moved one page of notes aside and looked at the next. "I finally talked with a Dr. Gruber at the CDC. It appears that he's one of the world's experts on this infection. It's true that in the past it's been universally fatal, but he told me that not long ago Argosy Pharmaceuticals talked with the FDA about getting approval for a new antibiotic. The folks at the FDA told them not to bother trying to continue testing it because it was no better than any of the existing drugs. Its—what did he call it? Oh, yes, its spectrum was essentially the same as several other antibiotics already approved and on the market."

Pearson leaned forward. "So what does this—"

"Let me finish," Karen said. "There was one important exception. The drug worked where nothing else did in infections with—what's this one's name?—with *Bacillus decimus*. But since there'd never been a case in the U.S., the FDA advised Argosy not to bother."

"So this new drug was effective?"

"They think so," Karen replied. "Gruber said the drug worked in the lab, and a few patients in South America had been through limited phase-two testing, whatever that is, against this superbug. But more research was needed, including long-term studies looking for late consequences from it. Those would come if the FDA gave a preliminary thumbs-up, which it told them wouldn't be forthcoming."

"But it worked in the few patients in whom they tried it," Pearson said. He seemed to cling to the idea like a drowning man clutching at a life preserver.

"Yes, it worked. And if you're willing to gamble on the limited data available, and if the pharmaceutical company still has some of the drug available, Gruber thought we might be able to get some. But it would probably be a very small amount."

"What are you saying?"

"Think it through," Karen said. "We don't know how much of the drug is still available. My guess is that most of it's gone. We may only be able to get enough of the drug to treat one patient." She looked straight at Pearson. "And if that's the case, you know who should be treated."

9

Rachel opened her eyes when she heard the door to her hospital room open and close. It seemed she was sleeping more and more. Was it the effect of the fever? Or was this the way someone died from whatever infection she'd contracted? Would she just go to sleep one time and never wake up?

In her head, Rachel knew that if that happened, she'd awaken in a better place, in the presence of her Lord. But she was surprised to realize that, although she was confident in her ultimate fate after death, she wasn't ready to leave this life yet. She wondered why. Was it because of the attraction between her and Josh? Did she want to experience more of that? Was her ultimate desire marriage, motherhood, a family? Well, whatever happened, God was in charge.

"Rachel, do you remember me?"

The voice, an unfamiliar one, came from above her bed. By now, she had a certain facility at looking beyond the isolation protection garb and discerning who was visiting her room, but this man wasn't one she'd seen there before. He was huskier and shorter than Josh. What she could see of his face above the mask wasn't familiar. "I'm afraid I can't—" Rachel was both frustrated and frightened when she discovered her voice had become so raspy she couldn't get the words out.

"I'm Josh's friend and colleague—Sixto Molina. We met a couple of months ago at a party." The man moved a bit closer. "Josh asked me to look in on you because he was afraid you were having some trouble breathing. I'm going to see if we can do something about that."

Despite her fever, Rachel felt a chill. *He's going to do a tracheotomy.* She had been trying to ignore that possibility for several hours now, but the nurse in her was well aware of the likelihood such a procedure would be necessary.

If Rachel's airway became compromised to the point where there was a danger, it would close off and smother her, the solution was an operation, a tracheotomy. A doctor would surgically open a hole in the trachea—her windpipe, a layperson would call it—and insert a metal or plastic tube into it. She'd be able to breathe freely through the hole in her neck, but with a tracheotomy tube in place there, no air would go upward past her vocal cords. Rachel would be reduced to writing notes and silently mouthing words until such time as the tube was removed.

She dreaded the possibility, but if the procedure was what it would take to keep her alive . . . with a silent prayer, Rachel mouthed the words, "Do what you have to." Then she added, "Thank you."

Sixto straightened from his exam of Rachel and looked down at her. "Rachel, your airway is borderline right now," he said. "We may be able to get by without doing a tracheotomy, but if you get much worse, what would otherwise be a scheduled, elective procedure might turn into an emergency one done at the bedside. As a nurse, you know that would multiply the chances for something to go wrong—bleeding, airway obstruction before we get the tube in, even post-op infections."

He waited to see if she would respond, but Rachel continued to lie perfectly still, her eyes closed, her breathing a bit more rapid than normal. The faintest sound of stridor accompanied every respiration, signaling impending obstruction of her airway. Sixto knew that Josh had been right to ask him to see Rachel, to make the decision that Josh was unable or unwilling to make. But it was still difficult to do, given the friendship that existed between the two doctors.

"Rachel," he said, when it was obvious she wasn't going to respond, "I think we should—"

"Dr. Molina, are you in there?"

The urgency in the voice over the intercom from the nursing station stopped Sixto in mid-sentence. "I'm here, but I'm trying to talk—"

"We need you in the room next door," the nurse continued. "Mr. Madison is having a great deal of difficulty breathing. I think he needs a trach, and we can't locate Dr. Pearson."

So now, he had two patients who needed him, one with an airway that might become compromised at any moment, the other who appeared to have reached that point already. Sixto patted Rachel's hand. "Can you hang on? If you feel any difficulty breathing, push the call button. We'll get help to you, stat. Do you understand?"

Rachel gave a minimal nod, and Sixto hurried through the door.

Josh was glad the person to whom he was about to talk couldn't see him. Undoubtedly he looked as grungy as he felt. It seemed as though he wasn't going to make it home to clean up. Maybe after this call he could take a few minutes in the surgeons' dressing room to shower. He might even borrow Sixto's razor and some toiletries from his locker there.

The thought of his friend brought Josh to the thing he'd been trying to ignore for the past half hour. Although he was happy to have another doctor make the decision about a tracheotomy for Rachel, Josh somehow couldn't rid himself of the guilt that went with abdicating that decision. He felt like he'd betrayed her by not handling that problem himself.

"Are you going to make the call, or have you changed your mind and want me to do it?" Karen Marks asked.

"No, I'll make it. I just needed to gather my thoughts first," Josh said.

"Are you sure I shouldn't be the one talking with them? After all, I can bring the former president's influence to bear."

"This is a job for a doctor," Josh said. "I'll put it on speaker and let you listen in."

When Josh had knelt at Rachel's bedside, it was the first time he'd prayed since his freshman year in med school. He didn't realize how far he'd gotten from God, and he regretted that it took something like this—something he couldn't control, something he couldn't fix—to bring him back. He vowed not to drift that far again. But meanwhile, he had to move forward. With a silent prayer for God's help once more, he found the number in Karen Marks's notes and prepared to dial.

Josh punched in the number, then while the call rang, hit the "speaker" button. Karen leaned forward toward the phone, as though by her posture she could make someone answer more quickly.

"Argosy Pharmaceuticals." The woman who answered seemed to have a smile in her voice, which Josh took for a good sign. Thank goodness there was no mechanical voice saying, "Press one for this and two for that."

"This is Dr. Josh Pearson in Dallas, and it's critical that I speak with someone about a drug you recently developed. It's not in production—the FDA didn't approve it—but it was effective against—"

"Sir, let me stop you right there. It sounds as though you may need to talk with our Chief Operating Officer, Dr. Gaschen. He's in a very important meeting right now, but I can ask him to call you in a couple of hours when he's available."

"You don't understand. I can't wait. This is literally a matter of life and death."

"Doctor, I'm sorry, but I have strict orders not to disturb Dr. Gaschen during the meeting. I'm afraid you'll have to wait until he's free."

Josh could see Karen move closer to the phone console, but just before her lips parted to speak, he thought of something that might help. "What about your medical director? Is he there?"

"Yes," the operator said. "Would you like me to see if he's available?"

Josh felt his heartbeat slow a fraction. "Please. Tell him it's urgent."

In the silence that followed, Karen asked, "What's this about? We don't have time for—"

At that moment, the phone came to life. "This is Dr. Johnson."

Josh couldn't believe it. If this was a fortunate coincidence, he welcomed it. Hope made Josh's hands tingle as though he'd touched a live wire. "Would that be Dr. Derek Johnson, who did his residency at Parkland Hospital?"

"Yes," a puzzled voice replied. "Who's this?"

"This is Dr. Josh Pearson—or, as you used to call me, JP."

"Josh, is that you?" The man's voice, a smooth bass that betrayed only the faintest trace of his roots in the projects of South Dallas, was warm and cordial. "I can't believe it. Are you looking for a job? Why don't you fly down here to Atlanta and we'll talk?"

Josh could just see Derek smiling—lips parted, white teeth gleaming in his brown face. He hoped that smile would still be there at the end of this conversation. "Nothing I'd love better than a visit with you Derek, but right now I'm calling on a critical matter. Remember how I used to kid you about selling your soul by going to work in pharmaceuticals? Well, I hope those words were soft and sweet, because I'm about to eat some of them."

◆

Sixto hurried out the door of Rachel's hospital room, deciding as he went that since both patients had the same infection, he wouldn't take the time to change his gown. He spent a few seconds changing gloves, then turned right toward the room ex-president Madison now occupied. He reached out to grasp the door handle when a man in a dark suit, white shirt, and muted red tie stepped in front of him and held up his hand.

"I'm sorry, doctor, but you're not cleared to enter this area."

Sixto's first impulse was to tell the man he was dealing not with a surgeon but with an ex-marine, skilled in hand-to-hand combat, and if he didn't want to eat that pistol concealed by his suit coat, he should step aside. But before he could act on his impulse, the door to the hospital room opened and the nurse inside spoke a few hushed words to the agent.

"Sorry, sir," the man said. "They need you in there. Please go ahead."

On the bed lay a man Sixto had only seen before on TV. However, in those situations he'd always seemed in complete control. Now, he was sitting straight up in bed, holding a mask to his face and gasping as he struggled to take in enough oxygen. His respirations were rapid and shallow, accompanied by a noise that told Sixto the man's airway was already severely obstructed.

The surgeon realized he had no idea how to address an ex-president. Never mind. In this situation, protocol gave way to medical expediency. "Mr. President, I'm Dr. Sixto Molina, a colleague of Dr. Pearson's. I'm aware of the infection both you and Miss Moore have. As you know, one of the complications of the illness is swelling of the throat that can block off the windpipe and suffocate a patient. I've been asked to look at you to see if we need to perform an emergency operation to prevent that. Is that all right with you?"

Madison nodded weakly. He opened his mouth, but only a faint squeak issued. His lips formed the word yes.

Sixto's exam took less than a minute. He straightened and said, "Mr. Madison, we need to do a tracheotomy, right now." Briefly, he described the operation, mentioned the reason behind it and the possible complications, and asked, "Do I have your permission to proceed?"

Again, Madison nodded. The nurse, whose name pin was obscured by her isolation gown, handed Sixto a clipboard and pen, which he put in front of Madison. After the ex-president signed and the nurse witnessed the signature, Sixto said, "No time to go to the OR for this. We'll do it now."

"Doctor, his wife was here not long ago. Shall we call her?"

"Ask the agent outside to notify her. And page Dr. Marple, stat, to come assist me. Then open that trach tray and some sterile gloves. We need to get moving."

Josh stared hard at the phone console as though he were face-to-face with the doctor in Atlanta, instead of eight hundred miles away. "Derek, I'm going to have to depend on your discretion to keep this between us."

Karen Mills opened her mouth to speak, but Josh shook his head sharply. He had to handle this one, and it was going to work better doctor-to-doctor, rather than playing the political card.

"Josh, I'm not sure what you've got yourself into, but it sounds like something a lot more interesting than what I had on the docket for this afternoon. Tell me what you need, and I'll help any way I can."

"Okay. I'm treating two patients—ex-president Madison and a nurse, who's also my girlfriend."

Beside him, Josh heard a sharp intake of breath, but to her credit, Marks remained silent.

"Here's what I've got." Josh went on to describe the infections, the diagnostic problems he'd run into, and the eventual discovery that the patients were infected with both the diphtheria organism and *Bacillus decimus.*

"I know all about your friend decimus," Derek said, pronouncing the *c* as if it were a *k*. "That's sort of why we went ahead with our research on robinoxine."

"We've pronounced the name of the bacteria differently."

"Not important. I'll tell you later about why that name was given and how to pronounce it. Keep going."

"Both patients have received diphtheria antitoxin and antibiotics, and that part of the infection should be coming under control, but clinically they're not responding. Unless I can kill out the other bacteria, they're going to die. They already have high fevers and are bordering on airway obstruction. That's why I need—"

"You want to give them RP-78."

"RP-78? I thought you called it robinoxine."

"We use a shorter name here when we're talking about what amounts to an experimental drug. By either name, I guess that's what you want."

"It's our only hope."

"You do know that the FDA essentially told us to stop trying to develop it because it wasn't any better than existing antibiotics. Of course, at that point they thought *Bacillus decimus* had died out except for one small area in South America."

"Yes," Josh said. "But now your drug is the sole chance we have to treat our two patients, both of whom have *Bacillus deci-*

mus infections. I recognize it's not fully tested. All that aside, it's the only hope these two people have."

"It's more than its not being tested. When the FDA told us unofficially there was no need to keep working on it, we got rid of what we had, or at least most of it. There might be just a bit still around, but it would take a while, maybe several weeks, to make more."

"I'll take whatever you have. Just get it to me ASAP."

"I'm going to have to clear this with Dr. Gaschen, our Chief Operating Officer."

"Call him, find him, do whatever you need to. But if I send a jet to Atlanta . . ." He looked at Marks, who nodded. "If I send a jet to Atlanta, can you get the drug—whatever you called it—can you get it on that plane?"

Derek's sigh sounded like a hurricane when it came through the phone line. Then he said, "How long will it take your plane to get to Hartsfield International?"

Marks leaned in toward the phone console. "Doctor, this is Karen Marks. I'm the administrative aide for President Madison. I can make a call and have a jet standing by at Dobbins Air Base, just north of Atlanta, in less than an hour. You get the drug to Dobbins; we'll take it from there."

After another silence, Derek said, "Okay, but tell whoever you talk to at Dobbins that they're going to have to fly more than some medication. I'm coming, too."

"Are you sure?" Josh asked.

"Yep. I probably know more about RP-78 and *Bacillus decimus* than anyone else in the world," Derek said.

"We'll take all the RP-78 you can find, and your help would be welcome," Josh said. "Just hurry."

"I'm not sure what Dr. Gaschen is going to say when I tell him I'm sending what he have left of the drug and going with it, but I guess the worst that can happen is that he fires me. I was getting sort of tired of working for a pharmaceutical company anyway."

10

When Josh ended his conversation with Derek Johnson, he had to resist the inclination to heave a sigh of relief. Yes, this was a positive step, but the battle had just begun.

"Good work, Dr. Pearson," Karen Marks said. "You handled that pretty well."

"Thanks, but we're a long way from being out of the woods here. Will you make the arrangements for the jet at Dobbins and someone to meet it here?"

"That's what I do," she said. "It's what I'm good at. Your job is to keep your patient alive until the ribo-whatsitsname arrives."

"Actually, I'm interested in two patients," Josh reminded her.

Marks narrowed her eyes. "While I'm only interested in one of them."

Josh didn't have a reply for that one. Besides, he was too wrung out to argue further. "I'm going to clean up and change into a scrub suit. Call me when you know something more about the drug's arrival."

Rachel came awake and noticed that some things had changed. Sometime while she was asleep, someone had adjusted her bed so she was sitting more upright. They'd also slightly increased the flow of moist oxygen being delivered by the mask that sat loosely on her face. She tried increasing the depth of her respirations and heard none of the squeaking stridor she'd noticed before when she tried to breathe too deeply.

The man standing over her bed spoke in a voice that was soft, somewhat at odds with his physical appearance. "Awake, are we?"

"Dr. Molina? Sixto? Is that you?"

"Sorry I had to leave in such a hurry, but they needed me next door."

"How is Mr. Madison?" Rachel asked.

Sixto didn't say anything, and it was as though Rachel could see him thinking, *Do I want to upset her, since she's got the same problem?*

The rush call for the doctor, her own fight with air hunger, plus her knowledge of the natural history of diphtheria, supplied her answer despite his silence. "Did you have to trach him?" Rachel asked.

"How are things in here?"

Rachel smiled at the familiar voice. In addition, she could almost see the relief on Sixto's face, despite its being partially covered by a mask. Now there was no need for him to answer.

Josh moved to her side and put his gloved hand into her own. There was tenderness in his touch, a tenderness she'd missed.

"I'm doing okay," Rachel said, being careful to speak gently and breathe slowly. She didn't want Sixto to have to perform another emergency tracheotomy today.

Josh turned to his friend. "Sixto, I appreciate your looking in on Mr. Madison and taking care of him. I was on the phone, lining up what I think may be the treatment we need to get these patients on their way to recovery."

"Can you . . . can you explain?" Rachel asked. She was concerned because her voice seemed to be weaker. She wasn't anxious for a tracheotomy, but she had to ask. Maybe the two men would leave soon, and she could rest.

Sixto looked at Josh and raised his eyebrows, the only expressive part of his face that Rachel could see. Apparently, he didn't know this part of the story either.

"Rachel, it seems that you and the ex-president are infected with both diphtheria and another bacteria—one everyone thought until now was confined to a few cases in South America."

Rachel raised her own eyebrows, hoping it would keep Josh talking while letting her conserve her energy and her breath. Evidently it worked.

"I've been in touch with the CDC," he said. "They mentioned that a pharmaceutical company was working on an antibiotic that could possibly work in this case. A friend of mine, a doctor who's the medical director there, will be on a jet in a few minutes with as much of that drug as he can put his hands on. As soon as we get it, we'll start treatment."

It was probably a good thing that Josh's features were partially obscured by his mask, because Rachel sensed that there was more to the story than what he was telling. But for now, she simply nodded and let her head fall back on the pillow.

"Look, I'm sorry I haven't been able to look in on you, but believe me, I've been really busy." Josh readjusted the mask to her face, turned up the oxygen level even higher, and said, "The nurses will keep checking on you. I'm going to shower, shave, and change into a scrub suit." He shrugged his shoulders in a way that told Rachel they were tense or tired or both. "I think I have another long night in front of me."

When Josh and Sixto had left the room, Rachel lay silent, breathing slowly, trying not to give in to the air hunger she was starting to feel. There was one thing she could do, something that wouldn't require exertion or speaking. She silently prayed.

Before finally heading for that long-awaited shower, Josh changed to fresh protective garb and approached the room now occupied by the ex-president. The agent at the door—Josh couldn't recall his name—said, "Sir, would you mind pulling your mask down so I can check your identity before you go in?"

Josh complied, and the man said, "Thank you, Dr. Pearson. I think you can see why that's necessary."

"Right," Josh said. "I guess I'm not used to all this security." He realized he'd gotten in the habit of deferring to anyone wearing a dark suit and an earpiece. He studied the agent's face carefully, and asked, "And tell me your name."

"Rutledge, sir."

"Thanks." Josh, vowing not to be as trusting as he'd been to this point, pushed through the door. His patient was lying in bed, evidently still recovering from the shock of what had just happened. "Mr. Madison, are you feeling okay?"

Before the ex-president could reply, a woman, her features hidden by a mask and facial shield like the ones Josh wore, stood up from the bedside and walked toward him, her hand out. "Doctor, I don't think we've had the opportunity to formally meet. I'm Mildred Madison."

Josh took the gloved hand. "Mrs. Madison, I apologize if I haven't talked with you before this, but I thought—"

"You had your hands full trying to save my husband's life, and for that I thank you. Jerry Lang and Karen Marks have kept me informed." She inclined her head toward the bed where David Madison was scribbling rapidly on a white dry erase board. "And please convey my thanks to the doctor who did the emergency operation on David. It not only probably saved his life, it left him dependent on writing his thoughts instead of voicing them . . . every one of them."

Josh couldn't see Mrs. Madison's expression, but he was willing to bet she was smiling. "I'd better see what my patient wants to say." The two of them approached the bedside.

David Madison held up the white board on which he'd written, "How long does this thing need to be in my neck?"

"Let me explain things to both of you," Josh said. "It's hard to tell how much of your airway obstruction is due to diphtheria and how much is from the secondary infection. The DAT we gave you plus the antibiotics you're receiving should take care of the diphtheria, probably by tomorrow." When Madison started to write, Josh hastened on. "We've determined the identity of the secondary infection, and at this moment a supply of a drug we think will treat it is on its way here via military jet, together with a colleague of mine who is something of an expert in its use."

Before her husband could write, Mrs. Madison said, "So . . ."

"You'll hear from me when we have the drug, and I'll keep you both informed as things go on." Josh had never been a good poker player, but fortunately his features were hidden when he delivered his next comment. "I think things are coming under control."

❖

"I'm sorry, but you'll have to show some identification."

Derek Johnson fixed the airman second class standing guard at the entrance to the flight line with a glance that would melt steel. He took in the airman's armband that said AP and the holstered pistol he carried. Realizing the guard was only following orders. Derek reached slowly for his wallet and brought it out using two fingers. He noticed that when he made a move for his hip pocket, the Air Police Officer stepped back and unsnapped the safety strap on his sidearm. Derek supposed that a large and somewhat intimidating man trying to enter a sensitive area might raise a red flag or two.

When he had his wallet in his hand, he pulled out two laminated cards and handed them to the guard. The first was a Georgia driver's license, listing Derek at six feet, five inches, the second an identity card for Major Derek Johnson of the Air Force Reserve. "Are we good now, Airman Potter?" Derek said, noting the nametape over the breast pocket of the airman's battle dress uniform.

In answer, the airman snapped a brisk salute and said, "Yes, sir. Thank you for providing the ID." He ducked back into the guard shack, consulted a clipboard, and said, "Your bird is that F-22 Raptor over there. The crew chief will fit you with a flight suit and a helmet. Good luck, sir."

In less than half an hour, Derek was strapped into the rear seat of the fighter jet. The small cooler containing all the RP-78 he'd been able to find after a thorough scouring of the Argosy facilities was safely stowed away. This was probably the last chance for the drug . . . and for Argosy. If RP-78 cured these two patients, one of them a former U.S. president, the FDA could almost certainly be persuaded to have another look at the compound.

Of course, if there are problems that arise from this off-label use of the drug—in other words, if this thing turns sour—I needn't bother coming back. They'll clean out my desk and send my things to me.

◆

Fresh from a shower—or as fresh as someone could be after twenty-four hours without sleep—Josh made use of the razor and toiletries Sixto kept in his locker in the surgeon's dressing room. Then dressed in a clean scrub suit, his dirty clothes crumpled into a pile in the corner of his hospital office, Josh tried to put his thoughts in order.

Doing what he'd done at the start of each new day during his residency training, Josh leaned back in his office chair, closed his eyes, and thought about the patients for whom he was responsible. In this case, it was a short list. David Madison remained his number one priority. Although the urgency of the past twenty-four hours had abated slightly now that Madison's airway was no longer at risk, there was still the knowledge that an infection of this sort had been universally fatal in the past. The only hope of avoiding that fate for Madison lay in a poorly tested drug that was in a jet headed for Dallas at this moment. For the third time in less than a day, Josh let his thoughts morph into a prayer—a prayer for healing for his patients and for wisdom and strength for himself.

Shame washed over him as he realized he'd put aside thoughts of the woman he . . . the word that he was about to choose brought Josh up short. He'd recognized for some time that he was developing deep feelings for Rachel. Her absence on the trip made him even more aware of them. And now her illness brought his feelings into full focus—he loved her. Yet Josh had been so caught up with the responsibility thrust upon him as physician for the ex-president that he hadn't told Rachel. But he would . . . soon.

That brought Josh face to face with another dilemma. RP-78, although virtually unproven, was the only hope to treat the fatal illness that infected both David Madison and Rachel. But what if there was only enough drug for one person? Karen Marks had made it manifestly clear that, so far as she was concerned, Madison's life was the only one that mattered. But the ultimate decision would rest with Josh. Whom would he choose? The ex-president dependent on him for care or the woman he loved?

A light tap on the door interrupted his thoughts. Before Josh could speak, Jerry Lang stuck his head in. "Do you have a minute?"

Why not? He was getting nowhere with his current problem. "Sure. Come in. Sit down."

Lang dropped into the chair on the other side of Josh's desk, stretched, and yawned. "I think we need to talk."

"If it's about treating Mr. Madison—"

"Karen Marks has already told me about the RP-78. I'll leave the medical end to you. I want to see what your opinion is about Dr. Lambert's death."

Josh shrugged his shoulders, wishing he could have stayed longer under the hot shower. "Honestly, I'm puzzled by the whole thing. I've reviewed Ben's medical records, and there was nothing there to suggest any heart problem."

"But without an autopsy we can't know, can we?" Lang asked.

Josh shook his head. "No. I've already told Rachel it's possible Ben Lambert was given a drug that would mimic a heart attack. But I don't know why anyone would want to kill him."

"Nor do I, and that's something to be investigated. I suppose we'll have to let it wait until later, though." Lang rose. "Right now, my primary job is protecting Mr. Madison. And I guess yours is to save his life. After that, we can look into Dr. Lambert's death. In the meantime, be thinking of why anyone would want to kill your colleague . . . or the ex-president." With that, the Secret Service agent turned and left.

Lang's question was the stimulus Josh needed to follow up on the question he'd been meaning to answer. Years ago he might have checked journals and textbooks. Now he hit a few keys on his computer, scrolled down the page, then peered at the monitor. There it was, from no less an authority than the National Institutes of Health. The article was headed "Aconite poisoning."

Aconite—sometimes called *wolfsbane*. Josh had heard of it, read about it (in Greek literature and Shakespeare), but never thought he'd see a case of poisoning involving it. His eyes danced over the words in the article, but stopped when he saw: "Highly cardiotoxic and neurotoxic." Josh read further until he confirmed that, in whatever manner it was administered, aconite did indeed mimic the signs and symptoms of a heart attack.

Of course, all this was academic, because without a body for an autopsy no one could confirm or rule out the presence of aconite in the deceased. Josh's mind moved on to other questions. Forget the manner of Ben Lambert's death. Why would someone want to get rid of him? And why would someone try to kill David Madison? And then there was the question that wouldn't leave Josh's mind. Would he be next?

At that moment, the door to Josh's office burst open and a tall, stocky man in a too-tight flight suit strode in. In one hand, he held a small personal cooler, one that might normally carry half a dozen soft drinks, in the other a duffel bag. The man tossed the bag in the corner and lowered the cooler gently onto Josh's desk. "Well, friend, here I am." He pointed to what he'd brought. "And, to my knowledge, this is the world's entire supply of RP-78. Let's hope it works."

The two men clasped hands and clapped each other on the shoulder. "Thanks for coming, Derek," Josh said.

"JP, you certainly know how to throw a party. I'm here, and I brought the stuff. How do you want to do this?"

"On the phone, you told me you were probably the world's expert on *Bacillus decimus*. Well, I've called you in to consult. Tell me about this however-you-pronounce-it."

"In Latin, the *c* in *decimus* would be pronounced like a *k*, but in English it sounds like an *s*. In our lab, we used the Latin pronunciation. But you can take your choice."

"Let's settle for the English, because that's how I've been pronouncing it. And why *decimus*? Was it discovered in December?"

Derek shook his head. "Remember your Bible, the plagues visited on Egypt?"

"Yes, sort of."

"The tenth plague was the death of the firstborn. The others ranged from bad to terrible, but this one was universally fatal. When Etienne Vandiver discovered the bacteria, he recognized that it caused death in every case. So he named it for the tenth plague."

Josh shivered as he thought of it. "Well, it appears that David Madison and Rachel Moore have both diphtheria and a *Bacillus decimus* infection. Would you like to see the cultures and slides?"

"I probably should, just to confirm. That way I can give you an official second opinion. And while we're heading for the lab, you can fill me in on the clinical picture of both patients. I doubt that you've made a mistake, but I suspect we'd better dot our i's and cross our t's for this case."

In a bit less than an hour, the two men were back in Josh's office. Derek eased into a chair and said, "Well, there's no doubt the diagnosis is correct. Now let's see what we can do to pull the patients through." He pointed to a dry-erase board on the wall. "Mind if I use that?"

"Anything that might help," Josh said.

Derek drew a line down the middle of the board and wrote Dipt on one side and Dec on the other. "You think both patients were given saline or something similar instead of DT boosters, so they were vulnerable to diphtheria infection. They've both received antitoxin and have been on antibiotics for about thirty-six hours. Right?"

Josh checked his watch and did some rapid calculations. "Closer to thirty hours on the antibiotics."

"Okay, although we can't see clinical evidence of a response because of the other infection, we can assume that by tomorrow they should be non-infectious from the standpoint of diphtheria." He entered a few notes in a sort of shorthand on the left side of the board. "That leaves *Bacillus decimus*. Madison has a tracheotomy, so his airway is safe for now. Rachel's is still borderline. It will take twenty-four to forty-eight hours for them to respond to RP-78, if it's going to work. Until then, the main thing to watch for is Rachel's airway closing off and either of them going into septic shock. If they exhibit high fever with convulsions, we've probably reached endgame."

"And if the drug doesn't work?"

"We'll cross that bridge when we come to it, won't we?" Derek said. "Now let's talk about dosing." He pointed to the cooler. "As I said, what I brought is what we have."

"Do you have data on optimum dosage?" Josh asked.

"We have limited dose-ranging studies in lab animals. The clinical studies were on seven volunteers serving life sentences in a South American prison. They understood the risks, but without treatment they were going to die. All of them recovered." Derek scribbled some figures in the otherwise blank right column of the board. "We think the dose is one milligram per kilogram of patient body weight, given once daily intramuscularly."

"For how long?" Josh asked.

"We have no idea. As you know, duration of dosage goes back to studies that show ten days is optimum for strep infections. Of course, some of the newer antibiotics, given for other infections, work well after three days, some after only one. But we always start with ten."

"How about in your volunteers?"

"We had enough of the medicine to give it for ten days, so that's what we did, but they all showed improvement within twenty-four to forty-eight hours. Unfortunately, we don't know if they would have relapsed if we'd stopped it then," Derek said. "If we had enough drug, I'd say give it for at least three days, seven would be better, and ten would be best."

"Let's check the medical records." Josh tapped some keys on the computer on his desk. In a moment he said, "Madison weighs one hundred eighty-five pounds, Rachel one hundred ten. That's about . . . let's see. That's one hundred thirty-four kilograms total for them both. Now to the most important question," Josh said. "How much do you have?"

Derek swung open the lid of the cooler to reveal a small, rubber-stoppered vial containing a pitifully small amount of clear, amber-tinted liquid. It rested amid three blocks of blue ice. He carefully lifted out the vial. "This is two hundred seventy milligrams of RP-78. That's enough for one dose for each of those patients or two doses for one of them. You make the choice."

11

David Madison opened his eyes and, for a moment, had no idea where he was. He could tell from his surroundings he was in a hospital room, but was he still in South America? Then it gradually came back to him, the whole story. He felt the fever. He heard the whistling as air moved in and out through the tube in his windpipe. He swallowed and felt the dull ache of the recent surgical incision in his neck. Then when he moved his eyes to scan the area around him, he saw Mildred sitting quietly at his bedside. Her eyes were closed, but her lips moved slightly. She was praying . . . undoubtedly, for him.

Madison tried to speak, but the only thing that came out was a rush of air. He lifted his hand. Mildred's eyes remained closed. He felt for the nurse call button at his side but didn't press it. It was ridiculous to call for help simply to get the attention of the woman who sat only six feet away from him.

For the first time in many years, David Madison, the man who at one time was leader of the free world, felt helpless. As he ascended the ladder of politics from local to state to national, eventually assuming the office of president, he'd grown accustomed to having people around him to do his bidding. He thought of the Bible story of the centurion who came to Jesus, begging Him to heal the man's dying daughter. The centurion had people he told to come or go, and they obeyed. But his power over men and events didn't translate into healing for his loved one.

Madison knew he was receiving the best possible medical care, but he was also struck by his helplessness in the situation. So, one of the most powerful men in the nation closed his eyes and joined his wife in prayer. It was all he could do.

Rachel tried to delay it as long as possible, but she realized she was playing with fire by putting it off. She'd tried to hide it from the nurse who checked on her every hour, sometimes every fifteen or twenty minutes, although she couldn't really say why. But her difficulty breathing was becoming more obvious. The nurse would see it the next time she came back, so Rachel pushed the call button to get her in the room now.

The nurse, Mary Wynn, hurried in. "Do you need something?"

Rachel nodded. She forced herself to speak slowly and quietly, fearing that if she pushed herself to any degree her vocal cords would go into spasm and close off her airway completely. "I think you'd better get Dr. Neeves or Dr. Molina. He was here earlier—"

The nurse frowned. "Don't try to talk." She pushed the button to elevate Rachel's head further, then turned up the oxygen even more. "I'll page them stat. Just hang on." As she hurried from the room, Rachel saw her cast a sidelong glance at the tracheotomy tray nearby, making sure it was ready.

Josh sat behind his desk with his eyes closed. He knew he had to make a decision, but another couple of minutes wouldn't hurt. He wished he could postpone it even more. "Derek," he said. "I appreciate your coming and bringing the RP-78. I never asked how Karen arranged everything."

"Once I got to Dobbins Air Force Base and got past the airman guarding the flight line, everything else was pretty simple." Derek stretched and yawned, then put his feet on Josh's desk. "A Secret Service agent, I think his name was Gilmore, met me at Love Field with a police escort to bring me to the hospital. That was kind of neat. On the way here, he told me that when I was ready to go back, Ms. Marks would arrange to fly me to Dobbins where I left my car."

"Won't your wife worry?"

The smile left Derek's face. "You haven't heard, have you? Robin died of ovarian cancer last year."

"Oh, man, that's . . . that's tough. I'm so sorry," Josh said. He hesitated, then decided to share his own news with his friend. "You may recall my wife, Carol. Well, she was killed in a car crash two years ago, along with our unborn child."

"It's rough, isn't it?" Derek said.

"And I'm not sure we ever get over it," Josh replied. "But now I have Rachel, and I hope there's someone out there for you as well. I know Robin would want you to be happy."

"Thanks," Derek said. "When we got the diagnosis, I'd just received an offer from a multi-specialty group in the Atlanta area. Good salary, great benefits, paid time for meetings and vacation. But when Robin's cancer was discovered, I decided to stay with Argosy."

Josh couldn't help but ask what to him was an obvious question. "Why?"

"To keep my insurance going. To avoid changing anything else in Robin's life. But mainly, I guess I was hoping I could come up with some sort of cure for cancer patients." He stood and began to pace. "I didn't, of course. I guess I was foolish to think I could succeed where some of the best minds in the world had been unsuccessful. But maybe RP-78 will turn out to be my magic bullet against *Bacillus decimus*."

Josh stood and picked up the cooler. "I guess I can't put off my decision any longer. It's time to give the RP-78 to . . . well, to one or both of them."

"I wish I could help you make the decision," Derek said.

Josh's cell phone rang. He looked at the caller ID, then answered. "Allison, what's up?"

Allison Neeves spoke in hushed tones, and Josh could hear voices in the background. "I'm calling from right outside Rachel's room."

Josh's pulse quickened. "What's happened?"

"Sixto just did an emergency tracheotomy on Rachel," Allison said. "She still has a high fever, but at least her airway is protected until you can figure out how to treat her."

Josh mumbled, "Thanks," and ended the call.

He was still faced with the decision of how to distribute the RP-78, and if anything, this new development hadn't made the choice any easier. Now both patients seemed to be in exactly the same situation. It came down to this—give two doses, which might be enough, to the woman he loved or to the former president of the United States. Or give each of them one dose and possibly sentence them both to death for lack of more of the drug.

Detective Stan Warren and Agent Jerry Lang sat in an isolated corner of the hospital cafeteria and sipped from cups of coffee that might have been fresh six hours ago. Warren had consumed so many bad cups of coffee over the years that he had come to accept whatever was available. Besides, he harbored the hope that, with the aid of the strong brew, he might be able to get through a few more hours without sleep as he tried to unravel the mystery surrounding this latest attempt on the life of David Madison.

"We caught a break on identifying the gunman," Warren said, his eyes on the surface of his cup. "We ran his fingerprints through the system and got a hit almost immediately."

Lang looked up with interest. Warren wondered how the Secret Service agent could be this alert despite little or no sleep for the past day and a half. The detective had snatched a few hours of shut-eye on a couch in his lieutenant's office last night while others worked on the case, but so far as he could tell Lang's head hadn't touched a pillow. Maybe the agents of the Secret Service really were a special breed.

"What did you find?" Lang asked.

"The name he gave Miss Moore and Dr. Pearson was Bill Smith, which was eminently forgettable," Warren said. He sipped from his cup, made a face, and put it down. "Of course, that was his intent. His fingerprints identified him as a Ukrainian named Leonid Malnyk."

Lang pursed his lips. "So there's a Ukraine connection. We'd better try to run that down."

Warren moved his hand toward his coffee cup, then thought better of it and rested it on the table once more. "Don't bother. Malnyk was for hire to anyone with enough money. It's unusual that he actually was the triggerman, though. Generally, he put together jobs, farmed them out, and kept half the money for himself. Someone must have really greased his palm well for Malnyk to do this on his own."

"What about the body-snatching, or whatever you want to call it?"

"I was checking on that when this shooting went down. There's a veterinary clinic in South Dallas that has a crematory oven. A dog owner went by there yesterday to pick up the remains of his dog and found the vet shot dead. The oven, which is big enough for large pets, was still warm."

"So . . ."

"So we think Malnyk took Lambert's body to this place, got the veterinarian out of the way, and reduced the body to ashes,"

Warren said. "That would take an hour or two at most. He took Lambert's effects, the wallet and jewelry, and delivered them along with the cremains to the local funeral home. A few phone calls would tell him which one he wanted. The note was designed to indicate that all this was a mistake, hoping that would satisfy the police and they'd let their investigation drop."

"How do you explain the absence of Lambert's class ring?"

"Who knows? Did the mortician in South America steal it? Did Malnyk decide to take it? Was it burned up in the crematory oven? I have no idea. But I feel certain that the cremated remains delivered to Sparkman Hillcrest are those of Ben Lambert, and thus there will never be an autopsy to show his cause of death."

Lang said, "So I need to backtrack and see if Malnyk's shooting attempt was related to the incident in South America that probably infected Mr. Madison and Ms. Moore." He looked at his watch. "I guess I'll start by interviewing the remaining members of the party, who should be returning sometime tonight or early tomorrow."

As though on cue, Lang's cell phone rang. He looked at the caller ID and said to Warren, "And wouldn't you know it, this is Dr. Dietz, the other physician who accompanied Mr. Madison on the trip."

Lang answered the call. Warren could only hear one side of the conversation, but it was enough. "I'm sorry your flight was delayed, but you know how that goes. Is the group about to leave for the U.S. now?"

There was a pause. "I'm sorry, Dr. Deitz, but Mr. Madison can't talk right now. But I'm sure he wishes you and the rest of the delegation safe travels. Call me after you get back to the U.S."

Lang ended the call and said, "Be glad you don't have to handle all these people."

"I think I have enough on my plate with the disappearance and reappearance of Dr. Lambert's body, plus this latest shooting episode." It appeared to Warren that the Secret Service agent had his hands full guarding the former president, investigating what happened almost three thousand miles away, and keeping a lid on the number of people who knew about it. *Better him than me.*

Warren took another look at the cold coffee in his cup. Oh, well. Maybe it would help keep him going. He finished the dark liquid in two large gulps.

◆

"Would you mind coming into the room with me?" Josh asked Derek. "I think President Madison would like to meet you."

"Sure," Derek said. He began the routine of donning a paper gown, gloves, and mask. "Remind me after we're through here to tell you some things about isolation precautions for *decimus*."

Josh let that slide. He had to concentrate on the decision he was facing. "I appreciate what you're doing, Derek."

"Just trying to help out a colleague. And, oh yes, a former president." He tied the strings of his gown. "And since I'm the one who brought the medicine and discussed its use with you, my presence might help you spread the blame around if what you're doing fails."

Josh had no answer for that, mainly because there was a grain of truth in it.

As they stood in the doorway, Derek said, "I suspect you know this better than I, but I notice that sometimes you call him Mr. Madison, sometimes President Madison. Isn't it correct to reserve that title for the current office holder?"

"Maybe, but there are times I'm in a hurry, others when my respect for him trumps what etiquette dictates. Only a few years ago this man was arguably the most powerful person in the world, and even though he no longer holds that office, he's still larger than life to me."

"No argument there." Derek stepped back from the door and gestured to Josh. "Lead on. I'll be right behind you."

Madison was lying quietly in his bed, but as Josh approached he noticed that his patient's bedclothes were soaked. The man's brow was dry, but the reason was soon evident, as Mildred Madison reached out with a washcloth and blotted her husband's face. Because of the continued presence of the fever, together with the airway obstruction that made an emergency tracheotomy necessary, Josh was more determined than ever to bring this man through the crisis he saw inching nearer.

"Mr. Madison, this is Dr. Derek Johnson. He's the chief medical officer of Argosy Pharmaceuticals, the developer of this new drug we hope will help with the infection you have."

Madison nodded. He lifted the whiteboard from where it lay on his bed and printed, "Whatever you have to do." Then he dropped the board and lay back, obviously exhausted.

"Mrs. Madison," Josh said, turning to the woman standing at the bedside. "Do you have any questions?"

She shook her head. Josh was certain she understood the gravity of her husband's infection. This was a last-ditch effort to save him. No one was interested in talking about alternatives and complications. RP-78 was the only chance they had.

Mary Wynn, the head nurse, handed Josh the papers giving permission for this latest treatment. Madison scrawled his signature and Mildred Madison added hers.

Josh handed the permit back to Mary. "Why are you still here?"

"We're working twelve-hour shifts. I go off at seven p.m."

Josh wondered if the move was to keep the number of personnel moving through the area at a minimum, or if the staff felt as he did: it was important to do everything to save the life of this man. "Thank you," he muttered.

Josh raised his eyebrows to request permission before he lifted the whiteboard and felt-tip pen from the ex-president's bed. He calculated the dose, then showed the work to Derek who studied it and nodded. With the limited supply of RP-78, there was no room for mistakes.

Derek handed Josh the vial containing the drug. He cleaned the rubber diaphragm with an alcohol swab, then inserted a needle attached to a syringe and carefully withdrew the proper amount of the clear solution.

Josh cleaned Madison's upper arm with another alcohol swab. He took a deep breath, said a silent prayer, and plunged the needle into the mass of the deltoid muscle in Madison's arm.

Mary Wynn reached to a side table and retrieved the pad and pen that lay there. She jotted the time and details of the procedure. "I'll enter these in the electronic medical record when we finish here," she said.

Josh nodded. "And now, Mr. President . . . we wait."

"And pray," Mildred Madison added.

Both Josh and Derek nodded.

When the two men were back outside Madison's room, Derek said, "I can understand the isolation precautions, but what about the people who were exposed to Madison and Rachel before you confirmed the diagnosis?"

Josh nodded. "When this started, we thought it was a straightforward case of diphtheria. I made sure all of us had been immunized. Since I had close contact with Rachel, I started on prophylactic antibiotics as well. If we were just dealing with diphtheria, we could stop the isolation protocol a couple of days after treatment started. For *Bacillus decimus*, I don't think anyone knows, but the people in close contact with Madison and Rachel when they were getting sick could be at risk, I guess."

"You've been so busy thinking about others, you ignored yourself. Let me put your mind at ease. It takes a massive exposure to *Bacillus decimus* to get an infection. The men in the prison in Colombia had such a massive exposure, but we didn't even isolate them once they got sick."

"Since the two patients have received treatment for diphtheria, are you suggesting we stop isolating them?"

"No," Derek said. "Since you started it, I'd suggest you continue it for now. Better safe than sorry, I guess. You can stop when their fever has been down for a day or two."

Not if . . . when. Josh loved Derek's optimism. But his relief was short-lived, because Derek's next words, words he didn't want to hear, brought him face to face with the major decision facing him.

"Now comes the hard part, friend. Now you have to decide whether to hold back the remaining RP-78 and give a second dose tomorrow to Mr. Madison, or administer it today to Rachel Moore."

Josh looked at Derek, hoping for some word of guidance, but in his heart he knew the decision was his alone. And whatever he decided, it was likely to be wrong . . . and the consequences would be huge.

12

Josh had read what he could about the infection, and authorities seemed in agreement on the way symptoms would present and progress. Initially the infection produced a clinical picture that was similar to diphtheria, with a membranous swelling of the throat and airway, along with fever and generalized constitutional symptoms. After about a week the bleeding would start—bruises after the slightest touch, a progressive cough producing bloody sputum. Then came internal bleeding, with vomiting and diarrhea, the products containing massive quantities of pure blood. At some point, the patient's fever would no longer respond to medications. After that came convulsions and bleeding into the brain. This could take the form of a massive event, in which case the patient died immediately. Still as fatal, but sadder, were instances in which slight, repetitive bleeds gradually affected multiple areas of the brain, sending the patient into a vegetative state before the vital centers shut down entirely.

Josh wished he hadn't read the details, yet he couldn't ignore them as he scoured the scant medical literature about *Bacillus decimus* infections in hope of finding some way to treat it. Now he had at his disposal a tiny amount of the drug that might reverse the otherwise-fatal disease. What if one dose wouldn't help but two stopped the march of symptoms? On the other hand, perhaps one dose was enough. Derek said that in the pitifully small sample, treatment had continued for ten days . . . but that was simply because most antibiotics were given that way, at least in early trials. It was only in later dose-ranging studies that the optimum length of treatment would be determined. And those hadn't been done with robinoxine.

Derek had declined Josh's offer to go into Rachel's room with him. "This is a decision you have to make," he said. "I'll pray for wisdom for you, and I'll pray for the recovery of those two patients. But as for the decision, you're on your own."

Now Josh stood silent at Rachel's bedside. He looked down at her, relieved that her breathing was easier now with the tracheotomy in place, worried because despite that seeming relief, her infection with *Bacillus decimus* was proceeding unchecked.

He hesitated to make his presence known. The longer Rachel rested, the longer Josh could put off the decision that continued to torment him. After what seemed like an eternity, Rachel opened her eyes and smiled. She picked the whiteboard and felt-tip pen up off her bedside table and wrote, "I'm glad you're here." Then, in a move that tore at Josh's heart, she added, "How's Mr. Madison?"

"He's doing about like you. The tracheotomy gives him an airway, but I have to stop the progression of the disease."

Rachel frowned. Next she wrote, "This is more than diphtheria, isn't it?"

Josh nodded. In a few sentences he explained about the *Bacillus decimus* infection. He honestly didn't know how far to go, but eventually he told her that he'd managed to acquire a tiny amount of a medication that had been effective in a very small series. "But we don't know how many doses it will take," he said. "And we don't have much at all."

Rachel closed her eyes, and for a moment Josh thought she was sleeping. Then she opened them, took the whiteboard, and wrote, "If you only have enough for one patient, give it to Mr. Madison."

Josh's reflex reaction was to shake his head, but Rachel wrote again. "He's done so much, and has so much more to accomplish. Save him."

Josh blinked to clear the tears from his eyes. He knew what he was going to do.

◆

The ring of his cell phone brought Josh from deep sleep to full wakefulness with a speed born of years spent practicing medicine. In the time it took for him to reach to the bedside table and retrieve the instrument, he reoriented himself—he was in a call room at Prestonwood Hospital.

A glance at his watch told Josh it had been almost twelve hours since Derek asked him how long he'd been without sleep. Josh recalled responding that it had been about thirty-six hours.

"Well, you'd better get some now," Derek had said. "That drug isn't going to act immediately. We probably won't see any change in anyone's condition for at least twelve hours."

"But—"

"You heard Dr. Neeves say she was going to spend the night in one of the call rooms at the hospital, in case she was needed. I'll be around as well. I suggest you get some rest."

Josh picked up the cell phone and pressed the button to answer the call.

"Josh, this is Derek."

"Don't you ever sleep?"

"Sometimes, but not much. Allison Neeves and I are at the nurse's station going over both patients' vital signs. I thought you might want to join us."

"Let me splash some cold water on my face," Josh said. "I'll be right there."

Fifteen minutes later, Josh, Derek, and Allison Neeves congregated at the nurse's station. "So the fever's going up?" Josh said.

"Just a little. It certainly isn't going down. It had been stable at about a hundred and three Fahrenheit," Allison said. Neither she nor Josh was a fan of the new tendency to measure body temperature in degrees Celsius. "This morning it's a hundred and four."

"That's not a big spike," Josh said.

"No, but it certainly doesn't indicate any response to the RP-78," Allison said. "Not a positive one, at least."

Derek thought a moment before speaking. "You know that our series was small—actually, tiny when compared with most clinical trials. But I seem to recall that there was a further spike in fever before patient temperatures started to drop. Sometimes it took a second dose of the RP-78 before we saw improvement. Remember I said twenty-four to forty-eight hours."

Josh felt the eyes of both doctors on him. "And if I hadn't given the remaining drug to Rachel last evening, we'd have another dose for the former president."

"We're not judging you, Josh," Allison said. "You might be the presidential physician, but you're also a doctor . . . and that woman means a lot to you. You did what you thought was right to give two patients the best chance to live."

"Okay, enough of that," Derek said. "Let's reconvene in the cafeteria and put our heads together over some breakfast to see what else we can figure out. Remember what Yogi Berra said— 'It' ain't over 'til it's over.' Well, the fat lady hasn't sung yet."

Rachel opened her eyes and tried to focus on where she was and why she was there. In the middle of her thoughts, she realized that her respirations were producing a raspy sound—her tracheotomy tube was partially occluded by secretions. There was no clock on the wall of this room, and she had no idea where her watch was, but the noise in the hall told Rachel it was about the time of shift change. One of the nurses had mentioned to her that they were working twelve-hour shifts—not complaining, simply mentioning it—but Rachel had no idea if this was morning or evening. Would someone come in soon? And who would it be? No, she couldn't wait.

She was reaching for the nurse call button when the door to her room opened and a gowned and masked figure walked softly toward her. The personnel that entered her room had been limited, and Rachel had become adept at identifying them despite their isolation garb, but this one was different. Remembering what she'd heard via snippets of conversation outside her door about the recent attempt on David Madison's life, she kept her finger on the nurse call button. It dawned on Rachel that since she couldn't cry out for help, this intruder might be able to harm or even kill her before anyone responded.

"Rachel, I'm Barbara Carper. I usually work on weekends, and I'm relieving Mary Wynn today. I haven't had the opportunity to work with you yet, so I thought I'd better introduce myself." The newcomer reached inside her isolation gown, and Rachel cringed but didn't move.

The nurse made a few motions with her gloved hand and pulled out a hospital ID badge. "See, that's me."

Sure enough, the name matched the one the supposed Barbara Carper had given. Seeing the questions still in Rachel's eyes, the woman shrugged. "Please don't cough on me while I do this." She flipped up her plastic visor and pulled down her mask for a moment, allowing Rachel to compare the face on the badge with that of the nurse. The nurse restored the visor and mask to their proper places, and said, "Now let's clean up that trach tube and suction you. That should help you breathe better."

Rachel wasn't used to being on this end of the nursing care she was receiving, but as best she could tell, Barbara was doing everything right. She relaxed a bit, yet wondered if she'd ever get over being suspicious of every new face that came her way. Was she being paranoid . . . or just cautious?

The group went through the cafeteria line, then found a table in the corner where there were no neighbors to hear their conversation. Josh looked down at the food on his tray and found that, despite the stressful situation in which he found himself, he was hungry. He thought back and realized he'd worked through lunch yesterday then dropped, exhausted, onto the bed in the call room before eating dinner. He'd missed a couple of meals before during his residency, but he was a lot younger then.

Josh was about to attack the scrambled eggs and sausage on his plate when out of the corner of his eye he saw Derek bow his head. Josh was used to a spoken grace before meals when he was with a group of family or friends, although it usually wasn't his idea to initiate it. However, he'd totally ignored it in this situation. He wasn't sure if he was reacting to peer pressure or a guilty conscience, but whatever the cause, he closed his eyes, bowed his head, and rectified the omission.

Josh wasn't sure what Allison had done about grace, but when he raised his head and began eating he saw that she was already well into her stack of pancakes. He chewed, swallowed, and said, "Okay, at this table we have three people with above-average IQs and a significant amount of experience practicing medicine. What solutions to the current problem have we ignored?"

"We're dealing with an unusual organism that in the past has killed everyone infected with it," Allison said.

"Tell me something I don't know," Josh said, not attempting to mask his sarcasm.

"I'm getting there." She nodded at Derek, who had almost finished eating the fried eggs and bacon he'd chosen. "You said the drug had been tried on humans only once in a very small series. But it was successful."

Derek nodded his agreement but remained silent.

"So Derek brought all the RP-78 he could find at Argosy," Josh said. "After one dose, which was all we had, neither Madison nor Rachel has showed signs of improvement. We need more of the drug, but the pharmaceutical company has stopped making it. So, I repeat, what can we do now?"

Allison looked over at Derek. "Were you prepared to run your series in South America for a larger number of patients than the ones that received the drug?"

"Yes. We sent down enough RP-78 to treat twenty-five men for ten days each. But, as you know, when we floated the idea of the drug past some contacts we had at the FDA, they said to forget it, because the drug would never get approved."

Allison looked around the table, waiting for the light to dawn. Josh saw it first. "But there should be a supply of RP-78 still in South America. All we have to do is contact the doctor who was doing the work for you down there and get it flown to us."

Derek was already shaking his head. "After Josh called me and asked for as much of the drug as I could lay my hands on, I thought of that." He lifted his coffee cup, then put it down without drinking from it. "After the FDA rained on our parade, our study coordinator at Argosy contacted the doctor in South America and told him to destroy the remaining drug. It's gone."

Josh frowned. "If you can give me the name and number of the doctor who ran that study, I have an idea."

Derek opened his smartphone and searched for a minute. Then he took a paper napkin from a dispenser on the table, pulled out a pen, and wrote something. Josh stuck the paper in his pocket and stood. "I'm going to make a phone call." And without another word, he hurried away.

Josh closed and locked the door of his office. He started to turn off his cell phone, but decided that an emergency might arise that required him. This call was going to require all his diplomatic skills to bring off. He'd never done anything this important before. *God, help me to get this right.* Josh realized that he'd never prayed so often as he had in the past couple of days. He'd have to think about that . . . but later. Right now, he needed to make one of the most important phone calls of his life.

He encountered his first problem almost immediately. His call wasn't simply long distance. It was intercontinental. Josh tried to convince the hospital operator this was urgent, involving the case of former president David Madison. Despite his protestations, the operator told him she'd have to get approval from the administrator on call. Josh replied that he couldn't wait. Instead, he picked up his cell phone and dialed Karen Marks. In a few short sentences, he told her what needed to be done.

"Why can't you persuade the operator to let the call go through?" Marks asked.

"I tried, but for some reason, she won't believe me, and I don't want to wait for her to track down the administrator on call. Can you help?"

"Give me five minutes, then dial it."

Josh spent that time rehearsing what he was going to say. He had to be convincing yet diplomatic. Finally, he thought he had it. After five minutes, he picked up the phone, and following instructions he found in the front of a phone directory from the bottom drawer of his desk, he dialed the number.

"Alo?" This was followed by words in Spanish spoken so rapidly Josh had no chance of understanding. However, the female voice seemed pleasant enough. Josh hoped it was a portent of success.

"Do you or anyone there speak English?"

"I speak English," the woman said. "How may I help you?"

"This is Dr. Josh Pearson, *Señor Dr. Pearson*, calling from the United States for Dr. Andres Chavez."

"I'm sorry, but this is the doctor's answering service. He's not in his office on Saturday."

Saturday. Days had become meaningless for Josh as the medical situation of his patients deteriorated. "Look, this is an emergency. I need to speak with Dr. Chavez. It's urgent—truly a matter of life and death."

"I can try to locate the doctor," she said.

Josh had been down this road with answering services here at home. Despite the urgency he tried to convey, he wondered if the message would reach the doctor. "Can you give me his home number?"

The conversation went on for another five minutes, ending when the answering service operator said, "I'll do what I can to locate the doctor. If I do, I'll give him your number and your message. That's all I can promise."

After he hung up, Josh sat at his desk and cradled his head in his hands. Why hadn't he thought of this before? Would Chavez call back? And if he did, would Josh be able to convince him to cooperate? And if he were willing to help, would he have what was needed? Josh checked his watch. If he didn't get a return call in half an hour, he'd have to ask Karen Marks to call in yet another favor and help locate the missing doctor. Meanwhile, all he could do was wait.

13

Jerry Lang stood at the door to David Madison's room. He'd
sent Agent Chrisman, who'd taken over guard duty there, to
get some breakfast. After he got back, Lang would try to snatch
a few hours of sleep. Mrs. Madison had spent the night in her
husband's room, resting in a reclining chair. Lang himself had
managed about three hours of sleep in an unoccupied patient
room. Once more, he wished the ex-president had listened to
his suggestion that he be flown to someplace like Walter Reed
or Bethesda, a hospital set up for treating high-profile patients
with critical illness. But he hadn't, so Lang would have to do
the best he could with the resources at his disposal.

Lang's cell phone rang. He saw the call was from Dr. Wayne
Dietz. When Madison and Lang flew back early, they had left
Dietz, an associate dean and professor of Internal Medicine at
Southwestern Medical Center, in charge of leading the remain-
ing delegation back to the U.S.

"Dr. Dietz, when did you get back?"

Dietz's voice was a rich baritone that, even over a cell phone,
carried with it a tone of authority overlaid with a thick Boston
accent. "The charter arrived at Love Field about four this
morning. How's David?"

How much did Dietz and the rest of the group know? Well,
better to say too little than too much. "He and Ms. Moore

are both down with an infection they apparently picked up in South America."

"So I guess I can't talk with him? Is that what you're saying?"

You don't know the half of it. "That's correct, sir. Mr. Madison isn't able to talk, but I'll certainly tell him you called."

"Maybe Monday he and I can get together and discuss the opinions of the group about the clinic David's foundation wants to fund—you know, the location, size, staffing." There was the briefest of pauses. "Now that poor Ben Lambert is gone, I imagine David will want to talk with me about becoming his personal physician. We'll straighten that out on Monday as well, I suppose."

Lang ended the call. He'd mention it to Mr. Madison as soon as he was better. If he didn't get better . . . well, he'd cross that bridge when he came to it.

◆

Rachel didn't have access to her medical records, but she'd learned to assess the presence or absence of her own fever, even estimate its magnitude, without the use of a clinical thermometer. No longer would she cast a doubting eye on patients who said, "I know what's going on in my body." She was learning that was often true, based on her own experience, not something she'd been taught in nursing school.

All things considered, Rachel knew she was no better. Although she wished it were otherwise, she knew her fever had not broken after the injection Josh gave her last night. If anything, her temperature was a bit higher. She'd argued with him when he told her he was going to give her a dose of RP-78. Josh wouldn't tell her how much of the drug he had, or whether this represented a decision on his part to treat her while withholding a dose from Madison. But she knew in her heart that was exactly what he'd done.

Part of her regretted Josh's choice, while the rest of her loved him for it. There it was again. She loved him. The feelings she'd had for him before her trip to South America had grown in her first prolonged absence from him. Then her illness, including its potentially fatal nature, made what she felt for Josh crystal clear to her. Oh, her clinical mind could argue it was simply due to the effect the fever and other constitutional symptoms were having on her. Rachel knew differently. She was aware that she could die from this illness, although she couldn't recall Allison or Josh coming right out and saying so. Even so, she determined that before she drew her final breath, she'd tell Josh of her love. And she'd speak the words, not write them on a whiteboard with a felt-tip pen.

◆

Josh was still sitting at his desk, deep in thought, when the ring of the phone startled him into full wakefulness. *Please let this be Dr. Chavez.* He cleared his throat, picked up the receiver, and said, "Dr. Pearson."

"Doctor, this is Dr. Andres Chavez. My answering service says you wanted to talk with me. They said it was urgent, and you were most insistent."

Josh had expected to hear a heavy accent on the other end of the phone. Instead, Chavez spoke flawless English with a hint of a mid-Atlantic accent, perhaps Philadelphia or Baltimore. Josh could have kicked himself for not using the time he had to check the background of this man. Well, that ship had sailed.

"Doctor," Josh said, "I appreciate your getting back to me. I realize this call is transcontinental, so if you'd like to give me a number, I'd be glad to call you back."

"Not to worry," Chavez said. "When I realized this was a U.S. number, I drove back to the hospital where I work to return your call."

Josh wondered what kind of hospitals were in Bogotá, and it seemed that Chavez had encountered this before. "In case you're wondering, that's the University Hospital of Fundación Santa Fe de Bogotá. We're a two hundred–bed hospital, offering residencies in thirteen areas of specialization. We are affiliated with the Johns Hopkins Hospital, which is where I received my own training in internal medicine." Chavez paused to let that sink in.

"My apologies, doctor," Josh said. This totally changed his mind about his approach. He'd pictured the man who ran the RP-78 study for Argosy as a minor functionary who would think nothing of holding back some of the drug for his own private use—and sale. This doctor didn't fit that mold, at least not based on what was evident so far. And if that were the case, Josh's plan to threaten him if he didn't give up any RP-78 he'd held back wasn't going to fly.

"Dr. Chavez, I'm sorry for my ignorance of your situation there. I didn't have time to do my homework, and I guess it shows. I'll put my cards on the table." Josh tried to protect the identities of his patient, although he was prepared to reveal it if that would help him get the drug he needed. He told Chavez he was treating two patients who'd come back from South America with a diphtheria-like illness that had turned out to be caused by infection with *Bacillus decimus*.

"Would that be Señor Madison and Señorita Moore? I accompanied their delegation to a couple of areas in the less-settled regions of our country. They seemed to be developing some respiratory symptoms when they left."

Josh shook his head. This was no small-time doctor, picking up a bit of extra money by running a drug study. Obviously, Chavez was what some of the people here in the U.S. would call a "wheel." Well, it seemed to Josh the ace he'd been holding—David Madison's identity as the patient—was useless. All that was left was to tell the truth and beg this man, professional to professional, for help.

"Dr. Derek Johnson gave me your name and number as the person who was running the RP-78 study for Argosy. He scraped together enough of the drug for me to give one dose to each patient. It hasn't been effective so far. I'm trying everything I can think of to get more. I was hoping you could help me. According to Johnson, the remaining drug was to be destroyed and the study terminated. But if you have access to any RP-78—however little it might be—I beg you to let us have it."

The silence on the other end of the line went on long enough for Josh to wonder if he'd been disconnected. No, because he still heard the faint echo that marked a phone call between continents. Then Chavez spoke. "Dr. Pearson, I think I can help you."

◆

The group gathered in Josh's office included Derek Johnson and Allison Neeves, but this time Jerry Lang and Karen Marks joined them. There were normally only two chairs besides Josh's desk chair in the room, and rather than bring in more and further crowd the office, Derek and Lang said they'd stand.

After making sure the door was closed, Josh brought the group up to date on his conversation with Chavez. "I fully expected the man to be someone who might put back some of the medication and sell it to patients with a *Bacillus decimus* infection. I figured I'd either be able to buy him off or frighten him into letting us have what little he'd held out. Instead, this man is a Hopkins-trained internist who works at a university hospital. He thought it was ridiculous to destroy a drug when it had worked so well in a small number of cases, so even though the study at La Modela Prison had been stopped, he put the remaining RP-78 back in case there was a need for it in the future. He'd been considering contacting Argosy to see if they'd underwrite resuming the study and then perhaps seeking a market for RP-78 in South America, since there is a small area there where *Bacillus decimus* is still around."

"Man, I shouldn't have taken the word of our research coordinator," Derek said. "I should have called Chavez myself."

"He might not have told you the whole truth. After all, Argosy had the power to insist that he destroy the rest of the RP-78. In this case, because two patients are in crisis—patients he had met, two people he immediately identified without any help from me—he reacted as any good physician would. He said he had several vials of RP-78. Some of the original shipment had gone out of date, but Chavez thought there were perhaps a dozen doses that were still good."

"So we have enough to give each patient maybe six more doses," Allison said.

"Or ten doses for Mr. Madison, and—"

Josh kept his voice low, but there was an intensity to his words that no one could miss. "No. That's already been decided. It came down to a medical decision, and I made it. These aren't an ex-president and a nurse; they're a man and a woman who have a potentially fatal disorder, and I want to save them both if I can. Both patients will be treated equally with RP-78."

"How do we get it here?" Derek asked. "Is there going to be a problem getting it out of Colombia? I seem to recall that when Argosy shipped the drug in, they had to grease some palms to get it past customs."

"Chavez said the Colombian Air Force has a base right outside Bogotá. I asked about our sending a plane there, but he said it would be better and faster if he could get on a Colombian military jet and fly the drug here. And he probably could bypass customs by doing it that way."

"Great," Karen said. "Every time we need something else to treat Mr. Madison, we acquire another doctor in the bargain."

Josh didn't raise his voice, but there was a new note of authority in it when he spoke. "I've made a medical decision. Now I'd appreciate it if you'd pick up the phone and make arrangements for one of our top Air Force generals to talk with his counterpart in the Colombian Air Force. When that's done, we'll call Dr. Chavez to make the final arrangements to get him and the drug here." He took a deep breath. "And I don't care how many other doctors it takes to save Mr. Madison—and Ms. Moore. Bring them on. We'll handle it."

◆

Josh had just finished checking on Madison and Rachel, whom he was now treating in tandem with Allison Neeves, when his cell phone buzzed. He finished drying his hands before he stepped to the end of the hall, away from the rooms of his patients, to answer the call.

"JP, we might have a problem," Derek said.

"We've had problems for several days," Josh said. "What now?"

"I kind of assumed that whatever Karen Marks set out to get, she got. But there's some kind of hold-up in getting Dr. Chavez and the RP-78 onto a Colombian Air Force jet."

"I thought she was going to contact a general and have him talk with his opposite number over there to smooth the way."

"Well, apparently no one in Colombia wants to take responsibility for letting a solid citizen like Dr. Andres Chavez leave the country, especially with no real advance notice. Even though his passport is in order, they seem to be afraid this is some kind of scheme for him to escape Colombia. They're not sure he'll come back."

"Why—"

"Because his wife is dead. His grown kids live in the U.S. already. And when you talk about 'brain drain,' losing Chavez would be a topper in that department."

Josh considered the matter for a moment. "Okay. There's one more thing we might try. I hate to do this, but if we don't get that next dose of RP-78 here in . . ." He looked at his watch. "If it's not here in another six hours or so, it may be too late to do any good. Wish me luck."

Josh ended the call and headed back for Madison's room. Jerry Lang was back on duty, and as Josh gowned, the agent asked, "Weren't you here just a few minutes ago?"

"Got to ask your boss for a favor."

"I'm not sure he's in any shape to be doing favors," Lang said.

"I hope he's up for this one, because it's about the last chance we have to make this thing come out okay."

Inside the room, Josh wondered if he should ask Mildred Madison to step outside. Other than brief breaks for food, she hadn't left her husband's side for a full day. No, she deserved to hear this, too.

"Mr. President . . ."

Madison took his whiteboard and scrawled, "You only call me that when there's trouble. What?"

"I need you to make a call for me."

Madison pointed to his tracheotomy tube and shook his head.

"I've thought of that. When you get ready to call, we'll have you breathe one hundred percent oxygen for a bit, then deflate the cuff on your trach tube, put a cork in it so you can breathe around it and talk."

"It must be serious," Mildred Madison said.

"It is," Josh said. "You might say it's a matter of life and death." He looked at the ex-president, who looked anything but presidential at that moment. His hair was mussed, he was sweating profusely, his skin was pale, and his weakness was obvious to Josh. He'd give anything not to ask this favor of the man, but it was all he had. "Will you do it?"

Madison started to write, then dropped the whiteboard and looked at Josh. He nodded and his lips shaped a single word. "Who?"

"The president of Colombia."

14

And it worked?"

"I think so," Josh said. He and Derek were back in his office, each with a cup of coffee in their hands, awaiting word of Chavez's arrival. "The president of Colombia seemed surprised to get a call from Madison, but it was evident he still holds the former U.S. president in high esteem. Madison could hardly talk, but he got the idea across that this was a personal favor for him. He didn't go into details, but he convinced the man on the other end of the phone that this was truly a matter of life or death."

"I'm amazed Madison could talk that long," Derek said.

"Actually, he laid it out to the Colombian president in a few sentences, then let me handle the details."

"I thought they were afraid Chavez would want to stay in the U.S."

"I told him that had he wanted to leave Colombia, Chavez had received invitations to speak at conferences all over the world. He turned down some of them, accepted others, but as Chavez told me when I talked with him earlier, he got his training in the U.S. so could return to Colombia and train other doctors. With his wife dead and children grown, his profession is his passion and his place is right there in Bogotá."

"So he'll go right back?" Derek asked.

"He plans to spend a couple of weeks here, visiting his kids and grandkids, renewing acquaintances with a few of his colleagues at Johns Hopkins. Then he'll take a commercial flight back to Bogotá." Josh looked at his watch. "Frankly, I don't care how long he stays. I just want him to get here with that drug."

⬥

Dr. Andres Chavez felt as though he'd been on the world's longest and fastest carnival ride. He was still a bit wobbly as he climbed down the portable stairs from the plane on which he'd flown. At boarding, the pilot told the doctor this was a two-seat variant of the Kfir C7 fighter jet, and followed that with information about range and speed, all of which Chavez promptly forgot. However, he recognized the pride in the pilot's voice, so he listened patiently as he was strapped into the plane.

Dr. Chavez had taken a dozen unsteady steps across the tarmac when he saw a man striding toward him. His greeter wore a flight suit with eagles on the shoulders. His garrison cap bore a similar badge of rank.

When he reached the doctor, he said, "Dr. Chavez, I'm Colonel Bryan Gardner. Welcome to Texas. Do you have the medication?"

Chavez held up the small cooler bearing the robinoxine. "Yes. I was told someone would meet me here and take me to the hospital to meet Dr. Pearson."

"And that's exactly what we're going to do." Gardner explained that the jet had landed at the Carswell Joint Reserve Base in Fort Worth, which was about thirty miles from Dallas. "There's a car with a Secret Service agent waiting to take you there." Gardner indicated a man in a charcoal grey suit who waited nearby. "And you can be assured that we'll extend your pilot every courtesy while refueling his jet for the return trip."

Then Gardner reached out to shake hands with Chavez. "Doctor, on behalf of everyone in our military, you have our thanks. Mr. Madison is no longer our commander-in-chief, but we continue to respect and appreciate him."

Chavez, feeling very much as though, like Alice, he'd stepped through the looking glass, followed his escort to a waiting black sedan where he was ensconced in the very comfortable backseat before setting off at a high speed with two motorcycle patrolmen leading the way. He thought he'd seen it all in twenty years of medical practice, but apparently he hadn't. Well, not yet, at least.

The light tap at the door of Josh's hospital office stopped him in mid-sentence as he and Derek were talking. He opened his mouth to speak, but before he could respond, the door opened widely and Karen Marks strode in.

"Well," she said as she pulled out a chair and sat, "your Dr. Chavez is en route here with the drug."

"He's not 'my Dr. Chavez,'" Josh said. "But he's the man bringing the drug that may save the life of our two patients. And thank you for helping with the logistics to get him here."

"I told you before—I'd do anything for David Madison. The fact that Rachel Moore happens to need some of the medication this man is bringing wasn't a factor in my actions."

She was silent for a moment, and Josh knew she was figuratively biting her tongue to avoid bringing up his decision to give Rachel the second dose of robinoxine. If he hadn't done that, they might already have enough of the drug to give Madison a second treatment. Josh nodded at her as though to thank her for her silence.

"Anyway," Marks continued, "as soon as the doctor arrives, I'll bring him to your office."

Josh looked at his watch. "Assuming the medication Chavez is bringing is what we need, we should be able to give both patients their second dose about twenty-four hours after the first."

"Then what?" Marks asked.

Derek spoke for the first time since Marks entered. "Then we wait . . . and pray," he said.

❖

Rachel knew her condition was worsening. She could breathe more easily after the tracheotomy, but her fever seemed to be going up even further, her limbs ached as though someone had beat her with a baseball bat, and it taxed her to even try to sit up.

She wasn't afraid to die. Her faith assured her that, for a Christian, death is simply passing from this world into a much better one. No, that wasn't the reason she kept fighting for her life. She didn't want to die before she told Josh she loved him. And so she willed herself to stay alive, to resist what the bacteria were doing in her body, until Josh could think of some way to save her . . . and Mr. Madison, of course.

Rachel closed her eyes for a moment, but tried not to drop off. She fought sleep because she was afraid she wouldn't wake—at least, not in this present world. For some reason, she thought that if she stayed awake she could stave off death a little while longer. Then she heard the door to her room open, heard footsteps pad across the floor, felt a presence next to her bed.

She opened her eyes, but her vision was hazy. She could see enough to know there was a gowned and masked figure at her bedside, but she wasn't able to identify him.

Then he spoke, and she recognized his voice. "Rachel, it's me. Josh."

Relief swept over her. Now she could tell him. Then, if death won the struggle that had gone on in her body for days without end, at least Josh would know she loved him. She opened her

139

mouth and tried to talk, but the only sound she produced was a loud whoosh of air through the tracheotomy tube. Rachel had forgotten for a moment that she was unable to talk.

Her hands scrabbled around on the covers seeking the whiteboard, but she couldn't locate it. She tried to sit up to look for her means of communication, but the effort was too much for her.

"Rachel, I want you to know that soon we should have more of the RP-78, the drug that we hope will get you through this infection. I'll be back to give you that injection, but in the meantime I'm going to pray . . . for you and for Mr. Madison."

She tried once more to speak. Her lips formed the words, "I love you, Josh," and even though her communication was silent, Rachel hoped the message came through.

Maybe it did, because Josh bent lower and whispered, "I love you. Hang on."

Josh was headed down the hospital hallway when the buzz of his phone against his leg stopped him. He checked the caller ID and saw a hospital extension with which he was becoming all too familiar. He ducked into a quiet corner and answered.

"Ethan, this is Dr. Pearson. What's up?"

"Even though it's the weekend, I decided to take a chance that the reference lab would have the results of the diphtheria antibody titers we sent them two days ago."

Josh felt his heartbeat speed up for a moment before he realized the titer wouldn't really tell him anything. The second infection, the one with the potentially fatal *Bacillus decimus*, was the problem now. Nevertheless, he said, "And the results?"

The technician cited some numbers, but Josh didn't jot them down. He only needed to know one thing. "I could look this up, but you can probably tell me. Are they low or high?" he said.

"They're quite low," Grant said. "I don't really know what to make of them."

Josh thanked the tech and ended the call. *I know how to interpret them. And they tell me that neither patient received a real DT booster.* As he thought it through, Josh realized the low antibody titer indicated something else as well. If Madison and Rachel had a diphtheria infection, and it appeared from their cultures they did, it was a mild one, already coming under control when the blood was drawn for the test, possibly because of immunizations they'd received in the past. The significant infection was with *Bacillus decimus*, an infection that would kill the two patients if the RP-78 didn't work.

◆

Derek was in a vacant conference room trying once more to reach Dr. Gaschen, the COO of Argosy, in order to give him a status report. "I don't know if I'll have a job when this is over," he'd told Josh, who replied that if Madison and Rachel pulled through, he was pretty sure Derek could write his own ticket in a number of areas.

Karen Marks was on her cell phone in yet another empty room, fielding calls and trying to minimize the number of people who knew David Madison was critically ill. When Josh asked her why this was so important, she told him it was Madison's specific request.

"But why?" he asked.

"David Madison may be an ex-president, but he's still a very powerful man in domestic and world politics. Leaders everywhere respect his opinion. His foundation dispenses huge amounts each year. There are people who'd like him out of the way, either to silence his influence or throw his foundation into chaos until someone else takes over." To Marks, it was a no-brainer that her boss be perceived as a strong leader, firmly in control of everything with which he came in contact.

Josh was dozing in his swivel chair with his feet on his desk when the door opened and Lang led a man into the room. The newcomer was a Latino in his late fifties, probably no more than five feet six or seven inches tall but weighing two hundred pounds or more. He was dressed in an embroidered white shirt and black trousers. Josh had a similar shirt in his closet, a gift from a friend who'd gone to Guatemala. Evidently, this was what passed for business wear in a tropical climate.

"Dr. Chavez?" Josh asked as his feet hit the floor and he pushed himself upright.

"Dr. Pearson?" The man stepped forward and extended his right hand.

The two men shook. Josh looked at Lang and said, "Thanks for getting him here quickly."

Lang simply nodded and walked out the door, leaving the two men in the middle of the room, each waiting for the other to speak.

"Doctor," Josh said, "let's get right to it. How much RP-78 did you bring?"

"I found a total of two thousand milligrams of the drug that was still usable."

"And no one has breached the rubber dam sealing each bottle?" Josh asked, his heart in his throat. He had visions of the precious drug being contaminated as patients with *Bacillus decimus* received treatment.

"No, these are in sealed vials that haven't been entered."

"Well, you've brought enough RP-78, but why did so little remain usable?" Josh asked.

"Argosy originally sent twenty-five individual bottles, each containing one thousand milligrams of drug. When we admitted a patient to the study, we weighed him and assigned a vial of RP-78 to him. When he finished his course, any remainder in that vial was destroyed. That accounted for seven thousand milligrams. Another sixteen bottles have become unusable for one reason or another, leaving two bottles—enough to treat your two patients for ten days each."

Josh started to argue that it was virtually impossible for sixteen sealed bottles stored in proper conditions to go out of date or become unusable this quickly, but then he saw what Chavez had done. The doctor had calculated how much RP-78 was needed for the two patients here, and had brought that much. Josh was willing to wager that the remaining drug was hidden away somewhere for Chavez to sell or barter. Maybe Josh's initial assessment hadn't been too far off.

"Very well," Josh said. "Let's get busy." He looked at his watch. "If we're to give the second dose of the drug twenty-four hours after the first, we have less than an hour to do it."

◆

Derek saw that the door to Josh's office was open, so he walked in. Josh was in earnest conversation with a man who had to be Dr. Chavez. "Sorry," he said. "Am I interrupting?"

"No, it's probably good that you're here," Josh said. After introductions had been completed, he asked, "What did Gaschen say?"

"No answer on his cell phone. I left a message, but I think he's pretty much decided that if this works, that's great. If it doesn't, there's not going to be a job for me at Argosy. And he doesn't want to be involved one way or the other until it's all over."

"Then that's one more reason it has to work," Josh said.

Derek perched with one haunch on Josh's desk and watched Dr. Chavez carefully remove two vials of clear, faintly amber liquid from the miniature cooler he'd brought. "I'd have thought there would be more of the RP-78 left," he said.

He caught Josh's tiny shake of the head, so he hurried on. "But you've brought enough to complete the treatment. I'm glad you ignored the communication from our study coordinator and didn't destroy all the drug."

Josh picked up one vial. "Why don't we assign one vial to each of the patients? That way, even though we're observing sterile technique, we'll avoid any possible cross-contamination." When no one voiced any opposition, Josh took a pen from his pocket and marked one vial with a "DM" and the other with an "RM."

"Dr. Chavez," Josh said, "we gave the first dose intramuscularly, because Dr. Johnson said that was the way Argosy suggested it be administered when they designed the protocol. But you actually treated the patients. Do you agree?"

"Yes, with one exception. If the patient was moribund, often their circulation wasn't adequate to carry the RP-78 where it needed to go. In those cases, I actually administered the drug intravenously."

"Good thought," Derek said. "That's why we like to let the doctors dealing with the subjects being treated make decisions like that."

"Each patient has already received one dose of RP-78 with no adverse consequences that we could see. Is there anything we should watch for with this second dose?" Josh asked Chavez.

"Acutely, no," Chavez said. "Long-term? We haven't followed the treated patients long enough to know."

When Josh looked at him, Derek shook his head. "JP, this is the ultimate off-label use of this medication. It's barely been tested, it's not FDA-approved, and we don't know about its long-term side effects." When he saw Josh prepare to speak, he hurried on. "Despite all that, it's your only chance. If you want a second opinion, someone to agree with your using RP-78, you have my vote. Because if this doesn't work, those two people in there are going to die."

Josh, gowned and masked once more, eased into the room where David Madison lay apparently sleeping. As had been the case virtually every time Josh entered the room, the first thing he saw was Mildred Madison, sitting quietly at her husband's bedside holding his hand.

She wore a gown and mask, and her hands were gloved, but despite the barriers, it seemed to Josh there was such a closeness between Mildred and her husband that he could almost feel the strength flowing from her to him. Josh longed for such a relationship in his own life. And maybe someday . . . No, this wasn't the time to think about that. He had to give Madison his dose of RP-78 and move on.

Josh knew that both patients were weakening rapidly. Their blood pressure had dropped despite IV fluids and the judicious use of medications to support their circulation. Chavez's idea of giving the medication intravenously to get it more quickly to where it needed to go made sense.

Using one of the needles and syringes from the equipment sitting near Madison's bed, Josh carefully withdrew the requisite dose of RP-78. He used sterile technique to inject the material into his patient's IV line, then flushed the drug into Madison's circulation with a syringe full of normal saline. As Josh dropped the used syringes into the safe container for biomedical waste, he caught the eye of Mildred Madison and a look passed between them. He nodded once, she did the same, and he tiptoed out—but not before uttering a silent prayer that the drug would work, and work soon.

In Rachel's room, there was no one sitting at her bedside holding her hand. She, too, appeared to be sleeping, but in contrast to the drawn expression on Madison's face, hers was peaceful, almost contented. He injected her dose of RP-78, said another prayer, and was about to leave when she stirred.

Although she was obviously so weak it took a maximum effort to do so, Rachel turned in bed until she was looking squarely at Josh. Her lips parted, a rush of air came out her trach tube, and she frowned. Then she shook her head oh-so-slightly, smiled, and closed her eyes once more.

Rachel, I promise that if it's within my power, you'll pull through this . . . you and President Madison, both.

15

Detective Stan Warren rolled his desk chair back from his computer, pushed his reading glasses onto his forehead, and looked around the empty squad room. Two detectives on this watch had caught a case less than an hour ago and departed. Two others were already on the street from an earlier call. It was what Warren, after twenty years on the job, had come to expect on a Saturday night in Dallas.

When David Madison decided to locate in Dallas after leaving the White House, the police department made plans to share the job of providing security for the former president with his Secret Service detail. Although the additional work mainly fell to uniformed police, Warren had been chosen to be the liaison between his department and the Secret Service agents. Until recently, this assignment was a plum, a nice, soft job for a detective nearing retirement—until recently, but no longer.

Although some detectives might have complained about this development, Warren relished the chance to do some real detective work. He'd rather go out having solved what was turning out to be a complex case than to simply slide into retirement. If nothing else, this was going to give him lots to look back on.

He replaced his reading glasses and leaned again toward the computer screen. Warren tapped a few keys, then pushed the print button. He'd caught a break when he started to search various databases for the assassin. Although there was nothing in the U.S., he got a hit on the Interpol site. Leonid Malnyk had been arrested and fingerprinted once, in Spain. Although he'd managed to escape from the Guàrdia Urbana, the police in Barcelona, he'd been in custody long enough for them to take his fingerprints and a mug shot as well as solidify their suspicion that he was an international assassin, a gun for hire to anyone with enough money.

There were further sightings of Malnyk in Europe, Asia, and even Africa, but there had been no arrest other than the one in Spain. It appeared that the man never had to resort to plastic surgery to change his appearance. Rather, he used a seemingly endless supply of passports in various names, and these, combined with his eminently forgettable appearance, allowed him to slip away each time the authorities seemed to be closing in on him.

As computers became the norm in police work, Warren soon realized he could fight the trend only so long before he had to learn how to use them. Now it was time to put that hard-earned knowledge to use. Thanks to the one brief arrest and fingerprinting, he had Malnyk's name. With that, Warren was able to determine the man's last known address: a fashionable apartment in London. After that, the computer gave him a list of people with whom Malnyk had associated in the past, both abroad and in the U.S. At this point, he'd normally question the subject, but that wasn't possible.

As he pushed away from the computer and began to study the printed sheets in his hand, the detective said under his breath, "Okay, Malnyk. Who hired you . . . and why?"

Karen Marks lay prone across the bed in her apartment, her cell phone pressed to her ear. "Yes, I'm alone. Are you in a secure location?"

"I'm not certain how secure it is, but no one can hear me," Jerry Lang replied. "Did you get the funeral director and the Widow Lambert calmed down?"

"Finally," Karen said. "It took some doing, but I think they're okay. At first, Mrs. Lambert didn't want to believe the cremated remains were those of her husband. I suppose that if I'd been smart, I could have told her the body was cremated in South America, but I've discovered the truth is generally the best way to proceed in sticky situations like this."

"If you had, we could have explained the absence of her husband's class ring from the personal effects delivered along with the cremains by blaming the funeral director in South America," Lang said.

"Too late now," Karen said. "But I think I've settled her down, and she's proceeding with plans for a memorial service. As it turns out, her husband wanted cremation anyway."

"And the funeral director?"

"I had to use my powers of persuasion, augmented by a bit of cash spent in the right places, but the man at Sparkman Hillcrest, the one who discovered the cremains on their doorstep, has agreed it's best to keep things quiet. So far as anyone else knows, they're the ones that did the cremation." She'd held the phone so long she was getting a cramp in her fingers. She moved the phone to her other hand. "I had to commit the foundation to bearing the costs of the funeral, but I think David would have agreed to do that anyway—if he were in any shape to make that decision."

"Well, he's not," Lang said. "He's had two doses of the magic drug. Now all we can do is wait."

Karen kicked off her shoes and squirmed around until she was leaning against the headboard. "I can hardly wait for this to be over. It's getting harder and harder for me to keep what we're doing a secret."

"I know. But I hope we're approaching the end."

Josh and Derek sat at a table in the almost-deserted hospital cafeteria. The trays before them held the remains of an evening meal that neither man had done more than sample. Josh picked up his coffee cup, found it empty, and put it back down.

"Want some more?" Derek asked.

"No. You?"

"No. Why don't you get some rest? It will be at least twelve hours, maybe longer, before we see results from that second dose of RP-78."

"I'm okay," Josh said. "I thought I'd hang around. If there's no change in either of their conditions by midnight or so, I might catch a nap in one of the call rooms."

"How about Allison Neeves? Has she gone home to her family?"

"Allison doesn't have anyone to go home to," Josh said. "She and her husband got married when she was in medical school, but he divorced her about the time they graduated."

"Children?"

"Nope, which I guess is a blessing."

Derek leaned a bit closer to his friend. "I know you're serious about Rachel Moore, but was there ever a time—"

"Derek, don't go there," Josh said, realizing where the conversation was headed. "Allison and I are colleagues, nothing more."

Derek held up both hands. "Just asking." He looked at his watch. "I think I'm going to take a walk around outside, get some fresh air. You have my cell number if something breaks." He picked up his tray and moved away.

Josh was almost alone in the cafeteria. He shoved aside his tray, bowed his head, and tried to pray a couple of times, but in each instance, he almost dropped off. *This isn't doing anyone any good.*

He deposited the remains of his dinner onto the conveyer belt and shuffled through the door into the hallway. Despite having pulled a few all-nighters in the past, the strain of the past two days was getting to him. Maybe he'd do better with a few hours' sleep.

As Josh passed the glass wall in the passageway outside, he glanced into the gathering darkness and saw a figure moving about. Curious, he stepped closer to the glass and stopped. Derek stood outside, his back to Josh, his cell phone to his ear.

Josh moved away before Derek could see him, but as he made his way back to the ward that held Madison and Rachel, he wondered about the call. Derek's wife had passed away. There'd been no mention of another relationship. And the COO of Argosy hadn't answered Derek's last call, apparently deciding to dissociate himself from this use of their experimental drug until and unless it was a success.

Josh realized it was none of his business, but still, he was curious about whom his friend could be calling.

◈

David Madison brought his wrist close to his face and checked the time. The watch he'd been wearing when he was admitted to the hospital was locked up along with the rest of his personal possessions, so he'd asked his wife to bring his spare from home. In contrast with the nicer watch he wore most of the time, his other watch was a plain Casio with a black plastic band that he used when he ran or played a rare round of golf.

"Why do you need a watch?" she'd asked.

"Because I'm used to checking the time periodically, and since there's no clock on the wall in here, I'm about to go crazy not knowing."

Mildred hadn't argued, but instead of asking one of the agents outside the door of her husband's hospital room to find the watch in question and bring it here, she'd slipped out and visited the gift shop downstairs. There, the clerk was finally able to dig up a cheap watch, which Mrs. Madison purchased. "I'm not going to ask an agent to run an errand for us," she'd explained. "That's not what they're supposed to be doing."

Madison's room was dark except for one lamp in a corner that emitted just enough light for him to tell the time if he squinted. Mildred was asleep in the recliner nearby, but since he'd been sleeping more than being awake during the past day, Madison's eyes were as wide open as if the lids had been spring-loaded.

He was about to turn on his side and try once more to fall asleep when he heard the door of his room open. Supposedly, no one without a reason was supposed to come in, but Madison had already had one unwelcome visitor, one who'd taken a shot at him. Since then, he'd been wary of everyone entering his room.

Like everyone else who came in, the newcomer wore a disposable isolation gown, a mask, and some kind of latex-like gloves. The figure was shorter than Josh Pearson or Derek Johnson, and stouter than any of the nurses. This was Saturday, so perhaps it was a member of the nursing staff he hadn't yet encountered. No, his watch had shown it to be a bit before ten p.m., and Madison knew the staff was working twelve-hour shifts, and the nurse who came on at seven this evening had already been in once.

As the figure crept closer to his bedside, Madison's finger hovered over the nurse call button. No, he didn't want to raise a false alarm. Maybe he could awaken Mildred. He tried to call his wife, but the result was only an exhalation of air from his tracheotomy tube. Then he remembered what Josh had done to allow him to talk with the president of Colombia. Madison couldn't deflate the cuff of his trach tube, but maybe he could force enough air past it to serve his purpose.

He took a deep breath, then put his finger over the tube and strained to get the words out. "Can I help you?"

Mildred stirred but didn't awaken. Just as Madison was about to try again, the figure stopped about five feet short of the bed and said, "President Madison, you may remember me. We were together a few short days ago in Colombia. Now we meet again. You may not know it, but I flew over two thousand miles to bring the medicine you received a few hours ago."

Was this the doctor he'd met toward the end of his trip? His fever-addled brain searched for the man's name. Gonzalez? Gomez? No, that wasn't it. Chavez. Yes, Andres Chavez. Madison nodded once and tried to fix a smile to his countenance.

"When you are well, we will talk more—about your trip and especially about the decision you must reach on locating the clinic, if you decide to place one in Colombia. I believe I have some insight I was not able to share with you at our brief meeting."

Didn't the man realize this was neither the time nor place for such a conversation? Madison nodded again, hoping Chavez would take the hint and leave.

"I'll let you rest, but I wanted to reintroduce myself." Chavez turned to go, but not before saying, *"Recupérate pronto."*

Get well soon? Well, I'm trying. After the door closed behind his visitor, Madison turned his head away from the room's faint light and closed his eyes, but as before, sleep would not come.

Josh stifled a yawn, something he'd been doing frequently for the past hour or more. It was after midnight, almost six hours since Madison and Rachel received their second dose of RP-78. Thanks to telemetry, he'd been able to sit at the nurses' station and follow the vital signs of both patients without entering their rooms. If they could sleep, if they could simply rest, he wanted them to do just that.

"Dr. Pearson?"

Josh managed not to jerk, but was definitely startled by the voice behind him. He turned and identified Barbara Carper, the nurse working the seven p.m. to seven a.m. shift tonight. "Yes, Barbara?"

"Both patients have been stable since you gave them the medication almost six hours ago. I promise I'll call you if there's any change. Why don't you take a break? Maybe get some sleep?"

Josh was ambivalent about what to do next. He knew his sitting and watching the vital signs of the two patients wasn't doing anyone any good. On the other hand, he knew that if he left for any reason, even for only a few minutes, he'd feel as though he'd abandoned his patients.

"Dr. Neeves came by a couple of hours ago while you were in the cafeteria. She checked both patients and thought they might be doing a bit better."

"Is she still around?" Josh asked.

"She said she was going home to clean up and get a little sleep. You may want to do the same thing."

"No," Josh said. "I don't want to leave the hospital. But I guess it would be okay for me to stretch out in one of the call rooms for a couple of hours. Why don't you call me—"

"I'll call you if there's any change," Barbara said. "Otherwise, I'll let you sleep."

Reluctantly, Josh rose from his spot in front of the telemetry units. With one last glance at the vital sign readings, he turned away. Maybe some coffee would help. He might even shower and change into a clean scrub suit. And . . . he paused to stifle another yawn . . . and maybe he should try to get some rest. He had a feeling that the turning point wasn't far away.

In the almost seventy-two hours since David Madison and Rachel Moore were admitted, ward Two West of Prestonwood

Hospital had gradually been emptied of other patients, either by discharge or transfer to another wing. This wasn't the result of any direct order from one of the doctors or the agents guarding the ex-president. It had simply been decided by the hospital's administrator that since the number of people coming in contact with the patients had to be limited, both from the standpoint of security and infection isolation, this was a logical course to pursue.

Head nurse Mary Wynn sat at the nurses' station and listened as nurse Barbara Carper gave her report. Now that the ward's population had been reduced, for the next twelve hours Mary and a couple of nurse's aides would be responsible only for the care of the patients in rooms 2211 and 2213. As a consequence, Barbara's report was short and simple: the condition of both patients seemed to be stabilizing, possibly with some improvement.

Mary scanned the figures and agreed. "The vital signs look better. Blood pressure is up and seems much more stable."

Barbara nodded in agreement. "You'll also notice their temperatures have started to drop. Since admission they've shown sort of an up-and-down, sawtooth pattern, but last night their fever dropped and has stayed down so far."

"What about the patients? How did they look through the night?" Mary asked.

"Better. Of course, since the tracheotomies, respiratory distress hasn't been an issue. But in general they seemed more . . . I don't know how to put it, but I'm sure you've seen it yourself. A patient seems to be struggling, restless, their vital signs all over the place. Then they reach a crisis point and almost immediately start to get better." Barbara tapped one of the monitors with her forefinger. "I think that's what we're seeing. It's almost as though the medication they received last night was a miracle drug."

"I don't know if the miracle came from the drug or the prayers everyone's been offering," Mary said. "But either way, I think the doctors will like what they see this morning."

◆

Josh Pearson and Allison Neeves stood in the hallway outside the hospital rooms of their respective patients. Josh was trying hard to keep his emotions in check, but apparently Allison was making no such effort. She smiled widely and said, "Well, so far, so good."

Josh's features remained neutral. "Maybe, but we've still got a long way to go."

"So, what's next? For instance, how long shall we treat?"

"I talked with Derek and Dr. Chavez, who probably have as much experience with the drug as anyone in the world. They agree that since there are really no dose-ranging studies and we have enough RP-78, it's safest to treat for ten days. But once the disease process seems to be under control, we can consider decannulation."

"I agree, we can remove the tracheotomies once the danger of respiratory obstruction is past. Then what?"

"Once the patients have been free of fever for forty-eight hours, isolation won't be necessary."

"Are you certain about that?" Allison asked.

"No one is certain," Josh said. "There's not enough experience. But Chavez says it takes a massive exposure to infect a patient unless the bacteria are delivered by injection. Some of the convicts in the treatment study were infected by bites from wild animals acting as a host for *Bacillus decimus*. Others had huge exposure from inhaling the bacteria for one reason or another. In our cases, it took someone throwing a whole flask full of bacteria-laden culture medium onto Madison and Rachel to infect them."

"So it sounds like things are coming under control."

"From a medical standpoint? I think so. But there are still some questions from a law enforcement standpoint."

"Such as?" Allison asked.

"Did Ben Lambert really have a heart attack, or was he killed? Why did someone want to steal and cremate his body? Who wants David Madison dead? And why?"

16

Rachel was surprised to see the door to her room open and Josh enter. Not that she was surprised to see him—for the past four days, since the crisis had passed, he'd visited several times a day. But this time there was no mask obscuring Josh's face, no plastic shield that made it difficult to see his sparkling blue eyes. And since no yellow isolation gown covered his clothes, she could see he looked quite handsome in a fresh white coat over a pale blue dress shirt and tie with blue and yellow stripes.

Force of habit made her place her index finger on the bandage that covered the site over her windpipe where the tracheotomy tube had been removed three days earlier. But that incision had already closed to the size of a pinhead, and she knew in a few days it would be fully healed over. Maybe a minor surgical procedure to minimize the scar would be necessary, but she'd worry about that later. In the meantime, she had no trouble speaking normally.

"Josh, am I officially out of isolation?"

"You are indeed. It looks like you're recovering well, and the only reason we'll continue treating you for a full ten days is because we don't have any hard data saying a shorter course is enough."

"How's Mr. Madison?"

"He's recovering as well. We'll probably keep you both here until we stop the RP-78. After that, you can be discharged, but we'll continue to keep an eye on you."

"Why is that?" Rachel asked.

"Just being cautious," Josh replied. "Our problem is that we don't know if there are any long-term effects of the medication."

Rachel thought about that for a moment. What a roller-coaster ride this had been. A trip overseas, a potentially fatal infection, her life saved at the last minute by what amounted to an experimental drug, and now the prospect of waiting to see if there were any long-term ill effects from that treatment. "I guess I should be—"

Josh held up his hand and reached into his pocket for his cell phone, which was buzzing. "Dr. Pearson."

Rachel could hear only one side of the conversation, but the frown on Josh's face told her what she needed to know. Finally, he said, "I'm on my way. Are Drs. Neeves, Johnson, and Chavez aware of this? They should be at the meeting as well."

Josh stowed the phone and said, "Rachel, I came in here to tell you something important, but it's not anything I want to rush. I'll be back as soon as I deal with this situation. And we'll talk then."

As Josh left the room, Rachel smiled. *I've already heard it, Josh. I don't know if it was a fever dream or if it was real, but in either case, I'm pretty sure I know what you're going to say.*

◆

Josh had practically lived at the hospital for the past week, and during that time this room had been his office. He'd sat behind that desk, used that phone and computer. But today he wasn't the man in charge. When Josh opened the door and entered, Jerry Lang sat behind what Josh thought of as his desk, with Karen Marks beside him.

"Have a seat," Lang said, gesturing to one of the four chairs arranged today on the visitor's side of the desk.

Josh looked around and saw that Allison Neeves already occupied one of those chairs. He took the one next to her, but before he could speak, the door opened and Derek Johnson entered, followed closely by Andres Chavez.

When everyone was seated, Josh said, "I think I know what this meeting is about, and—"

Lang opened his mouth, but Karen held up her hand to stop both him and Josh. "Jerry, let me do this." She scanned the doctors sitting before her. "On behalf of David Madison and his wife, thank you for your efforts. The Secret Service, in cooperation with the Dallas Police Department, continues to investigate this obvious attempt on former president Madison's life."

Josh wondered if Karen realized she was talking as though this were a press conference. He started to say something, but she gave him no opportunity, pressing on with what seemed to be prepared remarks.

"Meanwhile," she said, "it seems evident that Mr. Madison's condition has stabilized. He appears to have passed the crisis point and is moving steadily toward recovery. Now he thinks it's best that he leave the hospital and return to his home."

Josh was halfway out of his chair before Karen stopped speaking. "But he's—"

"We're not here to argue," Lang said. "Mr. Madison indicated to Ms. Marks and me this morning that he's carefully considered the matter and made up his mind. He wanted us to convey his thanks to each of you for your role in helping him recover. Now he's anxious to leave."

"I talked with him when I made rounds earlier," Josh said. "I explained to him that even though we've lifted the isolation precautions, we needed to keep him here for at least a full ten days' treatment. If he continues to do well, I can follow him on an outpatient basis to watch for recurrence of symptoms or late complications from the medication."

Karen Marks spoke this time. "After you were there, Mr. Madison had a long phone conversation with Dr. Dietz. The two men mutually agreed it would be best if Dr. Dietz took over Mr. Madison's care, seeing him as an outpatient at Southwestern Medical Center. After all, it's quite a prestigious medical institution, with all the resources necessary to care for almost any problem. And Dr. Dietz is a well-known internist."

"But—" Josh tried to interject.

Karen continued as though Josh hadn't made a sound. "Mr. Madison originally chose Dr. Lambert as his personal physician because the two men had been friends since childhood." She turned her gaze directly on Josh. "Dr. Pearson, we have no idea why Dr. Lambert chose you to succeed him. Be that as it may, we're now asking you to transfer Mr. Madison's care to Dr. Dietz."

Derek Johnson stood with Josh Pearson in front of Prestonwood Hospital and watched the motorcade pull away. "Well, JP, I guess our moment of glory has passed."

"I don't care about the glory. Matter of fact, I think I'll rest easier not having a critically ill patient with so much riding on my care of him. But I still don't understand it."

"What don't you understand?" Derek asked. "It's politics trumping medicine. We don't know the reasons behind it, but I've worked in the pharmaceutical industry long enough to recognize behind-the-scenes pressure."

"Still—"

"Josh, it's out of our hands," Derek said. "You and I tried to explain to Lang and Marks why this was premature. Even Allison Neeves came down on your side. Dr. Chavez didn't have much to say, but you could tell by his expression he was shocked."

Josh shoved his hands into the pockets of his white coat and turned back toward the hospital's front door. "Well, I guess I'll talk with Rachel. I still think we should keep her here under observation for a bit longer." He shrugged. "Of course, that decision rests with Rachel and Allison Neeves. I guess I'm back to being just another internist at the clinic."

Derek shook his head. "Not simply another internist," he said. "An internist who saved the life of two people with a potentially fatal disease—the first time it's been done in the U.S., by the way. And whatever else happens, you should be proud of that." He fell in beside Josh. "I know I would be."

◆

Rachel sat in a recliner facing the door of her hospital room. For the first time in a week, she wore her own nightgown, covered by a satin robe. There were no IVs in her arms, only a tiny coil of plastic inserted in a vein and filled with heparinized saline, a heparin lock, allowing access for intravenous drugs should it be needed. She looked up from the book in her lap when Josh tapped on the doorframe.

"May I come in?"

"Of course," she said. "I've been wondering when you'd make it back."

He dragged a straight chair from beside her bed and sat facing her. "It turned out to be a more complicated problem than I thought, but it's out of my hands now."

"Can you tell me about it?"

Josh shrugged. "Sure. I don't think there's anything classified about what's happened. It seems that Mr. Madison, whether on his own or with some persuasion, has decided to fire me, go home, and let Dr. Dietz care for him in the future."

Rachel listened quietly as Josh recounted what he and the others had been told and the arguments, sometimes heated, which followed. "The bottom line is that I'm no longer the personal physician to the former president of the United States."

"And how do you feel about that?" Rachel asked.

Josh stood and began pacing. "Relieved, I guess, although I think he's making a wrong decision."

"So, even though you're glad you no longer have that responsibility, you hate to see it taken out of your hands."

Josh shrugged. "Rachel, when I found out I was going to be the presidential physician, even if it was for an ex-president, I let it get to me. I became so consumed with that task and the position I held that I ignored other things that are important to me." He sat again, reached out, and took her hand. "But I'm clear on my priorities now. Yes, I hate to be dismissed this way, but it might be the best thing that could happen. Because it allows me to focus on you."

Rachel leaned forward but remained silent. If Josh was going to say it, now was the time.

"Seeing you deathly ill, realizing I might lose you, brought it into focus for me. Rachel, I love you. And I don't want anything to come between us in the future."

"You know, it's the funniest thing," Rachel said. "While I was racked with fever, I thought you came into my room to tell me you loved me. And, even though I couldn't speak because of the tracheotomy, I told you I loved you as well." She smiled. "Now I can actually say the words to you. I love you, Josh."

Before Josh could respond, Rachel saw his hand dart toward his pocket. He pulled out his cell phone, frowned, and said, "It's Karen Marks."

He started to reject the call, but Rachel stopped him. "No, answer it. It might be important." She nodded. "You and I will have lots of time in the future to continue this conversation."

The call was brief and, judging from Josh's responses, mainly one-sided. It ended with Josh stabbing his finger at the button that ended the call as though he were slamming down an old-fashioned phone. He shook his head. "And I thought it ended when Madison left the hospital."

"What?"

"They've reached the president's home and can't find the RP-78 to give him his next injections. Everyone is looking at someone else and saying, 'I thought you had it.'" Josh took in a deep breath through his nose and blew it out between compressed lips. "Karen the same as accused me of hiding the drug until Mr. Madison changes his mind about leaving my care."

17

Josh, Mr. Madison's no longer your problem," Rachel said. "Let it go."

"I'll try," he said, but she knew he couldn't turn it loose. Maybe this was a good time to ask her question. "Madison's gone home. What about me?"

"I think you should stay in the hospital for the full ten days of treatment," Josh said. "And before you ask, Dr. Neeves agrees."

"Then, so long as I'm out of isolation and you promise to visit me regularly, I guess that'll have to do," Rachel told him.

"I'll be in here so much that the hospital will assign the room to me and start charging my insurance company," Josh said. "But right now I have some things to do. I'll see you soon."

In the hallway outside Rachel's room, Josh dialed Derek Johnson's cell phone, but the line was busy. Josh wondered to whom Derek was talking. Well, no matter.

Although it would be easy enough for him to wash his hands of the whole matter and resume his day-to-day practice of medicine, Josh felt a connection to Madison—not because of the man's position. Thank goodness he'd moved past that. No, as a physician it troubled him that someone for whom he'd expended so much time and energy to pull them through a potentially fatal infection might now be put back in danger by something so simple as misplaced medication.

He wasn't certain how much longer he'd be able to use what he'd come to regard as "his" office here at the hospital, but for now no one else seemed to have moved in. Once seated behind the desk, he pulled a notepad toward him and began making a list of people who might have taken the robinoxine.

Until Madison left the hospital, a small refrigerator in the corner of their rooms held the vial of RP-78 used to treat each patient. After isolation was discontinued, both patients were moved to new rooms and orderlies were brought in from another part of the hospital to thoroughly clean and disinfect the rooms they'd occupied. The vials were moved with the patients, and last night both patients received injections, their sixth, so Madison's medication couldn't have disappeared before then. But as he thought about it, Josh found no clue as to who might have taken the medication—either by accident or on purpose—and he eventually balled up the paper with his list and dropped it in the trash.

His phone conversation with Karen Marks had consisted primarily of her not-so-subtle accusation that Josh had the RP-78 and was holding it as a sort of blackmail in return for Madison's returning to his care. Josh was certain Karen and Jerry Lang would have compiled the same type of list he'd started and were already busy trying to solve the mystery of the missing drug. He'd leave that to them. If they found the vial, the problem was solved. If not? Well, it really wasn't up to Josh . . . but he still wanted to give it a try.

First, though, Josh wanted to talk with Dr. Dietz. The doctor taking over Madison's care needed to know all that had gone before. Only then would come the big decisions. As of last night, Madison had received six doses of RP-78. Was that going to be enough to prevent a recurrence? And if not, where could they get more of the drug?

Josh had the main number he needed, but his call was transferred three times before he got through to the doctor now caring for David Madison. "Dr. Dietz? This is Dr. Josh Pearson. We need to talk."

Derek Johnson stuck his head inside the door of Josh's office. "Got a second?"

Josh waved him in with one hand, while holding the phone to his ear with the other. "You have all my numbers if you need me," he said to the person on the other end of the call. "And I'm sure you'll find that between Karen Marks and Jerry Lang, you have lots of resources you can call on."

After the call ended, Josh gestured to the chairs in front of his desk. "Have a seat, and I'll bring you up to date on what's happening now."

Derek screwed up his face at the news, but kept silent until Josh had finished his narrative. "And Dietz isn't alarmed?"

"I don't think he fully realizes the situation yet. He freely admitted that he doesn't know anything about *Bacillus decimus*. He's going to call a contact at the CDC and ask him for a crash course on the infection. I offered to put him in touch with you, but I think unless the information comes from either a government entity or one of his department chairs, he'll have a hard time accepting it."

"So the question to be answered is, will six days of treatment be enough? If not, where can he get more RP-78? Right?"

Josh nodded at his colleague's ability to get right to the meat of the problem. "If the answer to number one is yes, no worries. But if it's no, he won't know until the patient starts showing symptoms again. And at that point no one can be certain another course of RP-78 will help."

"And even if it does help, don't forget we have no idea what the long-term effects of that much drug will be." Derek leaned back in his chair and looked at the ceiling. "Are you going to keep working on this, even though Dietz has officially become Madison's physician?"

Josh swiveled in his chair to face the bookcases to his left, cases left empty by the departure of the office's last occupant. "Derek, if you had a patient you pulled through the acute phase of an infection, would you be willing to walk away and let someone else manage the rest of his care, especially if they didn't seem to have an idea what to do next?"

Derek didn't even have to think about that one. "No. Once I started, I'd want to finish it. I guess any doctor would."

"Then you have your answer," Josh said. He turned back to face his friend. "So, if you're still willing to help, it's time for us to put our heads together and start trying to dig up another four doses of RP-78 for David Madison."

"When can you get the vial of medication to me?"

The voice on the other end of the phone call was faint, probably to forestall anyone eavesdropping. "I'm not certain when I can get away. Isn't it enough that I have it?"

"No. You have to get it to me, and I need it tonight." There was a moment of silence. "Meet me at the loading dock in the rear of the hospital at six this evening."

"I don't know. I'll try."

It was time to be more forceful. "If you want the other half of your payment, you'll do more than try. I'll see you at six."

The caller's voice was faint, but there was steel in the words. "I don't think the amount we discussed is enough."

"We can talk about it when we meet. Be there. And be certain no one follows you."

Josh shrugged his shoulders and spread his hands in a gesture of defeat. "I don't know where Dr. Chavez can be. I've called his cell phone number three times now, but he doesn't answer."

Derek stood in front of Josh's office window and looked out at the hospital parking lot. It was mid-afternoon, and cars were streaming in and out as visitors arrived and departed. "Could there be a problem because his cell phone is from Colombia?"

"Doesn't matter," Josh said, joining Derek at the window. "When he arrived, Karen Marks provided him with a cell phone that had a local number so I could stay in touch with him—mainly for situations like this."

Derek stretched and yawned. "Man, I was hoping to get one good night's sleep before I head back to Georgia, but it looks like I'll be right here again tonight."

Josh held out his keys. "No need for you to stay up. You're welcome to crash at my place. It's a bachelor pad, but it's nicer than one of the call rooms."

"We'll see." Derek pulled out his cell. "I'm assuming that Marks and Lang would let us know if they locate that missing vial of RP-78. Meanwhile, since you can't find Dr. Chavez, let me try my boss at Argosy once more."

Josh slumped into the chair behind his desk and watched his friend dial. After a moment, Derek pocketed his cell phone. "No answer. I guess when he sees my number on caller ID, Dr. Gaschen lets it roll to voicemail because he doesn't want to be responsible if this off-label use of RP-78 flops."

"So he's willing to take the credit if it works, but put the blame on you if it doesn't. Right?"

"That's pretty much what I think he was saying as I left the plant."

"Who actually developed RP-78?" Josh asked.

"I guess you could say it was mine. I told you, I wanted to do something to cure the same type of cancer that took my wife. Matter of fact, I named it after Robin—robinoxine. And RP-78 are her initials—Robin Paige—and the year of her birth." Derek sighed. "As it turned out, robinoxine wasn't effective to kill tumors, but it was as an antibiotic."

"So if it's successful, you should get the credit."

Derek frowned. "Poor, naive JP. That's not how it works in the world of industry. If the drug works, Dr. Gaschen will label it the latest development from Argosy. Our stock will go up. He'll get a bonus. And, if I'm lucky, my name will be mentioned somewhere in the press release."

Josh reached for the phone. "Let me have Dr. Gaschen's cell phone number. I want to see if he'll answer a call from this number, one he doesn't recognize."

❖

Karen Marks sat behind a cherry wood desk in her office in one wing of the Madison home. The desk was larger, the office more nicely appointed than the one she'd had for eight years on Capitol Hill. Of course, in that situation she'd had to be more circumspect, ever aware that her actions were subject to scrutiny by both the public and agencies like the General Services Administration. Here, she was free to make her own decisions. The furnishings of her office, the appointments of the room, even her salary all came out of the generous allowance afforded ex-presidents. And so long as she kept a low profile, no one would challenge any of her actions.

"I thought that when we left the hospital, you or one of your agents would make sure you had the vial with the remaining doses of RP-78 for David Madison," Karen said.

There was no rancor in Jerry Lang's voice as he replied, "And I thought you had taken it."

"Well, let's not sit here playing the blame game," Karen said. "Have you located it?"

"Not yet."

"Are you saying your agents haven't been able to find out who took that drug from David Madison's room when we left the hospital?"

"They're still interviewing the people who had access to that mini-refrigerator over the past twenty hours, but they've had no luck thus far. Karen, it's an impossible task," Jerry Lang said. He patted his shirt pocket, remembered that he'd given up cigarettes years ago, and allowed a sardonic smile to cross his face.

"We discovered the vial was gone when we arrived here," she said. "That was shortly before noon today. According to the schedule Dr. Pearson was following, the next dose should be given in about two hours. You've had five hours to question perhaps a dozen people, yet your agents haven't a clue as to who has the drug." She frowned. "Jerry, that's unacceptable."

"What do you want us to do?" Lang asked. "Shall we drag them all in and forcibly administer a polygraph to everyone? We don't have enough evidence to ask for search warrants for each person's house and automobile. There's not a judge in this county who'd authorize our checking these people's bank accounts for large deposits. We're still sweating a couple of them, but right now all the thief has to do is keep saying, 'I don't know anything about it.' And apparently, that's what whoever's responsible is doing."

"Let me call Dr. Pearson again. Maybe he has some ideas."

Lang shook his head. "I wouldn't have the gall to do that—not after the way he was unceremoniously dumped earlier today. If I were in his position—"

She lifted the phone and began to dial. "But you're not. And I'm willing to do anything, including begging, if it means David Madison will get the medicine he needs."

Josh gave a thumbs-up gesture to Derek who was slouched in the chair across the desk from him. "Dr. Gaschen?"

"Yes? Who is this? The caller ID says Prestonwood Hospital in Dallas. Is there some sort of problem with one of our drugs?"

"You might say that," Josh said. "I'm Dr. Josh Pearson, personal physician to David Madison." Josh caught Derek's raised eyebrows at this stretching of the truth, but that didn't matter right now. "For reasons I can't go into, we need about another three hundred fifty milligrams of RP-78 to complete a course of the medication, which has been successful thus far in treating a *Bacillus decimus* infection. Can you help us?"

Josh held his breath. "What . . . Why . . . Well, I'm certainly glad the drug has helped your patient. But didn't Dr. Johnson explain to you that he was bringing all the RP-78 he could find here?"

"That was all he could find several days ago," Josh said. "Surely since that time you've thought about where you might be able to put your hands on a bit more. Dr. Gaschen, this is critical. If we complete the course of treatment, I can almost guarantee that the FDA will take another look at RP-78. And even if they don't, you could look into marketing it in South and Central America. I'd be surprised if there weren't more cases of *Bacillus decimus* infections there once you start looking for them."

Josh could almost hear the wheels turning in Gaschen's mind. Did he feel a humanitarian tug, an altruistic urge to leave no stone unturned to assist in saving the life that was at stake? Or was his focus on what it would mean for his company if RP-78 worked in this situation? Whatever Gaschen's motivation, the reply when it came was what Josh hoped to hear. "I think perhaps I can help you."

"I don't know why you're going to all this trouble," Derek said when Josh finally ended his call. "You've proven that the drug works, and that's great. And you have enough RP-78 to treat

Rachel. As for what happens with Madison from here on out, you can't control that. He essentially fired you as his personal physician after you made a diagnosis most physicians would miss and then worked hard to round up enough of the only drug that might possibly treat the infection."

"Same answer as before," Josh said as he pushed away from his desk. "Once I start dealing with a problem, I want to finish—and I want the patient to recover."

"So are you going to call Karen Marks or Dr. Dietz?"

"I've been thinking about that. Dietz isn't a bad man, but he's much more an administrator than a clinician. It won't surprise me if he designates someone familiar with clinical medicine as his right-hand man in dealing with the ex-president. If I get the word to Karen Marks that we've located enough RP-78 to finish Madison's treatment, she can arrange to get it here and see that it's given."

Josh still had Karen Mark's number on his cell phone's speed dial. He wondered how long it would be before he would remove it—either at her request or his desire. His call rang only once before she answered.

"Karen, this is Josh Pearson. I've located another five hundred milligram vial of RP-78. That should be enough to finish Mr. Madison's course of treatment. Dr. Gaschen at Argosy has the drug. I'll give you his number, and you can arrange to get it here."

There was a somber tone to her voice as Marks said, "Thank you. I'll call him, but in the meantime Jerry Lang's been contacted by the person who has the missing drug."

"So this isn't necessary after all," Josh said, disappointment coloring his words.

"Oh, that's not really true. As a matter of fact, it will probably save the Madison Foundation a million dollars. That's how much Dr. Chavez seems to want for the remaining RP-78 he's holding."

18

Allison paused at Josh's office door. She gave a couple of tentative taps, then waited until she heard him say, "Come in."

She took a few steps inside before she stopped. "Am I interrupting anything?"

Josh sat at his desk, staring out the window behind him. He looked up and said, "No, no. Come on in."

"Where's Derek? You two have been sort of inseparable the past few days."

"He's gone to my apartment to clean up and try for a good night's sleep. Matter of fact, he took my car, so I'm going to have to ask you for a ride."

"No problem," Allison said.

Josh gestured to the chairs across the desk from him. "Have a seat. I don't know how long it will be before they take this office back, but for now I guess it's still mine."

Allison eased into a chair and crossed her legs, her crisply starched white coat making a brief crunching sound as she settled in. "Why don't you go home, too? Your one active patient fired you. Rachel is doing well, and besides that, in case you've forgotten, I'm the one who's taking care of her."

"I guess she's had her daily dose of RP-78," Josh said.

"Just got it. I think Chavez's idea about giving it intravenously until the patients were past the crisis point was good, but she's received the last few doses of the drug by intramuscular injection. Her tracheotomy incision is almost healed already, she's gaining strength every day, and I think she'll be ready for discharge after she's had her last dose, which should be . . ." She counted in her head. "That would be on Sunday."

"Good. I'll go by and see her before I head home, if you can wait that long."

Allison leaned forward. "Josh, I know we've gotten cross-ways with each other a time or two during all this, but I attributed that to your frustration. It can't be easy, being given responsibility for the medical care of an important man only to find that he was infected with a fatal disease."

Josh grimaced. "Thanks for being so understanding, Allison, but I still owe you an apology. There were times I was a little too impressed with my own importance." He ran his hands through his hair. "I still wonder what Ben Lambert had in mind when he chose me to take over David Madison's care if something happened to him. Why was I the one?"

"Did you have any idea he'd done that?"

"He mentioned it in passing—sort of a casual reference. What were his words? Oh, yeah. 'In case something happens to me.' Did he have a premonition? Was there something in the wind he knew about? And if so, why didn't he leave me a message of some sort?"

"Maybe he did. Where have you looked?"

"I really haven't. I went over Madison's medical records. Then I looked through Ben's records, including his most recent physical. That's about it."

Allison stood. "Then I suggest we look, starting with Ben's office at the clinic."

Josh rose from behind the desk. "I guess we could do that, but somehow searching for some kind of message from beyond the grave makes all this seem like a scene from a novel."

Allison grinned. "And you think the rest of this is business as usual?" She moved toward the door. "Come on, Josh. Let's see if we can find the key that unlocks this puzzle."

◆

Jerry Lang sat in Karen Marks's office and listened as she arranged for an Air Force jet to ferry the last precious vial of RP-78 from Atlanta to Dallas.

"I'll have an agent at the airport to receive the medicine," she said. "And thank you again, Dr. Gaschen. I give you my word that Mr. Madison will contact the FDA to let them know how cooperative you've been and how helpful the drug was in this situation."

"How can you promise things on Madison's behalf?" Lang asked after the call was over.

"I've been doing that for years now. I've probably done it more since he left office than I ever did from the White House. He's given me a lot of responsibility, but with it comes authority, and I've learned not to be shy using it."

"Well, now that we know more of that drug, robo-whatever, is on its way, Detective Warren and I can put a stop to Chavez's little plan to extort a million dollars from the Madison Foundation."

Karen held up her hand. "Hang on. Tell me exactly what Chavez said."

"He said he'd 'found' the missing vial of medication, and he thought Madison would want to show his gratitude. I asked him how much gratitude he expected, and that's when he said a million dollars sounded about right. I'm supposed to call him back in half an hour to set up an exchange."

"Does he really expect a million dollars?" she said. "Obviously, we don't keep that kind of money around."

"I told him that. He said perhaps he could turn over the next dose as a good faith gesture. In return, he suggested we show our own good faith with something like fifty thousand dollars."

"And after that?"

"We haven't discussed how we'll exchange the rest of the drug for more money, but you can bet he's got something planned."

Karen looked at her watch. "I guess I'd better try to round up fifty thousand dollars so we can get that dose today."

Lang was already shaking his head. "Has it occurred to you that we have only Chavez's word that what he gives us isn't colored water? I think we should depend on the vial from the pharmaceutical company getting here—even a couple of hours probably won't make that much difference—and let me set a trap for Chavez. When we have him, we can sweat the details out of him."

Marks chewed on a fingernail. Finally, she said, "I'll have to leave that to you and Warren, then. In the meantime, I need to find out if Dietz is going to arrange for someone to give David Madison the remaining doses of the drug and follow him for any kind of complication or recurrence. That's something Dr. Pearson kept insisting was important."

"That's the other thing I need to tell you," Lang said. "Before the call from Chavez, I got a text from Dietz. It seems he's learned more about the infection Madison's had, and now he thinks Pearson should continue treating the ex-president until he's completely clear."

"I don't think that call to Dr. Pearson's going to be very pleasant," Marks said.

Lang got to his feet. "That's why I'm going to let you make it. Meanwhile, I need to get on the phone with Detective Warren and figure out how we're going to trap an extortionist."

Rachel was reading a novel when the door to her hospital room opened and both Allison and Josh entered. She laid the book aside and said, "Wow, two doctors visiting at one time. Should I be worried that something's gone wrong?"

"Not at all," Allison said. "I'm here as your doctor, just making evening rounds before I head home. Josh—well, I have no idea why he's here." She looked at her colleague and grinned.

Josh leaned over and kissed Rachel's forehead. "How are you doing?"

"Better each day," Rachel said. "Right about now, I must feel the way Lazarus did when he walked out of that tomb. I guess you have to almost die before you fully realize what a blessing life is."

Allison moved to the bedside, pulled her stethoscope from the pocket of her white coat, and listened to Rachel's chest. "Lungs are clear." She used a small pocket flashlight to check Rachel's throat. "No redness. No swelling. Good airway." Allison stepped back and looked at her patient. "No fever. Other than the healing tracheotomy wound, there's not the slightest suggestion you were literally at death's door less than a week ago. It's almost like a miracle."

"Not 'almost,'" Rachel said. "I prayed and I imagine some others did as well. The drug helped, I'm not doubting that, but I'm certain God had a hand in my healing as well."

"I remember a quotation from Ambroise Paré, the famous French surgeon," Josh said. "At the time I first heard this I was in pre-med, and I thought it was interesting but hardly accurate. Now I believe there's a lot of truth to it."

"What did he say?" Rachel asked.

"Paré's original quote was in French, but a rough translation is, 'I dressed his wounds. God healed him.' I think that's true in a lot of cases . . . including this one."

Agent Jerry Lang perched on the edge of a chair in a small, unused office in Madison's home. His cell phone was on the desk in front of him. He'd done a lot of things in his years in the Secret Service, but this one might have the most riding on it of any of them. He took a deep breath, then another.

Detective Stan Warren, sitting to Lang's right, said, "He gave you a number to call?"

"Yeah, and I've already checked. It's a prepaid cell phone. Probably picked it up at Radio Shack or Best Buy. Use it and toss it. No identity associated with it."

"What about using cell towers to triangulate his location?"

"We'll try, but if he's smart enough to use a 'burner' phone, I'd be surprised if he stays still long enough for us to do that." Lang looked at his watch. "It's time for me to call him. Ready?"

Warren nodded. He reached to turn on the small recorder that sat next to Lang's phone, connected to it by a thin wire.

The speaker of the cell phone buzzed with the rings. One. Two. Three. Four.

Lang's throat felt dry. Was Chavez playing a game with them? Would he call back later with more demands? Or had he changed his mind?

"Hello."

The voice was slightly muffled, probably due to either equipment or a network flaw. Surely Chavez wasn't trying to disguise his voice. It didn't matter, though.

"Doctor, this is Agent Lang. Let's finalize the details and get this transfer made."

"And we are in agreement on what I suggested?"

"Let's say we can put our hands on fifty thousand dollars tonight. We'll talk about the balance you want when we're face to face." Lang looked at his notes. "We have to have the RP-78 within the next hour. You know how important giving it on time is."

"Actually, there's no hurry. In our small study, the medication was often administered as much as two hours late, and sometimes more than that. After the first few doses, it didn't seem to matter that much."

That was good. Lang relaxed a bit as his fears of the time constraint eased. "Nevertheless, let's set up a meet so I can give you the money and you can turn over the drug."

"What do you propose?"

"The Foundation Board will provide fifty thousand dollars for you but insists that you personally hand the drug over to me before I give you the money."

Lang noticed Warren's eyebrows go up, but he didn't want to stop and explain.

"Agent Lang, I'm sure you're trustworthy, but in my home country we've learned to be suspicious of police and others with authority. I'd feel more comfortable if you rewarded me with the cash, after which I told you where to find the drug."

About five minutes into the conversation, a police officer tiptoed into the room and placed a note on the table. *Can't triangulate. He's in a car, moving at a high rate of speed. Goes from cell tower to cell tower too quickly.*

Lang cursed under his breath. The negotiations went on for another ten minutes, but at the end of that time Chavez had agreed to meet him at Reverchon Park in a half hour and make the exchange there. "The place I described is wide open," Lang said. "You can confirm I'm alone. It will still be daylight, and that's good, because I need to take a cell phone picture of you handing over the drug. That's the only way the Board will authorize payment."

"I still don't like that."

"I'll explain it when I see you." Lang scrabbled on the desk for his notes, and they fell to the floor. "But we need that RP-whatever . . . the drug."

"I'll see you in twenty-five minutes . . . alone," Chavez said. Then the line went dead.

Rachel sat on her bed, enjoying the sensation of breathing through her nose and mouth. Her tracheotomy tube had been removed only recently, but with closure of the residual defect with butterfly strips, the hole in her neck had already almost healed over. A small adhesive bandage covering the site was the only external evidence of what she'd experienced.

The door to her room opened, and Rachel turned so that she sat with her legs hanging off the side of the bed. What were Josh and Allison doing here again? "Not that I'm unhappy to have you both visit twice in one evening, but I'm betting something's up. What is it?"

Allison looked at Josh, but remained silent. Finally, he answered. "Nothing, really. As I said before, Allison is giving me a ride home. We're just finally getting away, and I wanted to stop by one more time."

"Ordinarily, I'd accept that explanation, but I've learned to read you pretty well," Rachel said. "My advice is never to play poker, especially with me. You're hiding something. So what is it? What aren't you telling me?"

"Allison here suggested that perhaps Dr. Lambert left something that would help me understand why I was chosen to take over the care of David Madison. I told her that made all this sound like a novel, and—"

"And she pointed out that's exactly what it sounds like," Rachel said. "And she's right. So, where are you going to look for this message?"

"Since Allison is giving me a ride home, she suggested we stop by the clinic and both look through Ben Lambert's office. I doubt that we'll find—"

"I'm coming with you," Rachel said. She slid off the bed and opened the room's tiny closet. "Where are my clothes?"

"When you went into quarantine, most of them were incinerated," Allison said. "But you can't come with us."

"I'm going stir-crazy here in this room," Rachel said. She looked at Allison, guessing that she'd be more sympathetic than Josh. "Please, please go to the nurses' locker room in surgery and bring me a scrub dress. Maybe the loafers I had on when I was admitted are still here."

"That's—," Josh started to say.

"Please," Rachel said. "Let me go with you."

"It's okay with me so long as we bring her right back here," Allison said. When Josh nodded his grudging approval, she said, "I'll be right back with a scrub dress. I'll try to borrow a pair of rubber clogs for her to wear, too."

"Why would you insist on going with us?" Josh asked Rachel after Allison had left.

"Because I've been right in the middle of this whole thing since I left for South America with Madison's expedition. Because I was one of the people who tried to revive Ben Lambert when he died. Because I've had an infection that took me to death's door until you managed to figure out how to save me." She drew herself up to her full five feet six inches. "So if you're looking for something to explain what's going on, I think I should be a part of it."

◆

"I don't like this. We're too far away."

Jerry Lang heard the words clearly through his earpiece. Keeping his lips as immobile as those of an accomplished ventriloquist, he spoke into the microphone concealed under the lapel of his jacket. "This is the only way not to spook Chavez. You can be here in less than a minute, but it has to look like I'm alone."

He squirmed in a vain attempt to get more comfortable on the wooden bleacher seat. Lang sat on the bottom row along the third base side of the Reverchon Park baseball diamond. Often there was a high school or pick-up game in progress, but today the area around him was deserted, partly because there were no games scheduled for that Wednesday afternoon, in part because the rain that had fallen for most of the day was continuing in the form of a light shower.

Lang had changed out of his usual suit into jeans, a dark blue tee shirt, and a Land's End waterproof jacket. His Texas Rangers baseball cap was pulled low over his eyes, not only to shield his face from the rain but also to make it more difficult to read his expression.

"Here he comes," Lang almost whispered as a car pulled up and joined his own vehicle in an otherwise empty parking lot.

"Ready," Warren replied.

"Ready," came the response of the second team.

Chavez wore brown slacks, a white dress shirt open at the neck, and a tan windbreaker. His head was bare. He looked left and right as he hurried to join Lang.

"Can we get this done?" Chavez asked as soon as he sat down. "The longer this goes on, the more it reminds me of something that might happen back in my native country."

"I have the money in my pocket," Lang replied. "And you have the medicine?"

Chavez reached into his jacket pocket and pulled out a tiny, unlabeled vial containing a small amount of a clear, faintly amber liquid.

"First, I have to take a cell phone picture of you and the drug," Lang said. He pulled a cell phone from his jacket pocket. "Hang on a second."

"This is ridiculous," Chavez said, but he moved his hand to display the vial next to his face.

Lang aimed the phone at Chavez. *Sure hope this works.* He took a deep breath, held it, and pressed the button. The cloud of gas released by the device was brief, but appeared to achieve the desired effect. The doctor slumped forward, forcing Lang to lunge to rescue the vial before Chavez tumbled to the ground.

"He's down," Lang yelled into his microphone. Not far away, car engines started and tires squealed as police responded.

Warren was first on the scene, followed by another car from which emerged two officers, one male, one female. While the two officers handcuffed the still stunned Chavez and drunk-walked him to their patrol car, Warren said, "I thought devices like the one you just used only existed in James Bond films."

Lang managed a smile. "Where do you think they got the idea? We had them first."

Warren pointed to the vial Lang held in his hand. "So, is that stuff really worth a million dollars?"

"Maybe, maybe not," Lang responded, "depending on whether it's really the drug we need or just colored water." He stood slowly. "And, of course, if it's genuine, we have to persuade Chavez to tell us where the rest of it is."

19

Dr. Ben Lambert's office at the Preston Medical Clinic had been closed and locked since shortly after the doctor's death, but Josh had no problem convincing a custodian to unlock it. "I might be moving in here," he said

Rachel stood with Josh Pearson and Allison Neeves in the middle of the office and looked around her. "Do you have any idea what we're looking for, or is this a fishing expedition?" she asked.

"I guess the latter," Josh said. "We may come up empty, but I'm looking for something that can tell us why Ben chose me as his successor if something should happen to him. Did he suspect he might not make it back alive from the South America trip? I don't know—I suppose I'm depending on our recognizing a clue if we see it."

The obvious place to begin the search was the desk, and Josh started there. Allison began pulling textbooks from the shelves that lined one wall of the office, shaking them to dislodge any loose papers before replacing each volume. Rachel went through the file cabinet that stood in the corner.

After fifteen minutes, they'd discovered nothing except that Ben Lambert hadn't considered dusting his office to be a major priority.

"All I'm finding in these books are a few notes, most of them a year or two old," Allison said.

"The file cabinet is filled with itineraries and receipts from professional trips, his continuing education certificates, some professional correspondence. Nothing that tells us what we want to know," Rachel said.

"And the desk drawers are almost empty," Josh said. "I suppose I could have guessed that as soon as I started searching and found none of them locked. You'd think that if Dr. Lambert had something important, he'd at least keep it in a locked drawer."

Rachel opened the closet door and pulled aside the three white coats hanging there. "No, I'll bet he put it here," she called. "There's a small safe on the floor of the closet."

"Why would he need a safe in his office?" Josh said as he and Allison crowded in behind Rachel. "You'd think he'd keep anything really valuable in a safety deposit box."

"Or a safe at home," Allison said. "But what would he keep here?"

The safe was a squat metal box, perhaps a foot and a half wide, about that tall, and perhaps two feet deep. The lock was controlled by a numeric keypad. Rachel figured the safe was not only secure from break-ins, but fireproof as well. "I would guess that what Lambert has in the safe is something he wanted to safeguard, but didn't want his wife to see," she said.

"If we can get a look inside, we may be on our way to that clue we were talking about," Josh said.

"Does anyone have an idea about what he might use as a combination?" Rachel asked.

"Maybe it's his birthday or wedding anniversary," Josh said. "I guess we could try the Internet or maybe the personnel office. I don't think I want to call his wife and ask her, though."

"I have an idea," Rachel said. She went back to the filing cabinet, pulled out the top drawer, and shoved the papers in it back until she could see the bottom. Nothing. She repeated the procedure with the middle drawer, and sure enough, there was a piece of white paper taped to the bottom front of the file drawer. On it were six digits she was willing to bet represented the combination to the safe. "Try these numbers," she called to Josh, who was kneeling in the closet, still fiddling with the keypad.

In a moment, the three were crowded together for a look at the inside of the safe. Most of the interior was taken up with hanging file folders in a rolling rack. Josh pulled it forward and flipped through the tabs. "Here's his current narcotics license, his most current Maintenance of Certification from the American Board of Internal Medicine, some other important papers I guess he wanted to protect in case of fire." He pulled the rack out further and gave a low whistle. "Here's something."

"What?" Rachel asked.

"This last file folder—it doesn't have anything written on the tab." Josh reached in and extracted several pieces of paper. "This is about a bank account in the Cayman Islands."

"I remember Ben saying he and his wife vacationed there last year," Dr. Neeves said.

"Well, he must have made a note of this bank while he was there," Josh replied. "There's only been one deposit to the account. It was made about a month ago."

"How large?" Rachel asked.

Josh scanned the pages he held. "Four weeks ago, the account was opened with a deposit of half a million dollars."

"Can that transaction be traced?" Dr. Neeves asked.

"Maybe the police or the Secret Service can shake loose the information," Josh said. He closed the file drawer. "I think we'd better tell them what we've found and let them get a warrant to do an official search."

Rachel pointed to the small shelf above the file folders. "Is there something on that shelf? Something shoved all the way to the back?"

Josh reached in and, using his handkerchief, extracted two small, maroon plastic-covered booklets with a complex design stamped in gold on the front. He held them up so Rachel and Allison could read the writing on the covers: British Passport Cayman Islands.

"What are the names on the passports?" Dr. Neeves asked.

Josh eased the passports open. "One is in the name of Byron Lester," he said. "But the picture is Ben Lambert's."

"And the other?" Rachel asked.

"I don't recognize the name, but the picture certainly isn't of Ruth Lambert, unless it was taken when she was twenty years younger and had red hair."

"Wow," Dr. Neeves said. "This certainly raises some questions."

"And this raises more," Josh said. He reached to the back of the shelf, and once more using his handkerchief to avoid leaving fingerprints, pulled out a vial labeled Tetanus-Diphtheria Toxoid. "I think this is the vial from which you and Madison received your immunizations. And unless I miss my guess, what it holds isn't the active toxoid. I imagine it's sterile saline."

"I don't understand," Rachel said. "This is evidence about Lambert's role in the plot. Why didn't he get rid of it as soon as it served its purpose?"

"I imagine Dr. Lambert put it here for safekeeping, intending to dispose of it as soon as he got back from the trip," Josh said. "Unfortunately for him, he returned in a coffin."

◆

The small room at police headquarters was stuffy because the air conditioning unit had gone out earlier that day. Warren was actually happy about that, because if he was sweating, he knew Dr. Andres Chavez had to be even more uncomfortable.

Warren looked to his left and gave a small nod to Jerry Lang, who returned the gesture of affirmation. The detective reached forward and punched a key on the small recorder sitting on the table in front of him. "This is Detective Stan Warren, conducting an interview with Dr. Andres Chavez. Also present is Special Agent Jerry Lang of the Secret Service." He added the date and time and once more read Chavez his Miranda rights. "Doctor, do you understand these rights?"

The doctor nodded, and Warren said, "Please give a verbal response."

"Yes, I understand them, but I maintain that I have done nothing wrong." Despite being in an interrogation room, one wrist handcuffed to a metal loop in the center of the table, Chavez was the very picture of calm. His guayabera—the short-sleeved South American shirt he wore—showed not the slightest trace of perspiration.

Warren's coat hung on the back of his chair, revealing his empty shoulder holster. His tie was at half-mast. Lang still wore his coat, and Warren wondered idly if the Secret Service agent slept in a suit. *I don't think I've ever seen him wear anything else. Oh, wait. He was in casual clothes when he met Chavez . . . and I almost didn't recognize him.*

"Doctor, I have to ask again if you are willing to speak to us without a lawyer present," Warren said.

"I am capable of defending myself," Chavez said. Apparently, in response to the lifting of Warren's eyebrows, he added, "In addition to my medical degree, I have a law degree from the Universidad del Rosario in Bogotá. In my position, it is quite useful for me to be knowledgeable in that area." Chavez said this flatly, not so much bragging as stating a fact.

"Very well," Warren said. "Why don't you tell us where you've hidden the . . ." He looked down at the wrinkled top page on the yellow pad that lay in front of him. "The RP-78. Where have you hidden it?"

"I have not hidden it," Chavez said. "I suspect that since you arrested me, you've obtained the proper warrant and searched my rental car. In the trunk is a cooler containing the drug in question."

Warren thought he heard a faint sound like a door closing. It was probably one of the police, watching via the interview via closed-circuit TV, leaving to check out Chavez's statement.

"All right. Then let's hear about your scheme to extort money from the Madison Foundation in exchange for the RP-78."

Chavez turned his hands palm upward, to the accompaniment of rattling from the handcuff chains. "I made no effort to extort money. Perhaps Ms. Marks or Agent Lang did not understand me. After all—" His smile was almost a smirk. "English is my second language. Perhaps there was miscommunication."

"I don't think fifty thousand dollars is something you'd miscommunicate. And certainly not a million dollars."

"I do recall mentioning that the Madison Foundation might wish to express its gratitude for my finding the missing RP-78—perhaps by a monetary reward. But I'm not sure of my exact words. I may even have given some suggested dollar amounts. I don't recall. But there was no demand." He smiled. "Unfortunately, we have no record of what was said by either party."

Warren glanced to his left and caught Lang frowning. In Texas, a phone conversation could be recorded if one of the two parties gave permission, but the initial call from Chavez had come to Lang's cell phone, and it was highly unlikely the agent taped his phone conversations. He'd have to check into that later. As for the second call, the one Lang made to Chavez, Warren searched his memory and decided that recording wouldn't help. The Colombian doctor hadn't really made an extortion demand.

"So how did you come to find the missing drugs?" Warren asked, anxious to move on.

"I was outside the loading dock behind the hospital having a cigarette," Chavez said. "I saw a cooler sitting nearby. I have to admit that, although it was none of my business, my curiosity got the best of me. I opened it, recognized the contents, and made my call to Ms. Marks."

There was a light tap at the door, and a patrolman entered. He bent to whisper in Warren's ear. "Say that again." The patrolman repeated what he'd said.

"Thanks. Be sure a crime scene crew is rolling to the scene. I'll be right behind."

Chavez's expression was one of puzzlement. This seemed like more of a response than finding the cooler in his car would cause. "May I ask what's going on?" he said.

"Dr. Chavez, in view of this new evidence, you may wish to reconsider your decision to represent yourself." Warren pulled a plastic-laminated card from his shirt pocket and read, "I'll refresh your memory. If you cannot afford an attorney, one will be provided for you."

"I don't understand," Chavez said. "What new evidence do you have? Explain."

Warren pushed back from the table. "How about finding a cigarette lighter with your initials engraved on it at the scene of a murder?"

"Murder? What murder?"

"The patrolman told me that one of the hospital staff was taking a smoke break outside the loading dock in the rear of the building when he found a body hidden behind one of the dumpsters there." Warren motioned Lang to follow him. He paused at the door and turned back to Chavez. "For right now, they're going to put you in a cell, but when we get back we'll talk about the murder of the night relief nurse on President Madison's ward—Barbara Carper."

20

Josh and Rachel were in Allison's car, on their way back to Prestonwood Hospital. "No answer," he said, stowing his cell phone in his pocket.

"Lang or Warren?" Rachel asked.

"Neither one is answering," Josh said.

They were near the hospital now, prompting Rachel to say, "I still don't see why I have to go back to the hospital."

Josh had been afraid that a taste of freedom would lead to this line of reasoning from Rachel. On the one hand, he'd been glad to have her along for the search. However, he knew that it would be best if she were kept under observation for at least the remaining four days of her treatment, with regular outpatient visits after that. After all, this wasn't a simple strep throat. This was an infection generally considered to be lethal. And despite the success of RP-78 to that point, Josh wasn't willing to consider the cure a certainty—nor forget the possibility of late effects of the experimental drug.

When Rachel reminded the two doctors that David Madison was already out of the hospital, they were quick to point out that he'd basically signed himself out against medical advice. "We think it's prudent to have you—and Mr. Madison, if he'd followed our recommendations—under close observation until you finish a course of RP-78," Allison said, her eyes never leaving the road.

Josh was about to mention the need for continuing exams, including blood tests looking for major organ malfunction, but he stopped when flashing lights caught his eye. To get to the physicians' parking lot at Prestonwood Hospital, they were circling around the side of the building. A number of cars with colored lights flashing—some on bars atop them or hidden behind their grilles—were parked helter-skelter around the loading dock. Although twilight was advancing, portable floodlights illuminated the area of the loading dock behind the hospital.

"Hang on," Josh said to Allison. "Stop for a second. I want to see what's going on."

Allison brought the car to a halt and everyone scanned the scene. "I wonder what all that's about." she said.

"I don't know," Josh replied, "But I think it's worth checking out."

Allison put her car in gear and drove slowly toward the assembly. They stopped at a strip of yellow crime scene tape that blocked the road. A Dallas police officer approached their car, and Allison lowered her window. "Sorry, folks." He looked at the decal on the car's windshield. "If you'll go back the way you came, you can circle the hospital in the other direction to reach the doctors' parking lot."

"Why can't we see what's going on?" Josh asked.

"Crime scene," the officer replied. "Now if you—"

"Wait," called a familiar voice. Detective Warren separated himself from the group near the loading dock and took a few steps toward the car. "Murphy, let them through. I have some questions for them. All of them."

"No need for you to see the body," Warren said as Allison, Rachel, and Josh exited their parked car. "The worker who discovered it has already identified her for us. Let's step over here so I can ask you some questions." He inclined his head toward an empty police car at the periphery of the activity.

"Who is it?" Rachel asked.

Warren consulted his notebook. "Barbara Carper. She was—"

"The night nurse who took care of David Madison and me," Rachel said. "What happened?"

"We'll get to that," Warren said. "Right now, I need each of you to confirm your whereabouts for the last three hours or so. You can come by police headquarters tomorrow to finish the process."

"I'll go first," Rachel said. She ducked into the passenger seat of the nearest police car, while Warren climbed behind the wheel.

Josh and Allison stood by, each lost in their own thoughts. After a couple of minutes, Josh said, "I wonder—"

"Should we be talking with each other?" asked Allison.

"He didn't tell us not to, which tells me he really doesn't suspect us," Josh replied. "As I was saying, I wonder if this ties in with the disappearance of the RP-78."

"I'm wondering if there isn't more to it than that," Allison said. "I think it's all tied together. It began with someone infecting David Madison and Rachel Moore while they were in South America."

"Then there was the disappearance of Ben Lambert's body."

"And the man who tried to shoot Madison."

"Now this nurse turns up dead, shortly after Madison's supply of RP-78 goes missing," Josh said. "It's certainly complicated."

"And what we found in Ben Lambert's office doesn't make it any easier to understand."

"Well, I intend to tell Warren about it when it's my turn to be interviewed," Josh said.

"Do you think we compromised the investigation by searching the office?"

"No, as Lambert's colleague and successor I had every right to look around there," Josh said. "Since there were three of us together, there's no way we could have planted anything. I'll just tell him about searching the office for notes about Madison's care and finding the safe in the closet. After that, we'll leave it up to him."

"What about the combination to the safe and the things we found in it?"

Josh shook his head. "If we discovered the safe and the combination, you can be sure the police will as well." He looked up as Warren and Rachel approached. Josh opened the door and climbed out of Allison's car. "Then we'll see how they think this all fits together."

Karen Marks frowned as she ended the call. She'd tried three times to contact Dr. Pearson, and each time there'd been no answer. Until she could get in touch with Pearson, the problem of treating David Madison remained partially unsolved.

As she often did when sitting at her desk thinking, Karen pulled a pad toward her and began doodling. First she drew a question mark, outlining it and shading the interior to achieve a three-dimensional effect. The question, of course, was whether the vial recovered from Chavez was a dummy of some sort. She agreed with Jerry Lang that that was probably the case. But that conclusion led to another problem.

Next, she drew a stylized caduceus . . . or was it a staff of Aesculapius? In either case, the next question was medical. She had to contact Dr. Pearson and see if he'd resume caring for David Madison until this illness was definitely controlled or cured or whatever the medical term was. Dr. Dietz didn't want to take over at this point, and Madison had discharged Dr. Pearson. Until she could contact Pearson and convince him to step back into the picture, her boss was a patient without a doctor.

On a second page of the pad, Karen drew an airplane—a representation of a fighter jet. A Navy pilot was waiting at Dobbins Air Base to receive the vial of RP-78 from Dr. Gaschen and fly it here, but Atlanta was experiencing terrible storms. Although rain wasn't a problem for airplanes, high winds and lightning had forced a ground stop, preventing flight line crews—even military ones—from carrying out the tasks necessary for planes to get on their way. The best predictions were that the weather would break in about three hours. But would that delay be a problem for Madison's continued treatment?

The solution to this last problem lay in using a dose from Rachel Moore's treatment vial, but that required the cooperation of Dr. Allison Neeves. Karen's last doodle was a telephone, with a line through it, because three calls to Dr. Neeves had gone unanswered so far.

Oh, David, if you only realized what I do for you. Well, one day he'd know. In the meantime . . . she reached for her phone to try another call.

◆

David Madison was home . . . and enjoying it immensely. Not even when he called the White House his residence did he luxuriate as he now did in the feeling of being "home."

Why had it taken him so long to exert himself and demand that Dr. Pearson discharge him from the hospital? He should have done it as soon as his fever broke. Well, maybe not at that instant, but certainly as soon as the doctor declared that isolation precautions were no longer necessary. Oh, he knew he'd need more injections of that drug, whatever its name, but surely he could arrange for a nurse to come by once a day to give them. Meanwhile, he had papers on his desk to read and sign, decisions to make, things that had been piling up for two weeks while he was in South America and then virtually incarcerated in Prestonwood Hospital. But that was about to change. He was back at home, back in charge.

He sat in his study, comfortable in jeans and a golf shirt, when his wife appeared in the doorway. "You're an idiot," she said. There was probably no one else in the world who could have called David Madison an idiot and gotten away with it, but Mildred could. She didn't do it often, but when she did, he listened—because she was generally right.

Madison removed his reading glasses and looked up at his wife. "Why do you say that?" he asked. His tone was casual. There was no need to argue. He'd learned to pay attention.

"Dr. Pearson saved your life, then you decided you know more medicine than he does."

"But—"

She continued as though he hadn't spoken. "He was handpicked by Ben Lambert, who you'd known since childhood, to succeed him as your physician. You were all set to let him punch and poke, take care of your everyday ailments, but when something really serious happened, you began having doubts. He diagnosed an illness that's unheard of in the United States, one that's been universally fatal for years. He found an experimental drug that might cure you. He worked miracles to get it and start treatment. Then when you were feeling better, you decided you wanted to go home. Not only that, you listened to that Dr. Dietz, who's more of an administrator than a physician, and let him persuade you to name him your personal physician."

Madison grimaced as his wife talked. What she said hurt, but what hurt most was that he realized she was right. Pearson had worked what amounted to a miracle to save two lives—his and Rachel Moore's—and David had shown his gratitude by walking away with the process unfinished. And Dietz had made a very convincing argument about letting someone with an impressive *curriculum vitae* take over the position as physician to the ex-president. Unfortunately, whereas Dietz had written numerous papers, contributed textbook chapters, and garnered teaching honors throughout the world, Pearson had produced results when it counted—when Madison's very life was on the line.

When he was sure his wife was through talking, Madison paused to chew on one of the temple pieces of his glasses as he considered her words. Then, as he'd done so many times in his life, both personal and professional, he said to his wife, "You're right. Tell me how I should fix this."

◆

Detective Stan Warren leaned forward in his chair as though to emphasize the earnestness of his words. "The Secret Service agent who heads Madison's detail keeps telling me how important it is that we keep a lid on this one. It's absolutely imperative that word doesn't get out that Madison's been terminally ill, or that he's anything but fit as a fiddle."

Lieutenant Pat Donovan glanced up to make certain the door to his office was closed. The blinds that covered the plate-glass window on one wall were drawn, separating him and Warren from the rest of the detective squad. The clock on his wall said it was almost nine at night, well past time for him to leave, but Warren had said it was important they meet. "Why is that?"

"He didn't say, but I've got an idea. Madison's foundation is about to choose a site for a clinic in Colombia. Some of the people who control medical facilities in that area aren't too happy about the competition. If the story gets out that Madison's not in good health, especially if rumor has it that he's not sound up here"—he tapped his head—"the Foundation Board might question his decision."

"And if he's critically ill? Or even if he dies?"

"The whole thing goes on the back burner."

"So where do you want to go from here?" Donovan asked.

"I think we've got four different crimes. There are the attacks on Madison—infecting him with some sort of unusual bacteria, then trying to shoot him. Then we have the Ben Lambert thing—the mysterious disappearance of his body, plus what Pearson found in his office yesterday. And we have Chavez—did he really try to extort money from Madison's Foundation in return for the last of that drug? Finally, the murder of Barbara Carper—is that related to any of this?"

Seeing Donovan nod, Warren continued. "Here's what I'm going to do. See if it makes sense to you."

The lieutenant tented his fingers and leaned back in his chair. "I'm listening."

"Although it's really his case, Lang can't backtrack the hired assassin who stole Lambert's body and took a shot at Madison without risking information getting out about the illness. The ex-president is adamant that we have to keep a lid of secrecy on the whole affair. We can do our own investigating, but it might involve some long-distance and international phone calls, and I may need your help getting access to some of this information."

"Okay."

"I want to follow up on what was found when we searched Lambert's office after Pearson's tip. I'd like you to put Robinson on that. He's sharp, and he's a whiz with the computer in case we need to chase down something. And he might be able to help find out who hired the assassin, too."

"Done."

"Meanwhile, I'm going to make Chavez my personal project."

"What about the Carper murder?"

"I can only do so much," Warren said. "You can let another team investigate it, but I want them to keep me in the loop."

"Okay," the lieutenant said. "Do it. And keep me posted."

◆

"Derek, thanks for flying back with the RP-78," Josh said. "And for your help in managing the two patients with *Bacillus decimus* infection."

Derek Johnson, fresh from a shower and dressed in clothes he'd pulled from his duffel bag, yawned. "No problem. Thanks for letting me crash at your place." He took a healthy swallow from the coffee cup that sat before him.

Although it was almost nine at night, the hospital cafeteria was as busy as ever. Around the two men, an auditory backdrop of a dozen conversations, a clattering of dishes, the occasional ring of a cell phone, all provided them with privacy for their conversation.

"Some things have changed since you left here a few hours ago, and I thought you'd want to stay involved." Josh went on to bring Derek up to date on what they'd found in Lambert's office, the disappearance of the RP-78, Barbara Carper's death, and the arrest of Dr. Chavez. "I think things are heating up."

"You realize, of course, that you're out of this," Derek said. "Madison has discharged you as his physician. Therefore, hunting for a clue about why Lambert chose you for the job in the first place is sort of moot. As for everything else you've described, it sounds to me like it's a police matter."

"You may be right," Josh said, "But I guess I'm enough of an idealist that I want to see this through to the end. Dropping out right now seems wrong to me. Besides . . ."

Derek drained his coffee cup and set it down carefully on the saucer. "Besides what?"

"I think I know why Ben Lambert chose me to care for David Madison. It's not what I thought. And I'm sort of angry about it."

◆

Dr. Josh Pearson tapped on the door of Karen Marks's office, then opened it and walked in. She stood and held out her hand. "Doctor, thank you for coming."

"Sorry for the late hour, and I apologize for missing your calls earlier," he said. "I'd turned off the ringer on my phone because we didn't want anyone to . . . that is, I was involved in something."

"Well, you finally called back. The reason I asked you to come here is that this is something you need to hear in person . . . and not from me."

The side door of her office opened and David Madison entered. He moved immediately to where Josh sat, reached down to shake the doctor's hand, and said, "Dr. Pearson, I'm sorry. I made a terrible decision, and I'm already regretting it. Will you take me back as your patient?"

Multiple emotions, from indignation to vindication, ran through Josh's mind. He looked at David Madison, still standing, an expression of pure apology on his face. Without turning his head, he saw Karen Marks leaning forward over her desk, her features frozen in a mask Josh couldn't interpret.

Josh took a deep breath before speaking. "This isn't just a matter of hurt feelings or fractured pride. Ordinarily when a patient discharges me, I consider the mutual trust between doctor and patient, trust I consider absolutely necessary, to be gone. And in that case it's best for all concerned that we not try to resume the relationship."

"I'm—"

Josh held up his hand. "Why don't you start by explaining your sudden change of heart?"

Madison, taking the initiation of a conversation as permission, pulled a side chair up next to Josh. "A couple of things, I guess. I'd been in that hospital room for what seemed like a month. True, you literally rescued me from death's door, but once it was evident I was going to recover, that somehow didn't seem so important." He looked down at his scuffed athletic shoes. "And then I got a call from Dr. Dietz. You know the man's credentials—recognized the world over as an expert in his subspecialty, he's visited with royalty, lectured to thousands, written or edited a number of textbooks. He expressed mild puzzlement that I'd chosen you as my personal physician instead of someone with his credentials, and I honestly didn't have an answer for him."

"For that matter, why did you choose Ben Lambert in the first place?" Josh asked. "He had more experience than me, but he's not on a par with Dietz."

"Ben was a good, average doctor. He didn't have all the answers, but he knew enough to get help if he needed it. The main reason I chose him was because I'd known him since we were boys together, and I trusted him."

"Yet he handpicked me to succeed him, but you didn't give me that same trust." Josh turned his head. He wasn't sure he wanted to look at this man who'd treated him . . . well, shabbily.

"I'll level with you."

Josh had learned years ago that when anyone, a politician or a plumber, prefaced remarks with that phrase, what followed was unlikely to be true. But he nodded as though he were ready to hear Madison's explanation.

"Dietz wanted the honor of being the ex-president's personal physician. But when he was faced with making some decisions about treating a potentially lethal disease, even after the worst appeared to have passed, he began to have second thoughts. And when he did, I did as well." Madison spread his hands. "That's the truth. So, will you take me back?"

Josh nodded slowly. "I'll care for you until you've had your last dose of RP-78. I'll follow you for a month afterward, to watch for late effects like changes in liver and kidney function. That will give you time to choose your new personal physician. I'll work with him to make the transition smooth. Okay?"

"If that's the best I can do . . ."

"That's it. And there are two things we need to do." Josh checked his watch. "I guess you can do this in the morning, but I want you back in the hospital, at least for another day or so—we can decide then whether you're ready for outpatient follow-up."

Madison started to speak, but Karen Marks overrode him with, "Done."

"The second thing is getting you the next dose of RP-78." Josh looked at his watch. "You're a couple of hours overdue for it. Do you have the medication?"

"That's another problem," Karen Marks said.

21

Although she had been gone from the hospital at the normal time for dinner, the nurses had put aside a plate and warmed it in the microwave for Rachel. Admittedly, it was much later than her normal evening meal—more of a midnight snack than dinner—but she was grateful for the gesture. She hadn't recognized the nurse who brought it to her, and because of this, she stifled her impulse to express sympathy for Barbara Carper's death. For all she knew, that news hadn't yet become common knowledge. Still, she shivered at the thought of the murder of a nurse who'd helped care for her during what could have been her terminal illness. She pulled the tray table closer and looked at what the hospital kitchen had sent up for her evening meal.

Rachel was toying with the food on her plate, the main feature of which was a dish that she thought might represent roast beef, when the room to her door opened and Josh Pearson entered. Before Rachel could say anything, Allison came in right behind him.

Josh said, "I know it's late, but I need to ask you something."

"Didn't we just spend a couple of hours together?" Rachel said, laying aside her knife and fork.

"Yes, and I'd hoped to let you rest," Josh said, "But something has come up . . . something that involves you."

She listened as Josh explained how he'd come to accept Madison as a patient once more and the limitations he'd placed on that offer. "My primary responsibility will be to finish treating him for the infection and do enough follow-up to assure the RP-78 hasn't caused any complications."

"But there's a problem with finishing the course of the drug," Allison said. "Chavez apparently had a small cooler in the trunk of his car with what he said was the balance of Madison's RP-78. But Josh here isn't sure that's what it really is. What's to say it isn't a dummy vial Chavez put together in order to get the money?"

"I called, and Dr. Gaschen, chief operating officer of Argosy, found another five hundred milligrams of the drug. Karen Marks arranged for it to be flown here via Air Force jet fighter, but there's a ground hold in Atlanta that will keep the plane from taking off for another couple of hours."

Rachel pushed her tray table aside and swung her feet off the bed. "And you want me to give permission to take a dose out of the RP-78 being used to treat me and give it to Madison. Right?"

"You're my patient, not Josh's," Allison said. "And at this point the decision to use what amounts to your medicine for him is up to me. But I want your permission, too." She looked at Josh, who nodded fractionally.

"I've said it before when there was a lot more at stake than there is now," Rachel said. "Whatever it takes to make sure David Madison is completely cured, even if it were to endanger my own health—I'm fine with it."

It was after eleven in the evening, but Detective Stan Warren was still at work. He yawned and reached for the Styrofoam cup of coffee sitting on his desk. He brought it to his lips, only to find it was empty. He, like many of his colleagues on the police force, believed coffee was the liquid that kept the wheels of justice turning. Warren heaved himself to his feet and headed for the pot in the corner of the squad room.

The detective took his coffee back to his desk and called across to a man in shirt sleeves, his tie loosened, who sat at a nearby desk tapping the keys of his computer. "Robinson, what did the officers find when they searched Dr. Lambert's office?"

"Just putting it all together," the other detective said. "Let me show you."

Warren moved to look over the man's shoulder at the computer screen.

"The combination to the safe was on the bottom of the middle file cabinet drawer—the same place a lot of people 'hide' theirs," Robinson said. "In the safe, there was a vial labeled diphtheria toxoid. There are several fingerprints on it, and we figure some of them belong to Lambert. The lab's going to do an analysis tomorrow, but we think it may be some sort of inert material, maybe even saline."

"And that would be the vial used to immunize Madison, so he really wasn't protected against diphtheria."

"And if you go back through the statements of some of the others involved, Miss Moore was immunized out of the same vial."

"On purpose?" Warren asked.

"No, probably that was luck of the draw. She came in for her immunization right after the nurse had given Madison his. The vial was there, so that's where her shot came from."

"What else?" Warren asked.

"Here's where it gets interesting. There's paperwork for a bank account in the Cayman Islands with a recent deposit of five hundred thousand dollars."

Warren nodded.

"The safe also held two Cayman Islands passports—one in a false name with Lambert's picture, one for a good-looking redhead."

"So Lambert was paid off for his role in all this. But if he and this redhead were going to ride off into the sunset, I'd imagine he'd want something like a million dollars. After all, he'd be leaving his retirement funds and bank account behind."

"I'm guessing the other half million was supposed to come after Madison died. But whoever was putting this together decided to get rid of Lambert instead."

Warren nodded. "And if he used some kind of injection that mimicked a heart attack, then got rid of the body so there'd be no autopsy, that would tie Lambert's part of it up with a neat little bow."

"Oh, and one more thing." Robinson turned so he was looking up at Warren. "Remember you asked me to try to backtrack the guy who took a shot at Madison? This was the same guy who dodged in ahead of the real funeral director, snatched Lambert's body, and delivered the cremated remains back the next day."

"Yeah. Leonid somebody," Warren said.

"Malnyk. Leonid Malnyk," Robinson said. "He entered the U.S. using a forged passport a couple of days before he pulled the body-snatching. We think we've found the room he was renting, but there wasn't anything in it that helped us. But we also found his car near the hospital."

"Were his keys in his pocket?"

"No, nothing that simple. We chased down the owners of all the cars in the hospital visitors' lot and found one rented with an alias that Malnyk sometimes used. The keys were in a magnetized box concealed in the left front wheel well. When the crime lab took the car apart, under the spare tire they found two things that might be of interest to you." He paused like a conjurer about to pull a rabbit out of a hat. "There was a Canadian passport with our guy's picture using the name Larry Miller and a bankbook showing a recent deposit of two hundred fifty thousand dollars in an account at the same Cayman Islands bank where our friend Dr. Lambert had his."

"Did you sleep well?"

Rachel opened one eye and saw Josh standing at her bedside. As she came more awake, she heard the sound of voices in the hospital corridor outside. After determining that Madison was to be readmitted after his brief absence from the hospital, Josh and Lang convinced the hospital administration to keep this wing unoccupied except for its two special patients. It made security much easier, but Rachel felt a certain amount of guilt at tying up nurses and aides who could be ministering to dozens of patients instead of two lone charges.

Josh drew a chair to her bedside. "How was your night?" he asked again.

"Surprisingly, I was able to sleep pretty well. As I told you earlier, once the crisis from the infection passed, I felt almost rejuvenated. And getting away from the hospital yesterday afternoon, even for only a couple of hours, was wonderful. I can hardly wait to leave here for good."

"What's the noise in the hall?" Rachel asked.

"Madison is back in the hospital."

"Complications?" she asked.

"No, conscience," Josh said. "The remaining RP-78 arrived during the night, and it appears to be in order, so we should have plenty of the drug for you and Madison to complete your ten-day courses." Josh crossed and uncrossed his legs. He rolled his head and flexed his shoulders, and Rachel heard bones cracking.

"Did you sleep at home last night?" she asked.

"No, I spent another night in one of the call rooms." He gestured to the scrub suit he wore beneath his white coat. "But

I plan to make it home sometime today to shower and change, maybe even catch a nap. And it won't be long until you'll be out of here permanently." Josh leaned forward. "And that brings me to the reason I'm here."

"That could mean a lot of things—some professional, some personal," Rachel said.

"Let's get the professional out of the way first," Josh replied. "Today is Friday. This evening you and Madison get the eighth of your ten doses of RP-78. As I've said before, it's possible you'll be fine without the additional drug, but we have no data to support that, and none of us see any need to take that risk."

Rachel felt her heart drop, because she still harbored hope that she'd get out of the hospital early—maybe even today.

"However . . . ," Josh said, and Rachel felt the ember of hope begin to smolder once more. "However, I've talked with Allison and Derek, and they agree with me that so long as you monitor your temperature, your other vital signs, and your general status—so long as you agree to report any changes immediately—then we can probably let you go home tomorrow. That's Saturday. What do you say to that?"

"Wonderful," Rachel said. "I presume Madison's wife will help watch him." She was silent for a moment. "Of course, I live alone. Do you still think it will be okay for me to be at home?"

"I've got that covered," Josh said.

Warning bells went off in Rachel's head. "Josh, I love you. We have a lot to decide about our future. But I don't think it would be a good idea for you to stay at my apartment, even for a good reason like this."

Josh smiled. "Not that I wouldn't like that situation, but I agree it's not the way we want to start this new phase of our relationship. No, I've talked with Allison Neeves about this. She's agreed to stay with you for a few days until we're completely certain there's no danger of a relapse."

"That's really nice of her," Rachel said. "Thank you for arranging it." She grinned. "Of course, I suspect I'll still see you every once in a while, even after I leave the hospital."

Josh nodded. "You can count on it."

◆

"So, I think we can let you go home tomorrow if things are still going well," Josh Pearson said.

David Madison sat in a chair in the corner of his hospital room. Rather than a hospital-issue gown, he wore maroon pajamas and a blue robe of some sort of light material. He fought down his initial response, which was to ask Dr. Pearson why he had to be dragged back to Prestonwood Hospital in the first place. Instead, he took a deep breath, counted to five, and said, "You're the doctor."

Pearson pulled his chair closer, so the two men were almost knee-to-knee. "I know. You're wondering why this sudden change of heart. The truth of the matter is that I've been taking this thing about being physician to an ex-president so seriously that I was afraid to trust my judgment. I didn't want to give some Monday morning quarterback a reason to criticize my decisions. After we got you back here last night and I gave you the seventh dose of RP-78, I sat down with Dr. Neeves and Dr. Johnson and discussed the case. None of us have definitive answers to our questions, but it seems reasonable that if we give the drug for a full ten days, then watch for signs of recurrent disease, you and Rachel—er, Miss Moore—will be fine."

"And how would you watch for those signs?"

Pearson went over his plan. He ended with, "And if this is okay with Mrs. Madison, I think we can let you go home tomorrow—to stay, this time. I'll still want to see you in the office a few times, probably get some lab work until we're sure you don't have any lasting organ damage. That will give you time to arrange with someone to be your personal physician for future care."

"I want to talk with you about that," Madison said. "But let me think about it first."

Pearson rose, then sat down again. "When we first met, you told me someone was trying to kill you. Obviously, I've seen evidence of that, but you didn't tell me why. I think you've seen I can be discreet. Are you ready to share that with me now?"

Madison stood up and began to pace. "I know a former president is soon forgotten, but it's interesting how much influence he wields. Legislators at all levels seek my opinion. My endorsement is invaluable when it comes time to make appointments or run for political office. I have a foundation that receives millions in donations each year and pays out about the same amount in grants, and there are some people who think it would be to their financial benefit if someone else headed that foundation. Sound like good enough reasons?"

"Vaguely, but I'm still not convinced. Any specifics you can share with me?"

"No, let's say that I have both friends and enemies everywhere—not just here at home."

◆

Detective Stan Warren had snatched a few hours' sleep on one of the cots in a room at the rear of the police station. He'd shaved and brushed his teeth using items from the shaving kit he kept in his desk. He'd changed into a clean shirt from the gym bag that resided in the trunk of his car for occasions like this. He hoped the change was enough to keep him from looking the way he felt.

Warren's only consolation, and a small one at that, was that he had little doubt Dr. Chavez had spent an even more uncomfortable night. He sat across from Chavez in a different interview room this time. Figuring that perhaps it was time to introduce the "good cop" into this scenario, the detective came into the room with two Styrofoam cups of coffee and placed one on the table in front of Chavez. "I don't guess you've had breakfast yet," Warren said.

Chavez reached for the cup with his free hand, the other bound by a handcuff shackled to the ring in the center of the table. "No, and I dread thinking what it might be if and when it comes." He took a swallow of coffee. "After I have been freed, I must send you some of our Colombian coffee. It tastes so much better than this."

So much for being nice. "Okay, Doc. Let's get down to business." The door opened and another detective joined them. "This is Detective Robinson. Now, let's go on the record." He pushed a button on the recorder in the middle of the table and identified everyone in the room. After he'd again recited the Miranda warning to Chavez, Warren said, "Why did you kill Barbara Carper?"

Chavez shook his head. "I didn't kill her. And when your officers complete their investigation, they'll confirm that. I presume she was shot, since as soon as you rushed off from our interview last evening, I was taken to another room where my hands were tested for gunshot residue. Undoubtedly the same type of test was done on my clothing." He gestured at the jail coveralls he now wore. "And since I didn't fire a gun, I know those tests were negative."

Warren opened his mouth, but Chavez held up his finger. "Let me tell you what happened. Yes, I knew Barbara Carper. We had met a few times behind the hospital to share a cigarette. She'd spent some time in Mexico and enjoyed speaking Spanish with me. Last night, she didn't have her cigarettes or lighter with her. I gave her a pack and loaned her my lighter, which she promised to give back to me today when we saw each other again. When I left her, she was very much alive."

"You left out one thing. Was she the one who stole the RP-78 from Madison's room? Wasn't she supposed to give it to you, in return for cash?"

"Of course not," Chavez said. "The drug I offered to Ms. Marks is some I discovered in my luggage. I'd brought one more vial than I thought, and I was willing to turn it over to Agent Lang. Naturally, I assumed there might be some kind of a reward for my help." He adopted a look of injured innocence. "And there was no attempt at extortion. I'm certain that was simply a case of you and Miss Marks misunderstanding what I said."

At that moment, the door to the interview room opened and Lieutenant Donovan stuck his head in the door. "Stan, a word with you?"

Outside, Warren said, "What? Do you have some more information for me?"

"Yes. Two patrol officers went to Barbara Carper's apartment to search it. In the refrigerator, they found this." He held up a plastic evidence bag that contained a small vial of a clear, amber liquid. Warren had to put on his reading glasses to decipher the label: DM. "I suspect Dr. Pearson can identify this as the vial of RP-78 used to treat David Madison."

22

Jerry Lang stood outside the hospital room of the former president. All this bouncing back and forth between Madison's home and Prestonwood Hospital was frustrating. He didn't understand how Madison could fire Dr. Pearson one moment and beg him to resume his care the next. Then again, it wasn't his place to make those decisions, or to question them. His responsibility was to protect the safety of this ex-president of the United States. *And so far, I've barely managed to stay one step ahead of the person or persons trying to kill him.*

He turned toward the door as it opened, and a nurse he'd come to know, Mary Wynn, exited the room. "He wants to see you," she said.

Lang shrugged. It was probably something to do with arrangements for Madison to leave the hospital and return home yet again later today. Well, that was part of his job. He'd better find out what the boss wanted.

"Sir, you wanted to see me," Lang said as he approached Madison, who was sitting in the room's recliner wearing his own pajamas and a navy blue robe with the presidential seal over the breast pocket.

"Yes, Jerry. I've been pretty much out of it since right after we got back from South America, but now I've had a chance to think back." Madison gestured to a chair. "Sit down. We need to talk."

Lang settled into the chair, turning it so that he partially faced Madison and partially the door. Agent Gilmore was on duty outside, but Lang still felt the responsibility of his assignment. "Yes, sir?"

"At the time it happened, I figured the woman who threw that flask of yellow stuff onto Ben Lambert, Rachel Moore, and me was just some crazy person striking out at the Americans who dared come to her village. Matter of fact, I originally thought it was a jar of urine or something. But obviously, she was trying to infect us."

Lang nodded. He could predict the question Madison was going to ask.

"You weren't with us that day. Agent Burkhardt was in charge of the protection detail. How did he let that woman get so close to us?" Madison took a deep breath. "And, for that matter, who was that woman?"

"Probably my fault, sir. I'd picked up some of the *turista* that others in our group were experiencing, and I stayed behind after Dr. Lambert gave me some medicine for it. Burkhardt fouled up, and I've already talked with him. As for the woman, when he tried to chase her down, she disappeared into a warren of alleyways crowded with people."

"Now we know that what she was doing was trying to expose us to a lethal infection," Madison said. "Thank goodness Dr. Pearson and Dr. Johnson were able to take care of that."

Lang waited, wondering if he was about to be criticized for letting the incident occur.

"The next question is, who was behind that attack? Was it the same person who tried to have me shot? And are there more surprises out there?"

"Sir, I know those are rhetorical questions, but let me say that it's hard for me to investigate any of this while protecting you, especially if I have to guard against an information leak.

Detective Warren is working on it, but he's having to use back channels as well."

Madison stood and moved to the window, looked out, and walked back to his chair. "I know. And the secrecy won't be necessary much longer. In the meantime, just know that I appreciate the job you and your detail do in protecting me."

"Is that all, sir?"

"Just keep me alive a few more days, Jerry. Just keep me alive."

Warren was at his desk when he saw a shadow fall across the papers in front of him. He looked up and saw Agent Jerry Lang standing behind him. "What brings you down here?" he asked, gesturing for the agent to sit down.

Lang hooked a chair from the desk behind Warren's and dragged it forward. He eased into it and said, "Look, we've each been busy looking at different aspects of this problem. Now I think it's time we tried to put it all together." He held up one hand to stop Warren from responding. "And let me say that if there are arrests coming out of what we find, they're all yours. My job is to protect David Madison. I'm not looking for a promotion. Matter of fact . . . No, never mind. Let's simply say I don't need any recognition for this."

"Okay, here's what we've got," Warren said.

He began by telling the Secret Service agent what they'd found in Lambert's office.

"So it's likely he was bribed to give Madison an inert substance instead of a diphtheria immunization. The fact that Moore got the same shot was simply an unfortunate coincidence," Lang said. "I wonder if the original plan was just to use diphtheria. If so, that should be curable, even with no immunization."

"No," Warren said. "I think the diphtheria was to cover the other infection. By the time the *Bacillus* whatever-it's-called was discovered, it would be too late to treat Madison, assuming there was any treatment."

"And do you know who was behind the shooting attempt?" Lang asked.

"No, but we suspect it was probably the same person who bribed Lambert." Warren went on to tell about the Cayman Islands bank account they'd found for the shooter. "Maybe the person behind this also had an account there. Then it would be a simple matter just to transfer money out of that account into new ones set up for Lambert and Malnyk."

"If Madison hadn't insisted we keep this quiet, I could make a few phone calls and try to find out," Lang said.

"I've got a detective working on it. If we find out the source of that bribe money, I'll let you know."

"What about Chavez? Have you gotten anything out of him?" Lang asked.

Warren shook his head. "We want to charge him with Carper's murder, but he tested negative for gunshot residues. However, those tests aren't infallible."

"Can you put him at the scene of the murder?"

"Chavez admits he met her for a smoke, but says she was alive when he left her. There's one thing, though." The detective told Lang about the vial of RP-78 found in Carper's refrigerator. "It's possible she stole it and Chavez was going to buy it from her."

"How? Why?"

"She had the opportunity to slip it out of Madison's room," Warren said. "Maybe she had a deal with Chavez, then wanted more money, so he shot her."

Lang shook his head. "There's too much we don't know."

"You're right," Warren said. "But we will. Meanwhile, you keep working from your end. I'll work this part. We'll meet in the middle." He brought his two hands together as though he were capturing an insect. "And when we do, maybe we'll have our bad guy."

Chavez, his hands chained to a wide leather belt, his feet shackled to allow him to shuffle but not run, moved along in a line with three other prisoners due to be transferred from the downtown jail to the Lew Sterrett Justice Center, from which he'd be arraigned on Monday. The four men were herded up through the back door of a van and directed to sit on a bench that ran along one side. The front area where the driver and another guard sat was separated from the rear by strong steel mesh.

Once inside, Chavez bowed his head, refusing to talk with the other prisoners. The compartment where he sat had no windows on the side, and the glass on the back door was so dirty as to allow almost no light to pass through. This suited Chavez. Once the door closed, he reached beneath the sturdy leather belt to which his chains were attached until his groping fingers found the paper clip he'd managed to find and palm shortly after he was first arrested. He straightened one half the clip and bent the tip against the buckle of his belt. If the lock to these shackles was like the one for handcuffs, he'd be free in a few moments. The dim atmosphere was no problem for Chavez, who kept his eyes closed as he worked. He'd learned to do this by touch, rather than by sight.

Although the facility to which he was going was only a couple of miles away, and Saturday traffic was light, an accident delayed the passage of the van. That was all right with Chavez, and by the time the vehicle came to a final halt he was ready.

He felt the van stop, then shouts came from outside. "You guys are almost an hour late. What kept you?"

"There was an accident. We were sitting in traffic."

"Well, you'll have to sit a while longer. The motor that opens the sally port is acting up. They're working on it."

The conversation became quieter, and it appeared some sort of compromise was reached, because it wasn't long before Chavez heard and saw the back door of the van opening. Evidently, he and his companions were going to be marched through a side door rather than the van pulling inside the complex. Perfect.

He'd been the first one into the vehicle, which meant he was the last in line to exit. The driver of the van was engaged with a Lew Sterrett guard, completing the paperwork for the exchange. The deputy, who'd ridden shotgun, both figuratively and literally, was standing at the foot of the single step that extended off the bumper of the van, saying, "Watch your step. Watch your step. Hurry up. Watch your step."

As he stepped down, Chavez appeared to trip. Suddenly his hands, which were free of his shackles, went out to wrench away the weapon the guard held. He hit the man one stroke with the butt of the shotgun, then turned to the driver and the other guard. "Take your guns out of your holsters with two fingers, slowly. One false move and I fire." He waited until they complied. "Now drop them by your feet and kick them over to me."

The men did as he said, although the looks they gave Chavez plainly said, "You'll regret this."

He stuffed first one gun, then the other, beneath his belt, from which dangled open handcuffs. "Now, into the back of the van. Quickly." He herded the driver in, then made the jail guard help the deputy from whom he'd taken the shotgun into the back of the van. He closed the door and twisted the handle to lock in the three men. That should give him a few minutes head start.

"Hey, man!" It was one of the prisoners who'd been in the back of the van with Chavez. "You can't leave without us."

Chavez threw a contemptuous look at the prisoner, casually pointed the shotgun at him, and pulled the trigger. As though lifted by an invisible hand, the man was thrown back four or five feet, landing on his back. His extremities jerked for one awful moment, and then he collapsed. The corpse lay on the pavement in a spreading pool of blood, its open eyes staring blankly at the sky.

The other two prisoners stood transfixed, not daring to speak or move.

"Anyone else?" Chavez asked. He pumped another shell into the chamber of the shotgun, then turned and sprinted the thirty yards to the adjacent street. He waved his shotgun at a passing car and when it didn't stop, fired a shot across the front of the vehicle. The driver skidded to a halt, opened his door, and took off running. Chavez nodded once with satisfaction before he climbed in and drove away.

◆

"You didn't have to drive me home," Rachel said as Josh pulled away from Prestonwood Hospital.

"Happy to do it." He could drive the route to Rachel's apartment by memory, and that's exactly what he did, letting his thoughts roam free. There were so many things he wanted to tell Rachel, but the first order of business was to get her home and settled. He'd told Allison not to come over until early evening, saying he'd stick around until then.

"Is my car still safe in the hospital parking lot?"

"It should be," Josh replied. "We can get it later this weekend. For now, Allison will be with you, and she has a car."

"Is Mr. Madison already gone?" Rachel asked.

Josh checked his watch. Eleven a.m. "He left about an hour ago. His staff will see that he's okay, and they've hired a private duty nurse, one who helped take care of Mrs. Madison when she broke her leg. She's going to check him twice a day and report any problems. She'll also give him his last couple of injections of RP-78."

Rachel frowned. "What should I do about mine?"

"Allison or I will give them. Don't worry. We'll take care of you."

Because Rachel had been in isolation, the flowers that some of her colleagues had sent at the time of her hospitalization had been distributed throughout the hospital. She wore the scrub dress Allison had procured for her the other day, along with a pair of rubber clogs left behind by someone in the nurses' dressing room. With virtually nothing to unload, Josh soon had Rachel settled on the couch.

"Would you like me to fix you some lunch?" he asked.

"Can we wait a while? Then maybe we can go out for a sandwich or something," Rachel said. "I feel like it's been a year since I was out among people."

"I think we can arrange that." Josh sat down next to her. "You were with us when we searched Ben Lambert's office. I've been thinking about that ever since then, and I'd like to run some ideas by you."

She nodded. "Sure."

"As I see it, there may be two things going on here. First, someone wants David Madison dead. The deadly infection didn't seem to be working, so they hired someone to shoot him. That failed, so there may be another attempt."

"Aren't—"

Josh held up his hand to stop her. "The police and the Secret Service are investigating that. I understand. But as a physician, I'm wondering about how I just 'happened' to find RP-78 when I needed it. I mean, the coincidences keep piling up. Karen Marks talks to someone at the CDC who mentions the drug. I call the manufacturer and talk with the chief medical officer, who turns out to be a buddy of mine. When the amount of drug he could bring wasn't enough and I was at my wit's end, I tried the doctor who was running the only drug trial Argosy had started for RP-78. He was able to bring some more, and so far it looks like it's working."

He looked at Rachel to see if she was following. When she nodded, he said, "Now, one coincidence is acceptable. Two? That raises suspicion, at least on my part. I'm wondering if someone who's behind all this didn't manipulate things so they came out this way."

"What are you saying?" Rachel asked.

"I took a philosophy course in pre-med, and we learned a lot of Latin phrases. For instance, *post hoc ergo propter hoc* means 'after this, therefore because of this.' And it's false logic. But there's another phrase that seems to apply here. *Cui bono?* Who benefits?"

"And what's the answer here?"

Josh took a deep breath. "I've done some investigating. Argosy Pharmaceuticals is on its last legs. Robinoxine, or RP-78, was its final hope. The FDA told them there was no need to continue studies on it because there was no way they'd approve it. The drug was no more effective than a couple of similar antibiotics . . . with one exception. There was a bacterium, *Bacillus decimus*, that didn't respond to any antibiotic except RP-78. But since that infection was confined to small pockets in South and Central America, there was no need to have anything available to treat it. That is, until a former president needed the drug, right here, right now. When this is over, don't you think Argosy is going to find that the FDA is now encouraging them to continue testing of the drug? And that may be the boost that company needs."

"I can see that," Rachel said. "But do you think Argosy contributed to Mr. Madison's being infected?"

"That's one scenario. I don't know how they would have done it, but I suppose it's possible." He changed his position on the couch. "There's another possibility, though. Derek's wife died last year after quite a struggle with breast cancer. I checked the insurance coverage Argosy provides, and it's poor.

I imagine he was left with a lot of debt. Could he have received a bribe, the same as Lambert?"

Rachel closed her eyes and shook her head. "He did everything he could to help treat both Madison and me."

"Of course," Josh said. "RP-78 had to work in order for him to profit."

"What about Chavez?" Rachel asked.

"I think Chavez is crooked—I don't know exactly how he fits into this, but I do recall one thing. He told me he did his residency in the U.S. . . . at Johns Hopkins. After Derek and I finished our training, I took this position with Preston Medical Clinic. Derek didn't go directly to Argosy, though. He took a year's fellowship in Infectious Disease in Baltimore . . . at Johns Hopkins."

23

Karen Marks sat to David Madison's right in his study. She crossed her legs and asked, "Are you ready for this?"

"I'm probably not at my best, but I think I'm good for a while." Madison wore a jogging suit. He was clean-shaven and his silver hair was neatly combed. Madison's recent ordeal had resulted in a weight loss of almost ten pounds, and his usual tan was fading. A small scar, one that was pink and prominent now, but which would fade and become less noticeable in weeks to come, was all that remained of his previous tracheotomy.

Karen opened a leather-bound folder embossed with the seal of the president of the United States. "I've managed to handle most of the phone calls from people who insisted they had to speak with you, as well as letters and e-mails with the same message."

"How . . . never mind. You've always done that well. Tell me the story you gave them, so it matches what I say when I get back with them."

"You came back from South America with a severe respiratory infection. Your doctor treated you, and you responded, although it was slow. He recommended you keep silent because your vocal cords were irritated."

"Sounds pretty close to the truth," Madison said. "What about the big stuff? What else is waiting for me?"

"You need to convene Dietz and the others who accompanied you on your trip to discuss their opinions on putting in a clinic there, and if so, where it should go."

"Contact them and see if we can all meet. . . . Hmm, this is Saturday. How about Monday or Tuesday?"

Karen scribbled a note. "Next, the ranking senator from Texas needs to speak with you urgently. He wouldn't tell me why, but it wasn't a staff member who called. He phoned personally. I think he wants to run something by you."

Madison looked at his watch. "I'll call him when we've finished. Next."

Karen went on with her list. Most of the things she'd handled . . . just as she'd done for years, from the time Madison was governor to his terms in Congress to his time in the Senate until she took her place at the head of his team in the White House. She looked at the seal on the folder she held and wondered how it would feel to stand behind a podium with that designation. *Put that aside and get on with it, Karen. You're in your place. Now do your job.*

Jerry Lang ended the call and stood for a moment with his cell phone in his hand, thinking and planning. It didn't take long for him to spring into action.

He punched a button on his cell phone, and the call was answered on the first ring. "Gilmore, this is Lang. I want all off-duty agents back here ASAP. As soon as you make those calls, I need you and Burkhardt to get Mrs. Madison and escort her to the safe room. I'm taking Mr. Madison there right now. When they're all together, stay with them until I tell you differently."

He listened for a moment. "No time to explain. Just do it."

Lang strode to the closed oak door of Madison's study. He could hear the murmur of voices inside. Normally, he'd wait for a break in the conversation, but this was different. He tapped sharply twice and immediately opened the door without waiting for a response. "Mr. Madison, I need your attention."

Karen Marks, who was in mid-sentence when Lang entered, frowned. She'd been through enough to know what this sudden entrance meant. The last time something like this took place was when the police received a credible threat that someone planned to detonate a bomb and destroy this house . . . with Madison and his wife in it.

"We need to go immediately to the safe room. Mrs. Madison will join you there. Karen, please come with us as well. I've assigned a couple of agents to guard you, and I'll be with you until they arrive."

Madison seemed calm enough. He rose from his chair but made no move toward the door. His usual smile had been replaced by a serious visage. "What's going on, Jerry?"

Lang shuffled his feet, anxious to leave, but he knew it would help if Madison knew what was happening. "I just got a call. Chavez managed to get out of his shackles while he was being transferred to the Sterrett Justice Center. He took a shotgun away from a guard, shot one of the prisoners traveling with him to the jail, and escaped in a hijacked car."

The ex-president nodded his understanding of the message, but his expression indicated he had a hard time believing it. "That's a lot more violence than I thought the man was capable of. Not that I didn't have my doubts about Chavez from the first time I met him in Colombia. He seemed a little too slick, a bit too . . . I don't know. He didn't ring true. And when I heard he'd been arrested for trying to sell back the RP-78 that disappeared from my hospital room, that wasn't out of character for him. But I had no idea he'd do something like this."

"Sir, we can discuss this later. Right now, I want you, Mrs. Madison, and Karen in a safe place. We think Chavez may target you."

As she passed Lang, Karen Marks said, "Do you think Chavez might be behind the other attempts on Mr. Madison's life? I mean, he flew here with the drug necessary to save the man's life. Why would he try to kill him?"

Lang shook his head. "We don't have a clue about the man's motivation. All I know right now is that my job is to protect Mr. Madison, and the best way to do it is to get him into the safe room."

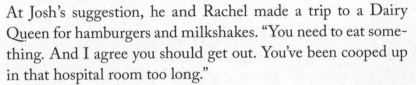

At Josh's suggestion, he and Rachel made a trip to a Dairy Queen for hamburgers and milkshakes. "You need to eat something. And I agree you should get out. You've been cooped up in that hospital room too long."

Rachel was unable to finish either her burger or shake, but Josh was sure her appetite would return, although it might be slow. This was a start. In the meantime, even the weight she'd lost and the residual pallor of her skin did nothing to dim his love for her.

After they returned, the two spent a quiet afternoon together, talking and making plans for their future. The consensus seemed to be that their personal lives would have to be on hold until the present situation was brought to an end. Despite that, both of them had no doubts that this was, for each of them, true love.

When Rachel's doorbell rang, Josh motioned for her to stay seated on the couch. "That'll probably be Allison. I'll get it." He looked through the frosted glass inset of Rachel's front door, and although he couldn't make out the exact features of the person standing on the other side, he was able to discern a woman with dark blonde hair. "Allison?" he called.

"Sorry. If there's a password, you forgot to give it to me."

He opened the door. "I guess I wanted to make certain this wasn't someone waiting to douse me with a flask of culture medium swarming with dangerous bacteria."

Allison carried a small soft-sided suitcase into the living room and set it in the corner. "How's my patient?"

"I'm okay," Rachel said. "Just weaker than I thought I'd be."

"It takes time," Allison said. She turned to Josh. "I'm going to be here with Rachel through the weekend, so you can stop worrying about her. Besides, I know you'll need to check on your number-one patient."

"He'll be fine. A private duty nurse the Madisons have used before is coming by to give him his shot today and tomorrow. After that, it's simply a matter of watching for recurrence of the infection or for late side effects from the drug."

Allison said, "I have Rachel's vial of RP-78 in my bag, and I'll give her today's dose later on. What about Madison's?"

"Madison has the drug that Dr. Gaschen at Argosy sent. We still don't know about the vials found in Chavez's car trunk and Carper's refrigerator." He thought a moment. "I know it takes a while to do an analysis that involves stuff like gas chromatography, but I wonder if they have any preliminary ideas about whether either of those was the real thing or a vial of saline."

Josh pulled out his cell phone and dialed a number he was getting to know all too well. "Detective Warren? Josh Pearson. I know you're busy, but do we know anything about the vials of RP-78 from Chavez and Carper?"

He frowned as he listened. Then he said, "Say that again." In another moment, he said, "Thanks," and ended the call.

"Dr. Chavez escaped as he was being transferred to the Sterrett Justice Center. He's armed, and Warren thinks he'll make a run at Madison," Josh said.

"Are we safe?" Rachel asked.

"I think so long as we stay here with the doors locked, there's probably no danger from Chavez."

"What about the vials?" Allison asked. "Does the lab have any preliminary information about them?"

"They did the simplest test first. They checked the specific gravity of both samples. A serum or any kind of drug will have a higher specific gravity than plain water, which measures out at 1.0."

"And?" Rachel asked.

"The sample from the trunk of Chavez's car had a specific gravity of one. It was water, probably with a drop of food coloring in it."

"What about Carper's?"

"They'll have to complete the analysis, probably on Monday, but so far it looks like the real stuff. Warren's guess is that Barbara Carper stole the RP-78 from Madison's room. Whether she was going to sell it to Chavez and changed her mind, or if she had another reason to take it, we don't know."

◆

Chavez parked the stolen car a block away from his motel. He needed to change out of the jail garments, grab some clothes and a few other things from his room, and put some distance between him and his pursuers.

He regretted pulling the trigger on the shotgun. It was a stupid mistake, undoubtedly a result of the anger he'd been holding back since his arrest. Well, it couldn't be helped now. Besides, if his knowledge of U.S. law was correct, and he was certain it was, his role in the attempted murder of Madison would make him as guilty as the person who threw the bacterial culture or pulled the trigger. Raising the charges from attempted murder to manslaughter or even murder, along with all the other counts he was certain they'd throw at him, made little difference. If he didn't succeed, he was a dead man anyway.

There appeared to be no police activity around his motel yet. He probably had a half hour before the news got to Warren and another fifteen minutes before the police could begin their manhunt. He slipped in a side door and took the elevator to the third floor. At his door, he started to reach for his key card, then realized that it, together with his wallet, watch, and keys, was still in the possession of the police.

He stood in in the hall, wondering how to get past the locked door, when a middle-aged Hispanic woman pushing a cart rounded the corner. Chavez saw her eyes widen. He had to work fast. He pasted a smile on his face and told her in Spanish that some of his friends were playing a trick on him. They'd abandoned him near his hotel dressed like a convict. If he could get into his room and change, he'd win the game they were playing.

She reached for her master key card and opened the door, all the while saying she didn't understand. As soon as the door was open, Chavez put one hand over her mouth, pulled her inside, kicked the door shut, and moved his hands until they were around her neck. He kept up the pressure until she stopped struggling.

Ten minutes later, Chavez hefted his suitcase, picked up his shotgun, and looked around the room. He wondered if he'd forgotten anything. If so, he'd have to get along without it. Now he needed to confuse the police a bit.

Chavez grabbed covers off the bed and towels from the bathroom and piled them on top of the maid's body in the middle of the floor, along with his jail jumpsuit and the leather belt with its chains and shackles. He automatically reached for his lighter before he recalled that the police had it. He looked around the room, then recalled seeing a suspicious bulge in the maid's pocket.

He rummaged past the pack of cigarettes he found there and pulled out a book of matches. *You won't need these any lon-*

ger. Chavez struck one and used it to ignite the whole book before tossing the flaming mass onto the pile on the floor.

As soon as he was certain the blaze was well underway, he put the Do Not Disturb sign on the door, closed it, and hurried away.

24

Are you going to check on Mr. Madison sometime today?" Rachel asked.

Josh leaned forward from his seat on Rachel's living room couch. "I've been thinking about that. I may not even be able to get in to see him. If the Secret Service has the information Warren gave me, and I have no reason to doubt it, they already have the area locked down."

"But surely they'll give you access. They know who you are. Agent Lang would recognize you, even if some of the others don't."

Josh shrugged. "I guess I should at least try. Truth of the matter, I'm a little worried about leaving the two of you here alone."

Without a word, Allison rose from her chair and went to her suitcase, which still sat in the corner of the living room. She turned it on its side, unzipped the flap, and rummaged for a second. When her hand emerged, it was holding a small, nickel-finish revolver. "By the time I left for Dallas to go into practice, I was already divorced. When I told my parents where I was going, my mother was worried because a woman alone in the big city would be vulnerable. My daddy was more proactive. He gave me this. Insisted I learn how to use it, too." She flipped open the cylinder to show cartridges in five of the six chambers, then flicked it closed again. "Empty chamber under the hammer, five shots I hope never to fire." Allison hefted the little gun. "I generally keep this in the glove compartment of my car, but I decided you and Rachel might feel better about my staying here if I showed you I'm capable of protecting myself and her."

Allison stowed the pistol back in her suitcase, but left the flap unzipped.

Rachel's feelings about Allison having a weapon were mixed, but in the end she decided it was a good thing. *Be glad she has it, and pray it's never needed.* "Call me when you're through at the Madison house," she said. "But don't worry. We'll be fine." Rachel just wished she were as confident as she sounded.

After the door closed behind Josh, Allison looked at her watch. "Do you want something to eat?"

"I really don't have much appetite," Rachel said. "Maybe later. Meanwhile, what would you like to do?"

Allison eased into the overstuffed chair she'd left a moment ago. "I'm ready to relax. It's so nice to be away from the hospital after all that's happened this past two weeks." She leaned back and looked toward the ceiling. "I guess I'll be going back to my usual routine in a couple of days. When do you think Josh will resume his regular practice?"

"He told me earlier today that he'll only follow Madison for a few more days," Rachel said. "I'm guessing that sometime tomorrow he'll talk with whoever's in charge at the clinic and arrange to get back to his practice early next week."

"So he's not going to remain as Madison's personal physician?"

"As I understand it, Josh insisted that Madison choose someone else for that title. I'm sure Josh will work to make the transition smooth, but frankly. . . . Well, honestly, I think he'll be glad to give up the position."

Allison rubbed her chin with her thumb and first finger. "You'd think being personal physician to an ex-president would be a good thing."

"He did, at first," Rachel said. "Josh's initial feeling was that he was named as sort of a backup to care for Madison if Lambert got sick or something. But after we found what Dr. Lambert had hidden away in his office, things changed. Lambert didn't plan on dying. He planned on taking off with his little redhead, enjoying the money he earned from his part in the scheme. In that case, Josh would be left to care for Madison. If the scenario worked, Lambert didn't want someone who'd see through the plot and expose it. He wanted someone who would probably miss the diagnosis, a doctor who would give the appearance of trying but whose best efforts wouldn't be enough to save David Madison."

"You mean . . ."

"Yes. Josh didn't think he was chosen because he was so talented. He believes he was selected because Ben Lambert didn't consider him to be quite smart enough."

◆

Derek Johnson paced his room at the Ramada Inn like a lion stalking back and forth in its cage. When he'd told Josh earlier today that he planned to stick around to observe for any late adverse effects from RP-78, his friend offered to let him continue to crash on the couch of his apartment. Derek figured that since Josh now had some free time, he'd be happier to have his apartment to himself, so he declined with thanks. No, if he were going to stay, he'd get a hotel room and rent a car. He didn't want to inconvenience Josh. Besides, he needed some privacy as well—because he had a decision to make.

Derek stopped his pacing long enough to bend backward, then rotate his torso a few times to work out kinks in his back put there by nights spent on call room beds and a few hours of sleep snatched on Josh's couch. He looked at the bed in his hotel room and silently gave thanks that he was sleeping in more comfort now.

He pulled out his cell phone, then replaced it in his pocket without dialing. Derek glanced down at the industrial-grade carpet of the room and marveled that he hadn't worn a path in it with his pacing.

He could call Josh, but what would he say? "Josh, I'm bored. Can I hang out with you?" No, he had to let his friend do his thing. Meanwhile, Derek wondered what his own thing really was.

He fell back onto the bed, totally at loose ends. He could go out to eat, but he wasn't hungry. He picked up the TV remote, then put it down without turning on the set. There'd been a local paper outside his door that morning, but it lay unopened on the dresser. He couldn't decide what to do.

He'd heard it said that having trouble making a decision represented a decision. Maybe his hesitancy to make the call should tell him something. Then again . . . Suddenly, Derek almost jumped off the bed, grabbed the room's card key that lay on the dresser, and headed out the door. Maybe a long walk would help.

❖

Rachel tossed the magazine she'd been reading onto the coffee table in front of her, got up from her sofa, and said, "Allison, I want to go out."

"We told Josh we'd stay here," Allison said.

"I don't think Chavez is going to come after us. Besides, you can bring your pistol."

"Did you decide you were hungry?" Allison asked. "I suppose we could eat somewhere."

"No," Rachel said. "Maybe after we get through with this I'll feel hungry, but there's a visit I need to make. It's been on my mind since I got back, but obviously I've been a little busy until recently trying to stay alive. Now it's time."

Allison shrugged. She picked up her purse, walked to the suitcase to retrieve her pistol, and dropped it into the bag. "Okay. I'll drive and try to keep you safe. Where do you want to go?"

"I need to talk with Ben Lambert's wife."

To Allison's credit, she neither argued nor asked for an explanation. Ten minutes later, both women were in Allison's car, headed to the address they'd found via the Dallas phone directory.

Lambert had been dead for over two weeks. Once the widow was convinced that the ashes returned to the funeral home were those of her husband, she arranged for a memorial service. That had taken place over a week ago. Now, Ruth Lambert was engaged in the tough task of putting together her life without the partner who'd shared it for many years.

"I don't have a black dress with me," Allison said. "Think this is okay?"

Rachel roused from her deep thoughts long enough to take in Allison's white blouse and dark brown slacks. "It looks fine to me. I don't think it's necessary to wear black when visiting this long after the funeral." At least, she hoped so, since she was wearing gray slacks and a red blouse.

They found the Lambert home easily and parked at the curb. There were no cars in the driveway and no activity in the yard. A small purple wreath was on the front door. Rachel opened the car door, but before exiting she turned to Allison. "You can stay here if you like. I don't think I'll be long."

Allison shook her head. "No, I'm going in with you."

The women walked to the front door, where Rachel rang the bell. In a few moments Rachel heard footsteps. A woman in her early sixties opened the door. "Yes?" Her response was curious, neither inviting nor off-putting.

"Mrs. Lambert?" Rachel asked.

"Yes? I'm Ruth Lambert." Mrs. Lambert wore a light gray dress. Her dark brunette hair showed a few touches of gray and was neatly styled. Her eyes were slightly swollen, but otherwise her face betrayed no evidence of what she'd been through. She wore her wedding ring, but no other jewelry.

"I'm Rachel Moore. I was on the South American trip with your husband. I . . . I'm one of the people who helped try to resuscitate him. And I . . . I accompanied his body home." She took a deep breath. "I came to tell you I'm sorry—for your loss, and for what happened to his body afterward."

Rachel held her breath, trying to read Mrs. Lambert's expression. For a few seconds, there was no response. Then the woman gave the faintest of nods, stepped aside, and said, "Please come in."

The house was probably quite nice, undoubtedly cheery and pleasant under normal circumstances. Unfortunately, these circumstances were far from normal. Rachel and Allison were escorted into the living room, where the drapes were drawn. The only illumination came from lamps on two side tables flanking the couch.

Mrs. Lambert gestured her guests to chairs opposite the sofa where she'd been sitting. On the coffee table in front of the couch were stacks of photo albums. "I've been looking at pictures . . . remembering our times together . . . trying to figure out where my life is going," she said after she was seated.

"I realize how difficult things are right now," Rachel said. "I wanted you to know that I was one of the people who tried to revive Dr. Lambert. It appears his terminal event was sudden, and if it helps any, he didn't suffer."

"Did you know my husband very well?"

Rachel wasn't sure how to respond. "I didn't meet him until this trip, if that's what you mean."

"But you'd recognize him. There's no doubt in your mind that he really died—that the man in that casket you brought back here was Ben Lambert."

"No doubt. There were four of us who worked trying to save him. We reached him right after we heard him fall, and he was already gone." Rachel started to reach over and pat Mrs. Lambert's arm, but at the last minute she withdrew her hand. "No, I'm sure it was your husband who passed away."

A single tear began to wind its way down Mrs. Lambert's cheek. "I didn't want to believe it. I've held out hope that this was all a mistake. I kept expecting Ben to call, to come in that door, to tell me it was all a big mix-up." She looked down at the albums in front of her. "But now what I have left are photos and memories."

Allison edged forward in her chair. "Mrs. Lambert, I'm Dr. Allison Neeves. I worked with Ben at the clinic, and I want you to know that all of us extend our sympathy to you. Is there anything we can do?"

Mrs. Lambert shook her head. "No. Ben and I didn't have children, but the people from our church have been very supportive. He had a huge life insurance policy, so money is no problem. It's just . . . it's just hard to think about life without him. Ben was due to retire at the end of this year. I wanted to travel. He didn't seem as interested as I was, but I felt sure that would change. But now . . ." Mrs. Lambert's lower lip trembled, but no more tears came.

Rachel thought about it. Obviously, Ruth Lambert had no idea about the passports and bank account they'd discovered in her husband's office. Was the lack of interest Ben showed in traveling with his wife simply a sign that, while she was planning their retirement together, he was preparing to run away with another woman?

As Rachel walked back to Allison's car, she tried to process what she'd learned. Was it still possible that Lambert had been framed? Or was he guilty? Had he been murdered to keep him quiet? And, if so, who was behind the plot?

Miracle Drug

◆

Josh drove slowly toward Madison's home. He was mentally reviewing the ex-president's case when his cell phone rang. He touched the button on his steering column that would route the call via Bluetooth to the speaker of his vehicle's radio. "Dr. Pearson."

"Josh, this is Sixto. Got a minute?"

"Sure. What's up?"

"I need to bounce something off you. I just did an exploratory laparotomy for internal bleeding on a middle-aged male who was in an auto accident. Wasn't wearing his seat belt, and the air bag didn't fully inflate, so he got thrown around quite a bit. He was bleeding mainly from a large laceration of the liver, but I sutured it and got everything controlled."

"Okay," Josh said. "So what's the problem?"

"The surgery went fine. His vital signs are stable, no evidence of further blood loss, but he's a lot slower coming out of the anesthetic than either the anesthesiologist or I would like. I mean, a lot slower."

"Neurologic status?" Josh asked.

"No localizing signs. I went ahead and got an MRI of the head, and it's negative. This isn't head trauma or a stroke."

"Medications?"

"Got the history from his wife because he was pretty well out of it when the paramedics brought him in. High cholesterol, controlled with Lipitor. History of depression, but not on any meds. Anything I might be missing?"

Josh thought a bit. "Any herbal stuff? A lot of people take St. John's Wort for depression, but don't consider it a medication because it's not a prescription item. Not sure if it helps, but it can really potentiate the effect of anesthetic drugs. That's why anesthesiologists ask patients to discontinue herbals of any kind prior to elective surgery."

"His wife said no, but given the way he's behaving now, maybe he's been hiding it from her. I'll check and call you back."

In fifteen minutes, Josh's cell phone rang again. "Sixto here."

"Yes?"

"The wife went home and looked through his medicine cabinet. She found an almost empty bottle of St. John's Wort and another full one next to it. My guess is he's been taking it for some time and not letting her know."

"And for whatever reason—embarrassment, insurance— he didn't want to see a doctor and get a prescription for an antidepressant."

"Exactly," Sixto said. "I've talked with the anesthesiologist. Now that we know this, I think we'll just watch the guy—his respirations are good, no circulatory collapse."

"I wish the people we deal with would tell us the whole truth," Josh said.

Sixto apparently chose to ignore that, because his next words were on a totally different subject. "While I have you on the phone, how are the two people I did emergency tracheotomies on? When I last saw them, they seemed to be doing okay after the trach tubes were removed. If there's too much scarring of the skin incision areas, I can do a revision. It's a fairly simple plastic surgery procedure under local."

"Both of them are fine. Rachel is at her apartment, and Allison Neeves is going to stay with her for a couple of days. I'm on my way to check Madison, but so far, so good with him as well. Thanks for your help."

"Thanks for yours," Sixto said.

By now, Josh was in the neighborhood of Madison's home. He'd been here only once before, and that time he was in the back of a car driven by a Secret Service agent, but he was pretty sure he could find it again.

This was an upscale area of town, although Madison's home was neither larger nor nicer than many of his neighbors' houses. Like theirs, his two-story house was situated on a lot a bit over an acre in size. As Josh recalled, the home was fronted by a long drive with a guard, a Dallas police officer, at the entrance. That shouldn't be too hard to find.

He was scanning the houses he passed for that guarded driveway when he heard a loud crack, and his windshield seemed to explode, throwing tiny shards of safety glass at him. Josh leaned against his seat belt, stretching it to its full extent as he flung himself to the right and downward until his head was below the level of the dashboard. He jammed his foot onto the brake, but the vehicle had already come to a sudden stop, apparently hitting something solid.

Josh jammed the gearshift lever into Park and turned off the engine. He'd ended up with the front end of his red Subaru Forester buried in a privet hedge that bordered someone's lawn. He wasn't sure what was behind or beneath the shrub, but whatever it was, his vehicle had hit it solidly.

His first instinct was to run, but then he thought better of it. Josh couldn't outrun a bullet, and if whoever had taken the shot wanted him, they probably wouldn't hesitate to try for a moving target. He could only hope this attempt was a one-and-done effort. Maybe it was simply calculated to warn him—but of what?

He pulled his cell phone from his pocket, and with his head still well below window level of his vehicle, punched in 9-1-1.

25

Mildred Madison watched and listened as her husband spoke to his chief of security, Agent Jerry Lang. Madison didn't raise his voice. He didn't stamp his foot or throw things. She realized this was essentially a *pro forma* protest, one that made him feel as though he was in charge. "Is this really necessary?" he said. "I've been confined to a hospital room for almost two weeks. Now I'm finally home, but you tell me I'm not safe, so I have to hide in a secure room."

Before Lang could answer, Mildred patted her husband's arm. "David, this isn't the first time we've had to go to this room or one like it. When we were in the White House, there were a few occasions when we had to do the same thing. And if it weren't necessary, we wouldn't have added a secure room like this one when we moved into the house." She smiled, a bastion of calm amidst a tornado of trouble. "It won't be too long."

"Mrs. Madison is right," Lang agreed. "This won't take long. As we speak, the Dallas Police Department is deploying additional officers to guard all the access points to this house. I've recalled all off-duty Secret Service agents, and when the detail is at full strength, we'll establish a perimeter inside the house in case Chavez manages to breach the outer security. When all that's in place, you'll be free to move about once more."

"I have no idea why anyone would think I'm this important," Madison grumbled.

Mildred remained quiet, but she knew that wasn't true. She realized exactly why her husband's life was currently in danger. And he did, too. Oh, well. In a few days, some of the pressure will have lifted.

Madison pointed to the briefcase Karen Marks had brought when she accompanied him here. "Might as well use our time doing something useful. Let's finish going over everything that piled up while I was out of circulation."

Marks pulled some papers from the case and spread them on the round table in the corner of the large room. Then she and Madison huddled side by side as she filled him in on various matters.

Mildred Madison retrieved the book she'd brought with her when the agent came to move her to the safe room. She made herself comfortable in a chair in the opposite corner from her husband and opened her book, a well-worn and dog-eared copy of Swindoll's *Hope for Our Troubled Times*.

Like so many of the years that had gone before, these were indeed troubled times. When they left the White House, Mildred thought perhaps that she and David could step away from the problems that beset the world and live a quiet life of retirement. Unfortunately, that had not been the case. Oh, well. God was in control. As she had for so many decades, she rested in that thought.

◆

Rachel saw that the call was from Josh. "I expected you to call earlier," she said.

"Everything okay over there?" he asked.

"We're fine," Rachel asked. "Why wouldn't we be?"

"Someone took a shot at me when I was on my way to Madison's home," Josh answered. "I wanted to make sure he hadn't bothered you guys."

"Are you all right?" Rachel beckoned Allison over and punched the speaker button on her cell phone. "Did the police catch the man who shot at you?"

Allison frowned and leaned closer to the phone. Rachel mouthed, "He's fine."

"Yes, I'm all right. No, the police didn't catch the man, but we all have a pretty good idea of who it was. I called Lang after it happened. Madison is fine. The private nurse has already been by and given him his shot. They're on lockdown until the police catch Chavez, and I'm not going to try to go there this evening."

"Where are you?" Rachel asked.

Josh explained that he'd been tied up, first with the police, then with the homeowner and his insurance agent. Now he was riding with the wrecker driver to drop off his car and get a rental.

"Well, let me hear from you when you have the rental car," Rachel said.

"Will do," Josh replied. "What did you all do after I left?"

"I went to see Mrs. Lambert."

"Why?"

"I wanted to express my sympathy for her loss," Rachel said. "After all, I was with her husband at the end." She went on to summarize her visit with Ruth Lambert. "She talked about the plans she had for the two of them to travel after his retirement. I get the impression he wasn't as enthusiastic as she was about it."

"Maybe that's because his idea of travel was going out of the country with a redhead who's much younger than her," Josh said.

"I don't know if that's it or not," Rachel said. "Maybe he was framed, maybe not. I'm going to have to leave it to the police to discover the truth there."

"I see that we've almost arrived," Josh said. "I'll call you after everything's settled. In the meantime, stay there with the doors and windows locked."

"Don't worry about us," Rachel said as she took the call off speaker. "You be careful, though."

"I will."

Rachel cleared her throat. "Josh, would you come by tomorrow morning and pick me up so we can attend church together?"

"Sure," Josh said. "Are you going to invite Allison?"

"I'd like to," Rachel said, "although from what I gather so far, I doubt that church is on her regular Sunday schedule."

◆

The next morning, Rachel wiped her mouth with a paper napkin and crumpled it onto her plate alongside the crumbs from an English muffin. She had one final sip of coffee and pushed back from her kitchen table.

Allison sat opposite her, paging through the Sunday paper and drinking a cup of breakfast tea. Rachel got the definite impression that her temporary roommate wasn't much of a morning person. Allison probably hadn't spoken a dozen words since rolling out of bed.

Well, now the woman was up. She was almost finished with her tea, and Rachel figured this was as good a time as any to broach the subject of church with Allison. "Josh is picking me up in an hour for church. I'd love for you to go with us."

Allison looked up from the Metro section of the *Dallas Morning News* and frowned. "I . . . I really didn't bring church clothes when I packed for the weekend."

"What you wore when we visited Mrs. Lambert would be fine," Rachel said. "At the church I attend, most people don't dress up for the services. Oh, some of them, especially the older generation, still wear nicer clothes, but by and large most of us don't even pay attention to what anyone is wearing."

"That sure wasn't the case in the church my parents attended," Allison said.

"You say your parents attended church. Didn't you go?"

"Oh, sure. I went every Sunday, at first because my parents made me. Then I got interested, mainly through our church's youth group. I still remember the summer I walked the aisle and made my decision for Christ. But things changed after I left home."

"What do you mean?"

"Like a lot of college students, I rebelled a little. By three months into my first year of pre-med, I'd decided I'd rather sleep in on Sunday mornings. After that, I guess I never looked back."

"According to Josh, that's not an unusual scenario among doctors," Rachel said. "I've certainly seen it among some of my nurse colleagues. But it's good to see so many have made their way back after what I call 'taking a break from God.'"

"I took more than a break," Allison said. "During my senior year in med school . . . well, never mind. I don't really want to talk about it."

Allison flipped the page of her newspaper, obviously hoping to drop the subject. Rachel decided to give it one more try. "Look, I don't want you to feel like I'm forcing you, but I can assure you this church is different. You'll feel at home five minutes after you walk in. The music is wonderful. The preaching is thought provoking. And I can almost guarantee you'll leave feeling better than when you arrived."

Allison looked over the top of her paper at Rachel, shrugged, and went back to reading.

As the congregation filed out of the church after the benediction, Josh whispered to Rachel, "You were right about this church. I felt right at home here."

"Do you like it better than the one you usually attend?" Rachel asked.

"To tell the truth, I've sort of let my church attendance slide for the past few years. Matter of fact, I'm not sure where my membership is. I guess it's back home in the church where I grew up."

Rachel looked around to make certain she wasn't disturbing those around her. "I'm glad you came with me today," she whispered. "But if there's a different church you'd like us to attend together, we can do that. I want us to be certain—not just about our church membership, but about the place God will have in our home."

They were outside now, squinting a bit in the noonday sunshine. Josh took Rachel's arm and steered her toward his rental car.

"Do you agree with me?" Rachel said. "I mean, about our marriage being founded on the relationship we have with God, not just what we have with each other?"

Josh seemed to think about that as he opened the car door for her. Then he said, "Yes. I think it's very important."

They were silent in the car as Josh pulled out of the church parking lot. When they were clear of the traffic, he said, "Would you like to get some lunch?"

"Okay, but let me call Allison. Maybe she'd like to join us— or we can bring her something."

"I'm sorry she didn't come with us," Josh said. "I think it would have been good for her. I'm not certain she's over the trauma of her divorce, and that's been three or four years ago . . . before she came to Preston Medical Clinic, anyway."

"Why do you say that?"

"Allison's a nice person," Josh said, "but her life pretty well revolves around her practice. She has no outside interests. I never hear her talk about her family. And she seems to have built some sort of a wall around herself, determined not to let anyone get too close. I think she was afraid someone would hurt her, like her ex-husband did when he left her."

"I thought you were her friend," Rachel said.

"We're colleagues, but I don't think she considered me a friend . . . until recently. And she seems to be getting comfortable with you recently, which makes sense, considering what you've been through together. But other than that, Allison's a pretty solitary person."

"Maybe I can help her come out of that shell," Rachel said. "Let me see if she wants something for lunch. We could even go by and pick her up." She pulled out her cell phone, dialed, and waited for a few moments without saying anything.

"Not answering?" Josh asked.

"No, and I'm surprised. What if this had been the hospital calling?"

Josh shrugged. "Maybe she was taking a shower. Maybe she was in the other room. Don't worry about it."

They drove on a couple of minutes longer before Rachel said, "Josh, I'd feel better if we went by my apartment. I want to check on Allison."

When they were in sight of her apartment, Rachel grabbed Josh's arm and pointed. There were two police cars parked head-in in front of her apartment, their revolving strobes alternately painting the side of the complex red and blue.

26

The first thing Rachel saw when she opened the apartment door was Allison, sitting on the sofa, pale as a ghost. A stocky blonde police officer with stripes on the sleeve of her uniform shirt sat next to Allison, nodding, talking in a low voice and occasionally jotting a few words in a leather-covered notebook.

Josh, who'd been a few steps behind her, joined Rachel on the stoop in front of the open door. At that moment, two uniformed Dallas Police officers, their hands on their holstered weapons, came around the side of the building and hurried toward the little porch leading into Rachel's first-floor apartment.

"I'm sorry, you can't go in. That's a crime scene," the first one, a muscular man, said.

Rachel glanced at the nameplate over his breast pocket before answering. "Officer Brown, I'm the resident here. What's going on?"

"Why don't you two step back here until Corporal Daley finishes interviewing the lady?" Brown said.

The little group walked back down the sidewalk and stopped. Rachel and Josh stood facing the still-open apartment door, while the two policemen barred their way without making it obvious what they were doing. "May I see some ID?" Brown asked.

After the police were convinced Rachel was indeed the primary occupant and Josh was present at her request, she asked once more, "What's going on?"

"The woman inside called 911 a little while ago. She said there was a prowler on the porch, trying to force his way in through the locked front door. We were dispatched, and by the time we got here the prowler was gone." He cocked his head toward the door. "And there was a bullet hole in that door."

Rachel's eyes followed the policeman's pointing finger. At about shoulder height, barely visible at the angle the door was open, was a small hole surrounded by splintered wood.

"I wonder if she hit him," Josh said.

Rachel inclined her head toward the four teardrop-shaped red splotches leading from the porch to the sidewalk to the grass beside the apartment building and around the corner of the building, each one marked with a numbered yellow plastic tent. "I guess you didn't notice these before, but I think they should answer your question."

"At first, the woman inside didn't want to let us in," Brown said. "When she finally opened the door, she told us the same story she'd given the 911 operator. A man was trying to gain entrance by forcing the lock. She says that after she hung up from the call she yelled at him repeatedly to stop, but he wouldn't. That's when she shot at him."

The police officer appeared in the open doorway, holding a plastic evidence bag. Inside it was a pistol. "You have my card," she said over her shoulder. "Call if you think of anything else. Either I or someone else will be back later today." She strode down the sidewalk, said something to the two police officers who stood there, and they climbed into their vehicles. In a moment, the cars—their lights no longer flashing—rounded the corner and were gone.

Rachel started toward the open doorway, with Josh hurrying after her.

Rachel and Josh entered the living room where Allison stood in stunned silence. Josh closed the door, while Rachel walked to Allison and gently laid a hand on her shoulder.

"Allison, what happened?" Rachel asked.

Allison shook her head. "I . . . There was someone . . . A man tried to break in. And I shot him."

"Are you hurt?"

"No. Just . . . just shaken up, I guess," Allison replied. Silent tears streaked her cheeks, but she wiped them away and fought to regain control of her emotions. "I'll be okay."

Rachel put her arm around Allison's shoulder. "Let's go into the bedroom and talk." She gave Josh a meaningful look. "Just the two of us."

❖

Josh and Rachel lunched on sandwiches, although neither of them was particularly hungry. As they munched, each listened for sounds from the bedroom where Allison had finally fallen asleep.

"I'll clean up," Rachel said. "Don't you need to look in on your patient sometime today?"

"Yes." Today was the day Madison was to get his final injection of RP-78. Josh looked at his watch and noted it was already mid-afternoon. He probably should leave fairly soon to visit his patient.

In a way, Josh looked forward to his visit today with Madison. After this and a limited amount of follow-up care, he'd have no further responsibility for the ex-president's health. The handling of future illnesses would be the responsibility of whichever doctor Madison chose. Josh was more than ready to shed this responsibility and return to his normal practice.

This, in turn, reminded him that he needed to call the Preston Medical Clinic's managing partner, Dr. Nadeel Kahn, to discuss his schedule. Nadeel would probably be disappointed that the clinic would soon lose the *cachet* of having the former president's doctor on staff. However, when Madison chose his new primary physician, perhaps he'd go with one of the other doctors from the clinic. So long as it wasn't Josh, that would be fine.

"You're fidgeting," Rachel said.

"I need to make a couple of calls," Josh said. "I think I'll step into the kitchen so I don't wake Allison."

"I doubt you could wake her with a cannon. She's been running on almost no sleep since I was admitted to the hospital. Now it's catching up to her."

Josh tiptoed into the kitchen, pulled out his cell phone, and called Nadeel's home number. The woman who answered didn't sound too happy that another physician wanted to speak with her husband on a Sunday. Night and weekend calls for a hematologist/oncologist apparently weren't common in the Kahn household.

"Josh, what's up?" Nadeel's tone, unlike that of his wife, was pleasant, almost welcoming. "I thought you had Mr. Madison's problems under control."

"They are. He gets his last dose of RP-78 today. After that, I'm done with him except for a bit of follow-up." Josh realized he hadn't kept Nadeel fully informed, so he hastened to remedy that omission now. Then he got to the reason for his call. "He's going to choose another personal physician, so I'm ready to come back."

"Problems between the two of you?"

"No, he seems happy." No need to mention the way Dietz convinced Madison to leave the hospital against Josh's advice and come under his care. That was water under the bridge. "I've found I'm not cut out for the pressure that goes with the job, and I get the impression Madison would like someone a bit more high profile. So, can you put me back on the schedule?"

"Let me see. One of the internists rescheduled his vacation so he could cover your practice and Allison's. It'll take a few days to get things changed back. Why don't you plan to start seeing patients again on Wednesday? Okay?"

"Fine."

"And if you see Allison, have her give me a call. We can probably get her started back about the same time."

"Will do. Thanks."

"It's part of my job," Nadeel said. "You know, when I did my fellowship at Johns Hopkins, they didn't prepare me for the administrative work I'm doing now. Would you like to take over some of it?"

Josh wasn't sure whether his managing partner was serious, but there was no question in his mind how to answer. "No thanks. I'm looking forward to getting back to patient care."

After Josh hung up, something Nadeel Kahn said popped back into his mind. He'd forgotten that, after his internal medicine residency, Nadeel had done his hematology/oncology fellowship at Johns Hopkins. Chavez said he'd trained there as well. Here was a link between Chavez and yet another player in the drama—more information to pass on to Warren.

◆

Derek Johnson came awake with a start. After his walk, which had done little to help him make up his mind, he'd stretched out on the bed in his motel room, intending to close his eyes for a moment. Instead, the bedside clock told him he'd been asleep for almost an hour. *Napping in the middle of the afternoon. Derek, you're getting old.*

He felt a bit more alert after splashing cold water on his face. Derek still hadn't made the phone call he'd been debating with himself about. However, there was one call he could make.

Josh answered on the first ring.

"JP, this is Derek. Are you busy?"

"Uh, a bit. I've got to go see my patient. What's up?"

"I was wondering if you'd like to get together this evening. Maybe share a pizza."

"I wish I could, but we've had a bit of excitement at Rachel's place," Josh said.

Derek started to say something, then decided there was more, and if he kept silent maybe Josh would tell him. Sure enough, after a few moments, Josh gave him the details of what had happened.

"Can I help? Shall I come over?"

"Not right now," Josh said. "Look, I've got to get going. I'll get back to you as soon as things quiet down. And thanks for your offer."

Josh was standing near the door of Rachel's apartment, one hand on the knob, when his cell phone rang. He eased onto the sofa and punched the button to take the call. The first thing he heard was a familiar voice. "Dr. Pearson?"

"Detective Warren. What's up?"

"It seems that you and your friends are trying to complicate my life."

"I take it you've heard about what went on at Rachel's apartment about noon today."

"Heard about it and learned some things you probably don't yet know," Warren said. "The police corporal who interviewed Dr. Neeves started calling all the hospital emergency rooms inside a couple of miles from Ms. Moore's place. She hit pay dirt the second place she tried. The triage nurse was getting ready to notify the police of a man who'd just come in with a bullet wound to his shoulder."

"Is he hurt badly?"

"Not much blood loss, but it tore up the shoulder to the point that he'll require surgery to put it together. Meanwhile, the two police officers who were at Ms. Moore's apartment questioned him at the hospital. It didn't take him long to confess that he was trying to break in when he was shot."

"Who was it?" Josh figured it had to be Chavez, trying to exact revenge on Rachel, maybe catch Josh there as well and kill two birds with one stone.

"No one you'd know," Warren said. "He's a junkie. He was looking for an apartment that was unlocked so he could grab some things and sell them for enough to buy his next fix."

"If that's the case, why didn't he stop when Dr. Neeves challenged him? She told us she warned him, but he kept trying to get past the lock. That's when she fired at him."

"Yeah, that's the same story Corporal Daley got from her," Warren said. "But the junkie says that's not how it went down. His story is that there was no warning. He jiggled the knob, pulled on the door a time or so, and was turning away when someone shot him through the door. "

"Do you believe him?"

"Not necessarily," Warren said. "I've questioned enough junkies to know we're probably not getting the straight story from this guy."

"Is Dr. Neeves in trouble?" Josh asked.

"I doubt that a Grand Jury will indict her for shooting someone who appeared to be breaking into the home where she was, and it's unlikely this guy is going to bring a civil suit, although I've seen crazier things. But we'll have to see if she wants to change the story she originally gave us."

"I'll mention it to her," Josh said. "I presume you or someone from the police will be by to talk to Allison about this."

"Probably later today."

"Uh, while I have you on the phone, I've been wondering about a couple of doctors from our clinic. If you haven't already checked them out . . ."

"Give me the names," Warren said.

"One is Dr. Nadeel Kahn, our clinic's managing partner."

"We've looked at him already. Not a hint of any involvement."

"How about Dr. Sixto Molina?"

"During the time frame when he could have substituted—what did you call it?—placebo for the diphtheria vaccine and later planted evidence in Lambert's desk, he was in Puerto Rico at a convention."

"You're sure?"

"There's a record showing he and his wife flew there. We've seen his hotel bill. And two hundred witnesses will swear he was at the meeting, where he presented a paper. I'm sure."

Josh relaxed. His friend was innocent, and he mentally chastised himself for his suspicions. "Then there's one more name to check. And he's not on the staff of Preston Medical Clinic." Josh hesitated. "Dr. Derek Johnson."

"Why him? He's a hero in this scenario. I mean, he put himself on the line to fly here with the miracle drug that saved Madison's life."

"I know this sounds far-fetched," Josh said. "But if you check to see who Karen Marks talked with at the CDC, you'll find it was a Dr. Gruber. Dan Gruber was a fellow in infectious disease at Parkland Hospital while Derek and I were residents. He and Derek were friends."

"So?"

Josh shared his thoughts about Derek. He tried to do this in an orderly fashion, as he had with Rachel, but even as he related them to Warren, the scenario sounded flimsy and the coincidences were almost impossible to imagine.

"That's quite a stretch," Warren said. "But I'll check into it."

Josh ended the call. He called to Rachel, who was in the bedroom with Allison, "I'm headed for Madison's."

Rachel appeared in the doorway. "Don't go quite yet. I think you need to hear what Allison just told me."

27

Allison sat on the sofa in Rachel's living room. Her head was bowed, and her red eyes and tear-stained cheeks were silent evidence of what she'd gone through today.

Rachel sat beside Allison and gestured Josh to an overstuffed chair sitting at right angles to the couch. Without looking at her, Rachel said, "Allison, I think it would be good if you told Josh what you've told me."

"Before you say anything," Josh said. "I just got off the phone with Detective Warren. They've already identified the man you shot."

Allison looked up. "Is he okay?" she asked in a small voice.

"He's going to need surgery on his shoulder, but he won't die, if that's what you're asking. Warren says he's a junkie, probably looking to grab something and pawn it. But the intruder tells a different story about how he was shot."

Rachel raised her eyebrows. She looked at Allison, who didn't say anything.

"The man you shot says he didn't try to break in," Josh said. "His story is that he rattled the doorknob and was about to take off when you shot him . . . without warning."

"Not true," Allison said, a bit louder. "I called 'stop or I'll shoot' at least twice, maybe more. I can't remember. And you

257

can look at the front door for scratches around the lock. He was trying to get in."

"But wasn't it overreacting to shoot him? You'd called 911. There was a locked door between you and the prowler. You had a gun to protect yourself. Why not wait for the police?" Josh asked.

"That's why you need to hear Allison's story," Rachel said. "Allison?"

Allison started out in a faint voice, but as she told the story her words became louder and more forceful. By the time she finished, she was speaking in tones that would have carried to the back of a large room. Her story of her father giving her the gun wasn't totally accurate, she said. Yes, he'd given it to her, but not because of his fear of her being a woman alone in the city. He'd given her the pistol because he'd already seen what could happen to a woman . . . anywhere.

"I was a senior medical student, coming home from the hospital late at night," Allison said. "A man jumped me in the hospital parking lot. He dragged me behind some parked cars, and he . . . he . . . he assaulted me at knifepoint."

"Did you report it?" Josh asked.

"I did, but the police never caught him. Mine was the fourth in a series of these attacks, but they stopped shortly afterward."

"Why?" Josh asked.

"The police said a number of possibilities existed. He could be in jail on other charges. He could have left town. He might even be dead. But for whatever reason, the assaults stopped." She looked away and her voice dropped. "I guess the case is still open. I haven't checked since I left town."

"Tell him about the effect on your marriage," Rachel prompted.

"My husband was devastated by what happened. After the episode he . . . he wouldn't touch me. It was as though it had been my fault. We were both due to graduate from medical school in six months, but by the time we got our diplomas, we had already split up. He went to California for post-graduate work, so I applied to facilities in the northeast for my residency. I did my internal medicine specialization at Columbia, then accepted the offer here."

Rachel looked at Josh, and she knew his thoughts were the same as hers. No wonder Allison seemed distant and withdrawn when people tried to initiate social contact. No wonder she'd built a virtual wall around herself. And today a strange man attempting to break into the apartment undoubtedly triggered memories and emotions strong enough to make her shoot the prowler, because she feared what he might do if he gained entrance.

Josh stood, but a brief shake of Rachel's head warned him to keep his distance. "I . . . I'm sorry this happened to you. I'm going to check the front door for scratches around the lock, and I'll take a picture with my cell phone camera to document them. Will you tell the police this story when Corporal Daley comes back?"

Allison nodded. "I hope the man is okay, but if I had it to do again . . ."

"I know," Rachel said. She nodded to Josh, who eased out of the room, closing the door behind him.

◆

Jerry Lang met Josh at the front door of the Madison home. "Sorry you had to work your way past all that security," he said as he ushered the doctor inside. "But I think you understand the need for it."

"No problem," Josh said. Although he'd seen the home from the outside, this was his first glimpse inside the Madison residence. He was a bit surprised to find that, although it was larger than most houses in which he'd been a guest, it was by no means opulent. However, occasional glimpses of men in suits, with wires leading to their ears and slight bulges beneath their coats, reminded him this was no ordinary home.

"Mr. Madison is in here," Lang said. He tapped twice on a door before opening it.

Josh entered a room that appeared to be what he'd heard called a den or a library. In his parents' modest home there had been no such room, probably because his father had no time to read. He'd been too busy working to feed and clothe his family. But Josh had heard about rooms like this, and seeing one now made him want one in his own home.

Bookshelves lined two of the walls, filled with books that appeared to be much more than simply decoration. These were books that had been read, then shelved—haphazardly in some cases—ready to be read again. Several comfortable leather chairs in one corner surrounded a large, round table. In another corner, a well-worn recliner sat beside an end table stacked with three books, each with a bookmark in it. A reading lamp was arranged so its light shined over the shoulder of the person sitting in the recliner.

David Madison, dressed in a sport shirt and jeans, sat in that chair, an open book in his lap. "Josh, thank you for coming. I feel fine, but I'm certain you want to check me over to make sure of that." He closed the book and laid it on top of the others on the side table. "How do you want to do this?"

Josh had brought a small leather bag, one he hadn't used since he was a medical student doing physical exams as a part of his training. From it he extracted a stethoscope and said, "Let's start by listening to your chest."

A few minutes later Josh stowed the last instrument. "Mr. Madison, you seem to be doing well. Have you had your last injection of RP-78?"

"About half an hour ago," Madison said. "Matter of fact, you just missed the nurse who gave it. Will there be any need for her to come back?"

"No, sir," Josh said. "Obviously, I want to hear from you if you have any problems. Otherwise, I'll want to see you in my office in another week or so. We'll get some lab tests at that time to be certain there's no problem with your liver, kidneys, blood count, any organ system. After that, you probably should be checked once or twice more, since we have no idea of the long-term safety of RP-78. But there's no evidence of any recurrence of the *Bacillus decimus* infection. I may be a bit overly cautious, but I think you can resume normal activities in another week."

Madison looked up at Josh, who was still standing. "I want to thank you for everything you've done. Are you certain you won't reconsider serving as my personal physician?"

"I appreciate the offer, but I don't think I'm cut out for the role," Josh said. "Have you decided who you are going to choose?"

"I have some thoughts but nothing final yet."

Josh picked his bag off the end table. Then he took the hand Madison extended. "Sir, I'm glad I could help."

◆

Shortly after Josh left for Madison's, Corporal Daley rang Rachel's doorbell and spent half an hour with Allison, getting the true story of the shooting and the woman's emotional state that contributed to it. "I don't imagine you have anything to fear from a Grand Jury," she told Allison. "You were defending your home—well, Ms. Moore's home—but the principle is the same."

"What about her pistol?" Rachel asked.

"Even though there's no question of who shot the prowler," Daley said, "the lab will fire a comparison round and match it to the bullet the surgeon removes from the man's shoulder. We'll need to hold the weapon until everything's settled."

After Daley left, Allison gave Rachel her last injection of RP-78. Now the two women sat together in the living room. "Penny for your thoughts," Rachel asked the silent Allison.

"I was thinking about that pistol," Allison said. "I thought I'd feel helpless without it, but I've decided that maybe I don't need the gun after all. I've taken a couple of self-defense classes. I carry Mace in my purse. And . . ." She hesitated. "And I don't feel so alone anymore."

"You're not alone," Rachel said. "Actually, you never were."

"I know," Allison said. "You and Josh have been friends. I know there are others who've tried to get close to me, but I kept shutting them out. But maybe I can change that."

"That's good," Rachel said. "But I'm talking about someone else. I don't know how long you've been shutting Him out, but I do know this. God's there for you. And when you decide to let Him into your life, you'll find He's been there all along."

Allison shook her head, opened her mouth, then closed it without saying anything.

Rachel wasn't sure what it would take to fully breach the defenses Allison had thrown up around her. But whatever it took, and however long it required, she was determined to be there to help.

❖

Josh made sure he stood well back from the door to Rachel's apartment after he rang the bell. He'd seen Corporal Daley take Allison's pistol with her, but he decided it was better to be safe than sorry.

He saw the frosted glass panel beside the door darken. Josh knew it was impossible to distinguish faces through it, so he held both arms wide as though to signal, "I'm harmless." In a moment, the security chain rattled and Rachel opened the door.

"Come in. I was wondering if you were coming back this evening." She pointed to the couch. "Let's sit here. Allison is resting in the bedroom."

Josh sat down, squirmed a bit, then pulled his phone from his pocket. "Let me just put this on the end table here next to yours."

"Why don't you take it and Ms. Moore's phone and toss them to the other side of the room?" The voice was familiar, and it sent a chill through Josh.

Dr. Andres Chavez stood in the bedroom door. His left arm was around the neck of Allison Neeves. In his right hand he held a semiautomatic pistol, the barrel of which was pressed against Allison's right temple.

28

Iow did you get in here?" Rachel asked.

"I suppose there are advantages to having a ground floor apartment," Chavez said, "But I must tell you it's not difficult to get past window locks like yours. A little maneuvering with a stout blade of a pocket knife, and I was into the bedroom before Dr. Neeves roused from her nap."

As soon as Josh saw Chavez with the gun, the image sent a message to his midbrain, triggering a fight-or-flight reflex. But before he could act, his frontal lobe, the reasoning part of his brain, intervened. He felt his muscles relax. *Not yet. Stay calm. There's got to be a way out of this.*

"What do you want?" Rachel asked.

"Ultimately, to carry out my orders and kill David Madison, of course," Chavez said.

"So it was you who . . . ," Josh said.

"Yes. I paid a local man to disguise himself as a female kitchen worker and infect Madison and Ms. Moore. I also paid him to go into the church bathroom and inject Dr. Lambert with aconite, killing him while simulating a heart attack." He smiled. "Unfortunately, he didn't live to spend the money he received."

"Why kill Lambert?"

"Haven't you heard the saying that 'dead men tell no tales'? Lambert gave assurances he wouldn't say anything about his role in the scheme, but—face it—there was only one sure way to guarantee his silence."

I've got to keep him talking. "Did you kill Barbara Carper?" Josh asked.

Chavez laughed dryly. "I bribed her to steal the RP-78 from Madison's room after his last dose, the night before he left the hospital. She was to give it to me in exchange for the other half of the money I promised, but she wanted more. I pulled a pistol, intending to frighten her, but she fought me for the gun. It discharged, and she died. Unfortunately, she didn't have the drug with her, so I had to improvise the rest of my little scheme."

"But you tested negative for gunshot residue," Josh said.

"I'm neither simple nor stupid," Chavez said. "The gloves and the shirt I was wearing when I shot her are in separate dumpsters, along with the gun I used."

"If you wanted to kill Madison, why did you offer to come to the United States with more RP-78?" Josh asked.

"Since I couldn't kill Madison long distance, this was a chance to get close to him, while ingratiating myself with everyone concerned."

"So now you've put some distance between you and the person who gave you your orders," Josh said. "Give me the gun. Maybe I can help you work something out with the authorities."

"No, I've merely bought some time. My mission is still to kill David Madison," Chavez said. "And that's what I plan to do next."

"You'll never get past Madison's security," Josh said.

"Not alone," Chavez said. "I'm sure the Secret Service and police think they have Madison protected. But I doubt they'll stop the car driven by his personal physician. And I'll be on the floor of the car behind you, covered with a blanket. You'll get me in."

"I can't—"

"You can and you will." Chavez indicated his pistol. "There are seventeen hollow-point bullets in this Glock. And if you say anything to anyone who stops the car, right after I kill him I'll shoot you. They may catch me, but you'll be dead."

Chavez moved the gun from Allison's temple and shoved her away. "It's a shame I have to kill the two women first, but I can't leave them here. What do they call this in wartime? Oh, yes. Collateral damage." He gestured with the gun. "Go over there beside Ms. Moore."

"Please don't," Allison said as she backed away from Chavez.

"I agree it's a pity. But if I were squeamish I wouldn't have gotten this far, would I?" Chavez motioned once more with the pistol. "Now I want you ladies to turn around and kneel. I promise you this will be swift and painless."

Josh knew it was now or never. He gauged the distance to Chavez. It was doubtful he could cover it before the first gunshot, yet he had to try. Rachel and Allison were already turning. Josh couldn't stand by idly, not without some attempt at resistance.

Then the sound of a passing car caught Chavez's attention and he looked up. The gun moved slightly, following his eyes.

Josh hadn't played football since high school, but he still remembered the fundamentals. He launched himself at Chavez, covering the ground between them in three quick steps and a leap. He heard two gunshots and felt a hot, stinging pain in his left shoulder, but he didn't stop. His right shoulder hit Chavez in the mid-section, causing a loud *woof* of expelled air. Josh tried to reach up with his left hand to grab Chavez's gun, but his arm wouldn't move. He crossed his right hand over and managed to deflect the weapon just as it fired two more shots. Josh didn't feel anything. Maybe the bullets went wild.

Josh struggled for a few moments before it became clear he couldn't hold out much longer. He was basically fighting one-handed against a man with a pistol. He decided to risk everything on one more move—one he'd read about in a Lee Child novel, but never practiced.

Josh drew back his right fist, and as he expected, Chavez moved to deflect the blow. That left Chavez's chin unprotected for the vicious head butt Josh delivered to the point of his jaw. The Colombian's head snapped back, and he went limp.

Working to summon the breath to speak, Josh said, "Allison, call 911." He snatched the pistol from Chavez's limp grip. "Rachel, use his belt to secure his wrists. Then take the laces out of his shoes and tie his thumbs together—tight." Josh inclined his head toward a lamp on the end table next to the sofa. "Pull off the cord and use it to secure his legs. If he starts to move, hit him with the base of the lamp."

The pain in Josh's shoulder had changed from burning to a deep, severe ache. Blood dripped in a slow stream down his left arm, which now hung limp at his side. His doctor's mind categorized his injury as a flesh wound, with no arterial bleeding. Then the doorbell rang. His injury could wait a moment longer. He had one more thing to do.

He shoved his left hand under his belt to support his injured arm. With the pistol in his right hand, Josh shuffled toward the door, where the frosted side pane showed the outline of the large man standing on the porch.

Josh opened the door and stepped aside, pointing the weapon at Derek. "Come on in. I've been expecting you."

Derek let his eyes take in the entire scene: Chavez was on the floor, apparently unconscious. Rachel was bent over him, pulling a belt tight around his wrists. Allison talked excitedly on her phone. And Josh, his best friend, was pointing a pistol at him.

"Hey, what's going on?" Derek asked. "And put that pistol down, Josh. It's me, Derek, your old buddy."

Josh waved him in and pointed with the gun to a chair sitting by the sofa. "Sit there. Put your hands on the arms of the chair and keep them there."

Derek complied, the quizzical look never leaving his face.

"Your partner tried to kill us, Derek. I was surprised you weren't with him. If you had been, he might have succeeded."

"What are you talking about?"

"The police will be here in a few moments," Allison said. Then she knelt to assist Rachel in securing Chavez's legs with the cord from the table lamp.

"Thanks, Allison," Josh said. He turned to Derek. "Here's how I see it." Even as Josh laid out the story, Derek could see by the look on his friend's face that he realized how far-fetched his scenario was.

When Josh finished speaking, Derek crossed his legs, relaxed in the chair, and shook his head. "You can check my bank account. You can look for overseas secret accounts all you want. You won't find any evidence of bribes or payments to me. And, by the way, I've paid off every penny of the bills I accrued with Robin's last illness." He blinked away the tears he felt forming. "I would have given twice that if she hadn't died."

Josh tried again, but it was evident he was running out of steam. "How difficult was it to get your friend at the CDC to direct us to Argosy Pharmaceuticals? Who else was in on it? And when did you join forces with Chavez?"

Despite the situation, Derek laughed—a full-throated roar. "Man, you've got it all wrong. None of that happened. So far as I know, this is all a big coincidence—a coincidence that ended up saving the life of an ex-president and your girlfriend, by the way."

"Have you been giving status reports to Gaschen back at Argosy? Is that why you've been on your cell phone so much lately? Is he already working on getting the FDA to have another look at RP-78?"

Derek leaned forward in the chair. He didn't think his friend would shoot him now. "Josh, I'm going to reach into my pocket for my cell phone. You can do it if you're afraid I'll pull out a gun." When Josh didn't say anything, Derek continued. "I want to show you the log of outgoing calls on my cell phone. I've been agonizing over this decision for a couple of days, maybe even a bit longer. During that time, I've made several calls about it. I finally made up my mind today."

He pulled out the phone and called up the screen to show his last few outgoing calls: Kahn cell, Kahn cell, Gaschen cell, Kahn cell, Gaschen cell, Kahn cell.

"What are you saying?" Josh said, lowering the gun.

Derek relaxed a bit. "You can check with these people if you want to. My last call today to Dr. Gaschen was to resign my position at Argosy Pharmaceuticals. Yes, what happened with RP-78 is good for the company, but I won't get a penny out of it . . . even though I was the one who developed the drug."

"What about the calls to Nadeel Kahn?" By this time, Josh was no longer pointing his gun at Derek. He'd put it down and was holding a folded handkerchief to his bleeding shoulder.

"I ran into him at the hospital several days ago. We discovered that we had some mutual friends at Johns Hopkins. With Ben Lambert's death, your clinic is an internist short. He liked me, was impressed with my background and experience. He checked my references, we talked some more, and he offered me a position. I've been going back and forth with him about it since then."

"I spoke with Nadeel earlier today, and he didn't say anything," Josh said.

"I asked him not to tell anyone, even you, until I made a decision. After I resigned my job with Argosy, I called him back to accept the position." Derek spread his hands. "Josh, I'm not one of the bad guys. I'm your new colleague."

29

Jerry Lang took a deep breath before he tapped on the open door of David Madison's study. "Got a minute?"

Madison, wearing jeans, golf shirt, and athletic shoes was at his desk, poring over the morning papers. He had formed the habit when in the White House of reading through, or at least scanning, several papers. Retirement hadn't changed that. The former president removed his reading glasses and laid them on the desk in front of him. "Come in, Jerry. What's up?"

"Sir, I need to talk with you."

Madison gestured Lang to a chair in front of his desk, but the agent said, "I'll stand, thank you."

"Okay. As I said before, what's up?"

Lang stood uneasily before the ex-president. "Mr. Madison, it's been my privilege to serve as chief of your protection detail since your retirement. There have been some close calls, but we've managed to keep you safe, and I'm proud of that record."

Madison held up his hand, palm out. "Before you go on, let me say I appreciate the job you've done. I realize you had one episode while I was in office when an armed man almost slipped through, but I never thought that was your fault. And when I retired, I specifically asked for you to head the detail. So far as I'm concerned, you have a clean record."

Lang felt relief of tension he was unaware was there. Yes, he'd thought this might have been a demotion, a move to get him away from the White House. Knowing that wasn't the case was comforting. "Thank you. But in a way, that makes this even harder." He swallowed twice. "I'll be resigning from the Service as soon as things are back to normal around here. I'm going to suggest that Agent Gilmore be promoted to chief of the detail—I think he'll do a good job."

Madison screwed up his face. "Does this have to do with the secrecy I've asked you to maintain about my brush with death? I can see where you might think my unwillingness to share information indicated a lack of trust, but that's not the case. And I can tell you the endgame is going on as we speak, so I'll soon be able to let you in on what it's about. Believe me, I didn't keep the details from you because I didn't think you could keep them in confidence. Only a very few people knew the real reason for all the secrecy."

"I appreciate that," Lang said. "But the fact remains that I need to resign. I've accepted a job with a private security firm here in Dallas."

"Is there anything I can do to change your mind?"

At that moment, a brisk knock on the door to the study preceded Karen Marks's entrance. "Is Jerry telling you he'll be resigning?"

"Yes," Madison said. "And I was asking if I might be able to change his mind."

Marks stopped beside Lang and put her arm through his, at which point he seemed to relax. "Sir," he said, "you'd have to change two minds." He nodded at Karen.

"I'll be resigning as your administrative aide," she said. "Not because I don't enjoy the work. Actually, it's kind of a rush. But I have other plans for the future."

"What plans? Whatever offer you have, I'll increase it."

"I don't think you can top this one," Karen said, smiling.

"Are you going to run for office?" Madison asked. "If you are, you know I'll back you."

"Tempting," Marks said. "But I'd have to clear it with my husband. Jerry and I will be married soon. We wanted to wait until you were back at full speed before we broke the news."

"And as for having a wife run for office," Lang said, "I think we're both going to enjoy being out of the limelight for a while."

Then Karen added, "Will a run for office come later? Who knows?"

Raul Moreno was eating dinner with one of his several girl-friends when pounding at the door interrupted him in the middle of a sentence. He frowned. Although many people might say that their home was their castle, in Raul's case it was not just figuratively, but literally true. He lived on a hill in the most exclusive section of Bogotá, in a home modeled on the castle of Miranda de Ebro in Spain. And everyone—from the people who worked for Moreno to the neighbors to tradespeople— knew not to come knocking without a specific invitation or reason.

Obviously the person at the double oak doors didn't know they were disturbing Raul Moreno, El Rey. If this were an honest mistake, his butler would quickly send the person on their way. If more force was needed to persuade the interloper to leave . . . well, Raul's bodyguards could manage that very well.

In a moment, the knocking ceased, and Moreno tried to recapture the thread of the story he was telling. His girlfriend leaned forward, evidently hanging on his every word, even though her attention might be due more to the lavish gifts she expected than to Moreno's personality. The reason was of no consequence to him. Money could buy almost anything, including companionship, and Moreno had a lot of money.

He paused to sip wine from the crystal goblet at his elbow. Then the carved double doors flew open and a cadre of police marched two abreast into the dining room. A dozen or more members of the *Policía Nacional*, in camouflage uniforms complete with helmets, each carrying a semiautomatic rifle at port arms, took up stations around the room, ringing the table at which Moreno and his companion sat.

Last in was an officer. In contrast with the other police, he wore a Class A uniform topped by a dress hat, its visor decorated with gold braid. He stood across the table from Moreno and said rather formally, "Raul Moreno, sometimes known as *El Rey*, you are under arrest."

Moreno drew himself up to his full height, a difficult feat when seated, and asked with as much dignity as he could muster, "On what charge?"

"Here in Colombia, there are many times you could have been charged with drug trafficking and numerous other crimes, but your influence with some of our politicians has protected you. But this arrest is made at the request of the authorities in the United States of America. You are to be extradited as quickly as possible to *los Estados Unidos* where you will stand trial for the attempted murder of former president David Madison."

"I will never be extradited. My attorneys will see to that."

"Oh, but you will. You see, the U.S. authorities have a witness willing to testify against you." He shook his head. "You trusted the wrong man this time." The officer nodded sharply to the police officers standing behind Moreno's chair. "Take him into custody."

Moreno knew better than to struggle. With one officer on each arm, he was quick-marched through the door, down the hallways, and out the door of his castle. He knew there would be legal battles. Well, such battles were nothing new to him.

He employed a cadre of lawyers, and this would simply be another instance when they could earn their money.

What bothered Moreno was that it appeared that his final legal battles wouldn't be fought here in Colombia, where he had many officials on his payroll and could buy more. Instead, he was being sent to the U.S. to stand trial. And for the first time in years, Raul Moreno was afraid.

◆

Josh Pearson sat at the desk in his office—not the one he'd used at Prestonwood Hospital, but rather the room he thought of as truly his office—the one he'd occupied for the two-plus years he'd been on the staff of the Preston Medical Clinic.

Josh was fortunate that the gunshot wound to his shoulder had caused only soft tissue damage, without hitting bone or damaging the joint. Three weeks had passed since the injury. His left arm was no longer in a sling. Now his only limitation was on the amount of stress he could put on that shoulder, and those restrictions would be lifted soon.

Allison Neeves had taken a week off to recover from the ordeal of being held at gunpoint by Chavez, but now she, as well as Derek, was at work, so the Preston Medical Clinic had its full complement of internal medicine specialists once more.

Josh and Rachel were still working through their plans for the future. Last weekend they'd gone together to buy her engagement ring. When his first wife died, when Rachel's fiancé left her, neither of them had felt they'd ever love again. But God had given them this second chance, and they were grateful.

When he heard his office door open, Josh looked up from the stack of forms he was signing. Allison Neeves and Derek Johnson walked in, looked around, and seemed surprised to find no one else but Josh in the room.

"Are we early? We were asked to meet David Madison in your office at noon," Allison said.

"That's news to me," Josh said, "but come on in." He motioned them to the two chairs across the desk from him.

"Is this where the meeting will be?" Rachel stood in the doorway, a puzzled look on her face.

"I guess so," Josh said. "Although this is the first I've heard about it. Come on in. Let me get a couple more chairs from the office next door."

"I'll help," Derek said. "You shouldn't be lifting with that shoulder."

The two men argued good-naturedly, and in a few minutes there were two more chairs in the office and everyone was seated, chatting while they waited for Madison to arrive.

"Sorry I'm late," David Madison said from the doorway. He turned to the Secret Service agent who stood slightly behind him. "Gilmore, you can wait in the hall if you don't mind. We shouldn't be long." With that, he closed the door and took the remaining vacant chair.

"Thanks for being here," Madison said. "I wanted an opportunity to thank you for your efforts and give you some information I couldn't reveal earlier."

There were murmurs of "you're welcome" and "it was nothing."

Madison looked around the group gathered there. "You've probably heard that the efforts to kill me were meant to influence the decision of my foundation to locate a clinic in Bogotá." He paused. "But that's not true. It was simply a convenient reason we floated, hoping people would believe it."

"So what was the real reason?" Josh asked.

"You may not recall this, but before I ran for president, I was a U.S. senator. While in the Senate, I was appointed to serve out the term of the U.S. Attorney General after he was killed in a plane crash. During that time, one of my priorities was strengthening border security and coming down on drug smuggling in the U.S. And I worked hard at it.

"As a result of those actions," Madison continued, "I made a number of enemies, especially in some countries to the south of the U.S. Although attrition and the actions of rival gangs took care of some of those enemies, a man in Colombia named Raul Moreno not only remained in power, but as rivals fell, his position strengthened. He eventually became known as *El Rey*, or The King. By that time, he was the head of the largest crime syndicate in Colombia. Unfortunately, during those years the grudge he held against me grew even stronger. After I left the White House, when he learned I was going to be in Colombia to evaluate clinic sites, he decided it was a perfect opportunity to get revenge."

"So he was behind all this," Josh said.

"Moreno himself, either directly or through an intermediary, arranged to bribe Ben Lambert to give me a fake diphtheria immunization."

"Why would Dr. Lambert do such a thing?" Rachel asked.

"It seems that my old friend, in the midst of a full-fledged midlife crisis, gave in to the temptation of a bribe Moreno offered him," Madison said. "He had to go with the group to Colombia in order not to arouse suspicion, but as soon as we returned, he planned to collect the rest of the money he was promised, then flee the country with a companion—but not his wife, Ruth."

"Was Dr. Lambert responsible for infecting us?" Rachel asked.

"No, that was Moreno," Madison said. "He used Dr. Chavez to obtain cultures of two kinds of bacteria—diphtheria and *Bacillus decimus*."

"Why two different bacteria?" Allison asked.

"I figured that one out," Josh said. "The diphtheria was supposed to mask the *decimus* infection until it was too late to do anything. Ben Lambert named me to replace him because he thought I'd be fooled by the diphtheria and never discover the other infection. But our head lab tech, Ethan Grant, figured out the identity of the second infecting organism."

"Dr. Chavez, acting on orders from Moreno, arranged for a man, disguised as a woman, to douse me with the bacteria. It was unfortunate that Ms. Moore and Dr. Lambert were there at the same time. That same man injected Ben Lambert with aconite to kill him while simulating a heart attack," Madison said.

"He wanted to make sure Dr. Lambert didn't talk," Rachel said.

Madison looked at the others to make sure they were following. "So you see, Chavez, acting on orders from Moreno, was behind everything."

"Why would Chavez do that? Money?" Josh asked.

"Partly for money, partly because Chavez was part of Moreno's drug network and thus under the man's control. When it looked like he wasn't going to be able to murder me with his original plan, Chavez decided to come to the U.S. and—excuse the expression—kill two birds with one stone. He could ingratiate himself with me if I lived, and he could get further away from Moreno in case he failed at his assignment."

"When did you figure this out?" Derek asked.

"Once it became apparent that someone was trying to kill me, I looked around at all the people who'd like me dead." Madison smiled without mirth. "You'd be amazed how long that list is. Then I asked the director of the Secret Service to put two agents—just two—to work investigating all these people. He and I, together with those two men, were the only ones who knew what was going on."

"Were you worried about your safety?" Rachel asked.

"I depended on my Secret Service detail and the local police to keep me safe, but I wasn't counting on them to find the person behind the attacks—although they were getting close."

"Why the insistence on secrecy?" Josh asked.

"So that whoever was behind this would have no idea how close they'd come to succeeding, or whether their scheme was still going forward."

"Why are you telling us this now?" Derek asked.

"Because I received a phone call about an hour ago. Moreno is in police custody in Bogotá. I've been assured he'll be extradited to the U.S. to stand trial, no matter how hard his lawyers try to avoid it."

"Is there enough evidence to convict him?" Rachel asked.

"Once we got Chavez in custody, he gave up Moreno and agreed to testify against him," Madison said. "The authorities have him closely guarded, and they're going to videotape his deposition just in case something happens to their prize witness. No, I think this affair is finally coming to an end."

There were a few more questions, but eventually Madison looked at his watch. He rose and said, "Thank you all. Now I've got to go. One of the things I have to do is reach a decision about a new personal physician." He scanned the room. "Any volunteers?" Madison let the silence build for a few seconds. Then he smiled. "I thought not."

He shook hands all around and left.

◆

Rachel stood in Josh's office chatting with the others until Allison and Derek left to grab a quick sandwich before returning to see patients. After she was alone with Josh, she said, "How much of what Madison told us was a surprise to you, and how much had you figured out?"

Josh waved Rachel to one of the chairs in front of his desk. He took the one beside it, turning it until he was facing her. "I didn't know the exact identity of the person or his reason, but I knew there had to be someone behind this. You may recall there at the end that Chavez told us he was carrying out orders."

"That's right. I guess I was so worried that he was going to shoot one of us that I forgot that."

"Then I had a hard time believing someone wanted to murder the ex-president to affect the location his foundation would choose for a clinic," Josh said. "Of course, when someone is trying to kill you, knowing his motivation becomes pretty academic. What you're interested in is surviving."

"Do you think this is really over?" Rachel found herself unconsciously running her finger over the slightly thickened scar at the base of her neck where the tracheotomy once had been. She quickly moved her hand to join the other in her lap.

"I think David Madison is no longer in danger from that particular man. However, I believe Madison and men like him will always have enemies. Anyone in the public eye, anyone who consistently tries to do the right thing, will. The good thing is that he doesn't worry about the opinion of others. He has his Secret Service detail to protect him, and Mrs. Madison will help him make the right decisions."

Rachel reached out and took Josh's hand. "I'm having lunch tomorrow with Allison Neeves," she said.

"You and she have sort of bonded, haven't you?"

"Yes, I guess you could say that."

"That's good," Josh said. "She needs a friend."

"I invited her to go to church with us this Sunday," Rachel said. "Is that okay with you?"

Josh smiled. "Of course."

Rachel twisted the diamond she now wore on the third finger of her left hand. She hadn't yet gotten used to feeling it there, but she didn't want to take it off—ever. "Are you still certain about where we're going with our lives?" she said. "You didn't let circumstances influence your decision?"

Josh looked up at the ceiling as though the answer lay there. "I'd known I loved you for a while before I ever said it. I came close to telling you when I met your plane that day at Love Field. I wanted to say it several times after that, but the time never seemed right."

"So it wasn't just the possibility I might die that made you say you loved me?"

"The danger might have been a catalyst, but the emotion was already there. And in case you have any doubts, I still love you."

Rachel wondered about that moment when Josh appeared to her in the middle of the night to say, "I love you." Was it real? Was it a product of her fevered imagination? Was it a dream? She could ask him, but she preferred to leave the question unanswered. Whatever the case, she knew how he felt. When he'd first said it was immaterial.

Josh took Rachel's hand and squeezed it gently. "We've both been through a lot in a fairly short time. I've watched how you acted through it all, and it was impressive. You were always so calm, never railing at God or cursing fate or blaming others for the bad things you went through. I've learned things from you—patience, the power of prayer, a belief that the ultimate outcome of every situation is in the hands of Someone much stronger than I. Thank you for showing me."

Rachel looked at her watch. "I've got to get ready for my shift at the hospital. Call me when you leave work this evening?"

After Rachel left, Josh sat quietly at his desk. Yes, they'd been through a lot in a short time, but they'd both grown from the experience. He'd meant what he told Rachel about learning from her. And he hoped he could continue to do so.

A voice on his intercom interrupted his reverie. "Dr. Pearson?"

"Yes?"

"One of Dr. Molina's patients is here for a post-op check, and he's complaining of severe chest pain. Could you have a look at him?"

"Get an EKG on him. I'll be right there." Josh rose from his desk, checked to make sure his stethoscope was in the pocket of his white coat, and headed out the door. It was good to be back.

Group Discussion Guide

1. At what point in the first chapter did you begin to sense how the story was going to develop? What would you have changed?

2. Before reading *Miracle Drug*, what did you know about the Secret Service protection of a former president? Do you agree with providing it? How long should such protection be furnished?

3. Prior to reading this book, have you given much thought to the steps through which a new drug must go for approval? Are you aware that the Food and Drug Administration must review new drug applications? In what ways do you think the process should change?

4. When did you first notice any evidence of the factors influencing Dr. Allison Neeves's behavior? How did you feel about these when they were fully revealed? Are there people in your circle of acquaintances whose past it might be helpful to know, but you just didn't ask?

5. What was your opinion of Dr. Derek Johnson when he was first introduced into the plot? How did your opinion change over the course of the story?

6. What about your impression of Dr. Andres Chavez? Do you tend to let race or background enter into your first assessment of people?

7. After reading the book, what do you think the takeaway message should be? How can a book be "Christian fiction," even though it contains no conversion scene or Scripture quotation?

Want to learn more about Richard L. Mabry, MD,
and check out other great fiction from
Abingdon Press?

Check out our website at
www.AbingdonFiction.com
to read interviews with your favorite authors,
find tips for starting a reading group,
and stay posted on what new titles are on the horizon.

Be sure to visit Richard online!

www.rmabry.com
www.rmabry.blogspot.com

We hope you enjoyed Richard Mabry's *Miracle Drug* and will look for his other books from Abingdon Press. Here's a sample of his upcoming novel, *Medical Judgment*.

1

The smell of smoke gradually nudged Dr. Sarah Gordon from a troubled sleep into a state of semi-wakefulness. Hours earlier she'd finally given in and taken a sleeping pill. Now it made her feel fuzzy and uncertain, as though she were moving through cobwebs. At first, she couldn't separate the odor of smoke from the dream in which she'd been mired. Sarah struggled to bring herself more fully awake. Had she really smelled smoke? Or was it a nightmare? She eased up in bed, resting on one elbow, and sniffed the air around her. There it was again. The smoke was real.

Her brain, still numbed by sleep and Ambien, took a few seconds to make the connection. Smoke meant fire. Something in her house was burning—perhaps the whole house was about to go up in flames. She had to wake Harry. He'd take charge. After she aroused him, they'd hurry down the hall together and get Jenny. Then Harry would lead them to safety.

Sarah reached to her left across the king-size bed, but when her hand touched a bare pillow, the reality hit her, forcing her fully awake more effectively than a bucket of ice water. Her husband wasn't there. He'd never be there again. He was dead. He'd been dead for eight months now. So had Jenny, their two-year-old daughter. Sarah was alone . . . in a burning house.

But was she alone? She had a vague recollection of hearing a noise about the same time she became aware of the smoke smell. Was someone out there, waiting for her? Or was that part of a dream as well? Should she stay here in the bedroom until she was sure? No, she needed to get to safety. The "someone" might or might not be real, but the fire wasn't the product of her imagination. She had to get out, and quickly.

She threw on her robe and shoved her feet into slippers. Sarah dropped her cell phone and keys into the pocket of the robe. She took two steps away from the bed before turning back to pick up the flashlight from the bedside table. Sarah flicked it on and checked the beam. It was dim—the batteries probably hadn't been changed since before Jenny died—but it gave off enough illumination to let her see a few feet in front of her. She hoped that would be enough. In several strides that displayed more confidence than she felt, Sarah covered the distance to the door leading to the hall. *Feel the door. If it's hot, find some other way out.*

Cautiously, she pressed her palm against the door. When she felt no heat, Sarah let out a breath she didn't know she was holding. She opened the door and looked around. No flames. Then she sniffed, and there it was again—a faint aroma of smoke wafting up the stairway—not enough to choke her, not an amount capable of blocking her vision, but sufficient nonetheless to send her hurrying toward what she hoped was a safe exit.

Guided by the faint glow from the flashlight, she descended to the first floor. As she got lower, she coughed a little, her eyes watered a bit, but she could breathe, could see through the tears. The smoke still wasn't bad. Maybe that was a good sign.

At the bottom of the stairs, she stopped to listen. Was that a noise? She strained her ears, but heard nothing more. Maybe there was no intruder. Maybe that was all in her imagination. Maybe.

But the smoke wasn't something she'd imagined. It was real, and where there was smoke, there was fire. But where was it? She heard no crackle of flames. She felt no pulse of heat on her face. She blinked away a few tears and sniffed again. The smoke was still there, and now it seemed to be increasing.

The light from the flashlight had become so dim as to be almost useless. *I need to see. Why haven't I tried to turn on lights?* Wasn't there something about electricity failing if the fire got too near the supply line? Sarah flipped the switch at the foot of the stairs and the overhead fixtures blazed into light. The power was still on—good. She turned off the flashlight but held onto it. *It might be a useful weapon.*

Sarah started to exit the house the way she habitually did, through the kitchen and into the garage. She turned to her right to go that way, but stopped when she saw tendrils of dark smoke drifting under the door from the garage and into the kitchen. The garage. That's where the fire was. She couldn't get out this way.

She turned back and scanned the area straight ahead of her, the living room. No smoke. No heat. No noise of flames. Best of all, there was no movement or sound that signaled someone there . . . at least, no one she could see. She could hurry through to the front door and make her escape.

Should she stop and call the fire department now? Was there any reason to further delay that call? Wasn't it important to call them immediately? *Get out of the house first. Call for help when you're safe.*

Sarah hurried to the front door, threw it open, and felt the fresh night breeze on her face. Her instinct was to run, to get out of the house as quickly as possible, but she stopped as yet another rule heard long ago surfaced in her mind. *Keep doors and windows closed. Air can feed the flames and make the fire grow.* She shut the door behind her.

Sarah hurried to the end of the sidewalk, her slippers making a soft shushing on the concrete. When she got there, she paused and turned back toward her house. At first she saw no one there. Wait! Had there been a flicker of movement in the shadows at the corner of the house? Or was it her imagination, fueled by the adrenaline of the situation, turning wisps of smoke into the shape of a prowler?

She watched for perhaps half a minute more, trying not to blink, looking with unfocused eyes into the middle distance. *Let your peripheral vision pick up faint images.* She saw no figures, no movement.

Enough. Get help. She pulled her cell phone from the pocket of her robe and stabbed out 9-1-1 before hitting "send."

"911. What is your emergency?"

"This is Dr. Sarah Gordon. My house is on fire. The address is 5613 Maple Shade Drive."

There was the briefest of pauses, during which Sarah heard keys tapping. "I've dispatched first responders. Is anyone injured? Are you in the house?"

"No injuries. And I'm outside, on the lawn."

"Is anyone else there? Or are you alone?"

Sarah hesitated before she answered.

"I'm alone." *At least, I hope so.*

◆

The call awakened Detective Bill Larson. He brought his wrist close to his face and squinted at his watch. Two fifteen a.m. The phone had interrupted a dream—not a pleasant one, but that wasn't unusual. Sleep that was troubled and dreams that were disturbing were part of the pattern his life had taken on during his struggle for lasting sobriety.

"We've got a fire at a private dwelling," the dispatcher said. "The fire chief on the scene thinks it might be arson, so I wanted to notify you. If you like, I'll send a patrol car by there now to do a preliminary. Then you can hook up with the fire marshal tomorrow. Would you like me to do that?"

Larson yawned. "Probably. Where's the fire?"

"The location is 5613 Maple Shade, the residence of Dr. Sarah Gordon."

The name brought him awake. Larson had met Sarah Gordon and her husband shortly after the detective moved to town. He'd been introduced to them at church. Realizing that being part of a church family would be important as he tried to get his life back together, he'd joined the First Community Church shortly after moving to Jameson. It was one of the larger churches in town, and Larson figured he could lose himself in a congregation that size. He needed to be just a taker for a while. Maybe after he had a few more months of sobriety under his belt he could find a place to serve. Maybe.

Larson called up his mental picture of Harry Gordon: a nice-looking man in his 30s, his blond hair always a bit tousled, a perpetual grin on his face. But the person his memory could more easily recall was Sarah. She had dark hair cut short, flawless olive skin, and always seemed to be laughing. Each time he saw the two of them together with their two-year-old daughter, Larson realized again what he'd lost when his own family was torn asunder.

After his initial meeting, he'd seen Sarah a few times at church, always at a distance and generally with her husband. Then she'd suffered the tragic loss of both husband and daughter, a loss that seemed to devastate Sarah. After that happened, Larson figured he should express his sympathy to her, but the time never seemed right. Then it wasn't long before she stopped coming to church altogether. He hadn't seen her since.

"Larson, are you there?"

"Sorry. Just thinking," Larson replied.

"So what do you want me to do?" the dispatcher asked.

"Tell you what," Larson said. "I know her from church. I think I'll head over there now." He ended the call and began to dress.

Sarah sat huddled under a Mylar blanket in the fire chief's SUV, her teeth occasionally chattering despite the warmth of the summer evening. One hand held an empty china mug, courtesy of her neighbor who'd brought coffee and offered to let Sarah spend the night—what remained of it—at her house. Sarah had declined with thanks. She wanted to be in her own home.

Her home. The phrase resonated in her mind. It was the house she and Harry bought when they were married. It was the home into which they brought Jenny over two years ago. It was full of memories. And now, although both Harry and Jenny were gone, she wasn't going to turn loose of those memories—or the house.

Sarah wasn't about to be driven from her home by fire or anything else. But was the house habitable? Just how bad was the damage inside? She'd soon know, because here came the chief. She decided that, no matter what he told her, she wasn't going to easily abandon her home. Sarah wasn't certain whether her attitude was based on pure stubbornness or a sentimental attachment, but whatever the cause, she was adamant.

The chief climbed into the driver's seat of his vehicle and half-turned to face her. Sara had a vague recollection of meeting him at some point in the past, although she couldn't recall his name. In her present condition, she wasn't sure she could even remember her own.

"Doctor, I'm Stan Lambert, the deputy fire chief," he said, answering Sarah's unasked question. "I know this is unsettling. Are you okay? The EMTs are here. I know you told one of my firemen earlier that you didn't need any attention, but maybe you should let them check you over."

Sarah made a conscious effort to still the shaking she felt inside her, shaking due not just to her ordeal but to the emotions it set churning within her. She put the empty coffee mug on the floor of the SUV. "I'm fine, chief. What I need to know is whether I'll be able to get back into my house tonight."

"That's the good news," he said. "The fire was centered in a pile of oily rags burning in the garage near the entrance door to the kitchen. It produced a lot of smoke, sort of like a smudge pot. Despite depositing soot around the area of the fire and leaving the smell of smoke in some parts of the house, the fire didn't do any real structural damage."

"Even in the garage?"

"There might be a little scorching of the wood in a place or two, but nothing that would make the house unsafe. By the time my men got to it, most of the rags were consumed. As soon as we arrived, some of the firemen unrolled the hose and hooked it to the fire plug down the street in case it was needed, but as it turned out, all we had to use was a hand-held fire extinguisher."

"So I can go back into the house?" Sarah said.

"Yes, that's the good news," the chief said. "But I think there's some bad news to go with it." He looked up. "And I think I'll let this man tell you about it."

The back door of the SUV opened. A man edged in and took a seat behind Sarah. In the illumination provided by the dome light, she could tell he wore a suit and tie. However, the suit was wrinkled and the tie askew. He closed the door, brushed his dark hair out of his eyes, and rubbed his unshaven chin. "I'm so sorry this happened," he said.

Sarah searched her memory. She knew this man. That is to say, she felt like she should know who he was. Then it came to her. She'd seen him at church, heard his name there. His name danced on the edge of her memory, and she found it at about the same time he held up a badge wallet and identified himself.

"You may not remember me, but we go to the same church. I'm Detective Bill Larson."

"Why are you here? Are you part of some group at the church that ministers to people who've had a fire?" She did a

290

double take. "Surely you're not here as a policeman. This was just a fire in some oily rags in my garage," Sarah said.

"No, I'm not here as a church member, although I'll do anything I can to help," Larson said. "And I'm very definitely here as a policeman. I'm sure the chief has already told you this was no ordinary fire."

"No, it was just some oily rags burning," she said.

"And where did those oily rags come from? They didn't just materialize and set themselves ablaze." Larson said. "Do you even keep such things in your garage?"

"No," she said. "I'm careful about that. They could catch on . . . Oh!"

"That's right," Larson said. "That fire was set. This is arson."

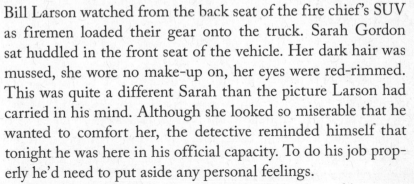

Bill Larson watched from the back seat of the fire chief's SUV as firemen loaded their gear onto the truck. Sarah Gordon sat huddled in the front seat of the vehicle. Her dark hair was mussed, she wore no make-up on, her eyes were red-rimmed. This was quite a different Sarah than the picture Larson had carried in his mind. Although she looked so miserable that he wanted to comfort her, the detective reminded himself that tonight he was here in his official capacity. To do his job properly he'd need to put aside any personal feelings.

He pulled a notebook from the inside pocket of his summer weight suit coat, clicked a ballpoint pen into life, and said, "Sarah . . . Dr. Gordon, can you think of any reason someone would want to do this?"

She pulled the blanket tighter around her shoulders. "No."

Larson waited for her to expand on that answer, but she just sat silent, unmoving. He figured she was probably in shock, and it was unlikely he'd get any useful information from her right now. But he had to try. However, his assumption proved correct as the answer to every question he put to her was the same—"I don't know."

Finally, Larson put his notebook back in his pocket. "Tell you what." He looked at his watch. "Tomorrow—or rather, today—is Saturday. Why don't I give you a call about mid-morning, and you can give me your statement then? Meanwhile, let the chief and me get you settled in with a friend or neighbor so you can get a few hours of sleep."

The chief said, "Doctor, where would you—"

She turned to face him, and her expression— the set of her jaw—stopped him in mid-sentence. "I'm perfectly fine to be alone," Sarah Gordon said. "I'm planning to spend the night—at least, what's left of it—right here. You've told me there's no structural damage to the house. Well, I can stand the smell of a little smoke. I've lived through much worse." She swiveled to look at her home through the windshield of the vehicle. "Nothing and no one will force me out of that house."

◆

Despite what she'd said about her willingness to be alone in her house, when the front door closed behind the fire chief and the detective, Sarah felt depression and loneliness descend on her. She dragged herself up the stairs, entered her bedroom, and—still wearing her robe and slippers—threw herself across the bed and buried her face in a pillow. She spent the next half hour sobbing into that pillow. She'd managed to hold it together in front of the fire chief and Detective Larson, but now she let it all out—not just the emotions caused by the fire, but her sorrow at the loss of her husband and daughter, the struggle she'd had since their death. She thought she'd be over it by now—she'd have moved on. But that's not what had happened.

Come on, Sarah. You're a grown woman. You're a physician. Every day in the emergency room you make critical decisions. Why can't you hold your personal life together?

That question had occupied Sarah for the past eight months, and she was pretty certain she had the answer. Before Harry's death, she'd gotten into the habit of shedding her professional persona at the door. At home she and Harry shared responsibility. They had been a team. If she didn't have an answer, Harry did. If one of them was unable to do something, the other one would. They could talk about things, make decisions jointly, lean on each other. But that changed with his death. Now she was alone, in every respect.

There was no more respite from responsibility when she came home from her work at the hospital. She simply moved into a different set of circumstances, another situation in which she had to make decisions. Wherever she was, whatever she was doing, it was all up to her. There were a few times when she thought she heard Harry's voice whispering, "Go ahead, Sarah. You can do it. You're strong." *But I don't feel strong— especially when things keep coming at me.*

And in addition to the burden she felt, Sarah was still subject to episodes of grief, interspersed with anger—at God, and (although she hated to admit it) at Harry for leaving her so alone.

The hardest times, times that seemed to tear her apart, came in the middle of the night. That's when she'd think she heard the sound of Jenny's voice. Sarah would roll out of bed, still half-asleep, and head for the room where Jenny slept before realizing that room was empty—just like all the other rooms in the house. Sarah was no longer needed as a mother. Jenny was dead.

Tonight the smell of smoke was pervasive throughout the house, but she could tolerate that. Her depression at the loss of her family nipped at the edges of her consciousness, but with an effort of will she put that aside to consider something of more immediate importance. What she couldn't get past was her fear that whoever set the fire would return. Every noise she heard seemed to represent footsteps on the stairs or movement in the next room.

Sarah wished she still had the pistol Harry kept in his bedside table. Right after they were married, she'd told him she felt uncomfortable with a gun in the house.

"I'm a nut about firearm safety," he'd said. "I want to have it to protect us, but I'm careful. Believe me."

After Jenny was born, Sarah renewed her objections. It wasn't safe to have a pistol in the house where there was a child. She'd read about gun owners who shot a family member or were wounded or killed themselves. Finally, Harry had given in to her entreaties to get rid of the weapon. But now she wished she had it with her. More important, she wished she had Harry beside her.

They'd worked together—she, an ER doctor, and he, a surgeon—to mesh their schedules so they'd have time with each other and with Jenny. Things were going well. They'd even talked about trying for a little brother or sister for their daughter. But one afternoon, as Harry drove home from the day care center with Jenny in the car seat, another driver crashed into them and snuffed out both their lives, as well as her own. And, so far as Sarah was concerned, her life ended at that moment as well.

Sarah told herself for the hundredth time there was no need to go over the past. Harry and Jenny were gone. She was still here, although she wasn't sure just why, and she had to concentrate on moving ahead. That had been her priority since her loss—moving ahead, one day at a time, one step at a time—even if she had to force herself. This fire was simply another roadblock she had to get past. *Harry, I'm trying. Really, I'm trying.*

The firemen had thrown the main electrical breaker to the house until they determined the location and severity of the fire. Now, although the electricity was back on, the clock at Sarah's bedside continued to flash 1:13, the time when all this took place. She'd fallen into bed without resetting the clock, so that now, when she opened her eyes and looked in that direction, she saw a constant reminder of what had happened tonight. She knew she should get up and reset the clock, but the effort was beyond her at this point.

It seemed to Sarah she'd done nothing but toss and tumble since dropping onto the bed in a state of exhaustion at almost four a.m. She untangled herself from the covers and punched the button to light up the dial of her watch. It was ten after five. Sleep wasn't going to come.

She slid her feet into the scuffs that had fallen at the bedside. She shrugged out of her robe, then went to the closet and wrapped herself in Harry's robe, one she'd kept because even after eight months she thought she could smell his after-shave lotion in it. Even now, it felt like she'd put on a suit of armor. It was a little like Harry was there with her. And she needed that.

Sarah padded down the stairs. In the kitchen, she flipped on the coffee maker and waited, hoping the scent of the freshly brewed coffee would overcome some of the smell of smoke that seemed to follow her wherever she went in the house.

She looked at her watch and wondered how long it would be before she could begin making phone calls. Sarah moved to one of the kitchen cabinets, opened a drawer, and withdrew a notepad and pencil. Then, armed with a fresh cup of coffee, she sat down at the kitchen table and began to make a list of the tasks that faced her.

The last emergency vehicle had gone. Clouds covered the moon and stars, and there were no streetlights nearby. He couldn't have planned better circumstances for watching unobserved. With the car windows partially open to let in the night breeze, he was comfortable leaning back behind the steering wheel. Other than a couple of officers driving by earlier, apparently the police had decided that regular patrols in the area weren't necessary for the rest of the night. That suited him just fine.

The house had been dark since he drove up, but he knew that didn't mean its occupant was sleeping. Sure enough, at that moment the light in an upstairs room came on. In a few minutes another window, this one downstairs, was lit, the illumination faint as though from a light in an adjoining room. He figured she'd been unable to sleep, had tossed and turned before eventually getting out of bed. Now she was probably sitting in the kitchen, perhaps drinking coffee or tea, wondering why this had happened.

Well, that was the point of the whole exercise, wasn't it? He didn't want to kill her—not yet. First, she had to suffer, but not necessarily physically. No, she had to suffer first. That's what this was about— the waiting, the wondering, the fear. The dying would come later.